CW01509180

Monaghan

Also available from Timothy O'Grady

Fiction
Motherland
I Could Read the Sky (with Steve Pyke)
Light

Non-fiction
Curious Journey (with Kenneth Griffith)
On Golf
Divine Magnetic Lands
Children of Las Vegas (with Steve Pyke)

Monaghan

Timothy O'Grady

With drawings and paintings by Anthony Lott

unbound

First published in 2025

Unbound
An imprint of Boundless Publishing Group Ltd.
c/o Ketton Suite, The King Centre, Main Road,
Barleythorpe, Rutland, LE15 7WD
www.unbound.com

Typeset by Jouve (UK), Milton Keynes

A CIP record for this book is available from the British Library

ISBN 978-1-78965-186-7 (hardback)
ISBN 978-1-78965-187-4 (ebook)

Printed in Great Britain by Clays Ltd, Elcograf S.p.A.

1 3 5 7 9 8 6 4 2

MIX
Paper | Supporting
responsible forestry
FSC
www.fsc.org
FSC® C018072

For Margaret Bernice (Welch) O'Grady and,
three generations along, Éabha Enver

With special thanks to Paul Cooper and John Trainor for
their generous support as patrons of this book

What was art, after all, if not simply giving out what you have inside you?

Émile Zola, *The Masterpiece*

Paintings described in this book along with additional artwork can be found at: www.anthonylott.studio/monaghan

New York City, 2013

You are leaving me, at last. I am at my window, in a dark room. Neither you nor Lydia know I'm here, you think I'm still in California slowly and wilfully losing my mind. I hear your shoes on our boards, I hear the rustling of clothes. A suitcase closes with a military click. You keep your voices low, as if this all has to be done by stealth, as if someone would stop you if you were heard. And you speak in Finnish. The further I slide, the more you speak to our daughter in that language. There is bile in my throat, a shortage of air, the feeling of metal bands tightening around me. The city throbs indifferently twenty-five storeys below. It is as if all of it, your sighs, the shadows, the emptying of our home, is being written across my back.

Yesterday I got your text – I can't go on. I'm taking her to Turku. Don't call. I was a month in that Tenderloin hotel where he had lived with the meek and desperate and had become one myself nearly. You might have thought I was too far gone to care. You were wrong. Care I could, express it I could not. But your text stirred me. I got the next plane I could to New York. Suitcases were already gathered in the hall when I got home. The door was ajar. I slipped in and came into this room where images and arrows and notes are all over the wall and postcards hang on strings and maps and texts are heaped on the desk and floor. I used to be so neat. Now it's like a cave where a madman dwells.

There is a pause. I picture you both having a last look. Ready? you say to Lydia, in English this time. Your voice is thin and strained. I want to bring a halt to this, I want to wind it all back to the time when we were well. But I cannot make myself move. You are like a tide receding. I hear you moving away along our hall. I hear Lydia struggle with her bag. If she knew I was here, she would come to me. I picture her tiny wrists, her fingers around the handle. What has she put in there to bring to her new home? Her ice skates? That dress I bought her, lemon yellow? I stand with my back to you, looking out the window, seeing nothing, just the grey opaque air over the city. The door clicks shut.

I stay still for a long time. I cry a little, I think. I hate you, I yearn for you, I pity you. The light dims. I walk through our rooms, the pots and pans on the walls, the furniture, the paintings, all without life now. A couple of drawers hang open like broken jaws. I keep walking, out the door and into the street. I don't know where I'm going. I forgot to put on a coat but won't go back now. I think of picking up a car, filling my pockets with cash and driving out over the hills and plains all the way to Guatemala or somewhere. People stare. It grows colder. Planes pass out on the horizon line and I wonder if any of them are yours. I walk without seeing, two hours, six, I don't know, I sense at some point that the density of things has changed.

Just beyond Gramercy Park, I think it is, under a lamp, words begin to fall, slender necessary words unbidden and both mine and not mine, falling in the only way they can fall, as a well-cut dress falls from shoulder and hip. I walk on through dark and light feeling them fall.

Laughter Soft as the Beating of Wings

Monaghan, 1984, 1988
Basque Country, 2012

I first saw the man who caused my downfall when I was thirteen years old, in Carrachor, County Monaghan, not six miles from my home.

I was high up in a tree, collecting apples. It was early morning, the sky was bright and sharp. I'd left my bicycle and our red dog with Generous McCabe, a relation of ours known all around the district for his wildness and his wealth and who was as old as the century itself. When I was small he'd get down on his haunches so we could meet eye to eye. No one else did that, not the priest nor the master nor my own father even. I took in the cool air in the crown of the tree. I dropped the apples into my sack. I looked all around me. Clouds ran in the sky. A white mist hung over a trough in the land like a rising of ghosts.

The mist rustled and waved and a man stepped through. I hadn't seen him coming. It was as if he'd been born in the mist. I thought I knew everyone in the townland, but I didn't know him. He was tall and fair. He moved through the grass to a stream lined with willows, splashed water on his face, drank from cupped hands. I held still and watched him. Arrows of light shot through the trees and flashed on the running water. He studied the light and I studied him. Still as he was he seemed to be doing something and whatever it was there was nothing else in the world for him but it.

After a long while he rose. He stepped into a small round arena bound by the trees. The air was blue there, the globs and shafts of light white and gold. They passed over his body, soft, dappling. He held out his arms. He began to move around the perimeter of the clearing like that, arms out, side-stepping. A little dip at the knees like he could hear music. He watched the play of light, on his body, in the air. His mouth was open, his eyes bright. He was like a saint in rapture. Then he stepped into the centre of the clearing and lifted an armful of fallen willow leaves and launched them up over his head. They fell around him like a shower of sparks, green and gold in the play of light through the trees. He did it again. And then a third time. What a thing to see, I thought, here in Carrachor, early on an autumn morning. Anybody doing something like that around here, you'd think they'd at least be laughing. But his face was serious, intent. I watched. I wondered what he'd do next.

But he stopped. He'd heard something. He stepped out from the trees and looked to his left. His eyes narrowed and the life left his face. I watched the line of his gaze. A white van I'd never seen before came off a lane and pulled in under the willows. The man moved towards it. And then, strange to say – it is still strange now to think on it even when I know so much more than I did then – I saw my brother Dermot step out of the driver's side of the van. Dermot could not be there. He was hauling bags of cement on a site in Birmingham. He'd been in it the past eight months. Or so I'd heard from people I thought had never told me an untruth. I squinted to get a sharper look. It was him. It had to be. The long arms, the helpless shrug, the way he wrinkled his nose like a rabbit when he was at a task.

Everything went very fast then. A blue car pulled up, the van doors swung open. Goods were shifted from van to car. Some were in boxes, others wrapped in blankets. I couldn't make out what they were. Then Dermot drove off the way he came and the car with the tall fair stranger in it set off to the east. Mist closed over their tracks.

I watched the spot, wondering if it had happened at all.

This is the place where I grew up, the Bough and Carrachor townlands, County Monaghan. The Irish borderlands. We had a farm of middling size. Hedge, lane, gable wall, church pew, barley field, I knew them all like I know your eyes. Or thought I did. We were Treanors out of Armagh. My father was Eamon, my mother Ann, the rest were Dermot the eldest, then Margo, Paddy, Ellen. I was the last. I arrived on a Christmas morning, emanating some kind of light, they said. They decided I was special. They went on telling me so.

In the borderlands then nothing was as it seemed and what was known or felt was not said or even implied, but rather encoded. Everyone knew a piece of something and vetted who they imparted it to. They nodded, whispered, spoke from the sides of their mouths. There was a war on. It was happening just up the road. We saw the military towers from our windows. We heard the helicopters. Men and women slipped through the shadows. Lines were indistinct, people mutated. Someone who sold you sweets or drove a tractor in the next field could be smuggler, tout, spy, partisan. But I was kept safe in the haven they made for me, far from cows and muck and secret organisations and guns. I grew, I found my range. I kicked balls through uprights and came first in exams. Our hopes rest in you, they said.

Generous was our chieftain. At least he was mine. I want to tell you about him now. Please stay with me. I know you know nothing of him, I never told you, it would be hard for you to think he could have anything to do with you now, or ever. But Bough to me was Generous, even if Generous was not just Bough. The catastrophe that has come down on us and what I've done to bring it about descend from that place and Generous's presence in it. I'd not have seen that man and my brother from the top of the apple tree nor heard the unforgettable laughter I will shortly tell you about were it not for him. The past has declined to relinquish its grip on me because of the onus Generous placed on me before he died. And because he took me more seriously than I took myself. I thought I'd transcended all that. I even thought I'd forgotten it. But it wouldn't let me. Generous is the dead man walking among us.

He was great-uncle to my mother. He lived in Carrachor just over the Blackwater River from us in an old lord of the manor house, leaky and grey and severe, with two wings, a lake and a glasshouse with little trees from China and Peru. Some say that the more disheartened he grew with the state the more he tried to make his own Ireland in his house. There were debates, home weaving, *feisanna*, a vineyard, the declaiming of poems. They came from Clare and Galway to dance sets in the kitchen. Politicians called for advice.

He was tall, wore long black coats and had a white beard and blazing blue eyes. He'd fought the British with the IRA in North Monaghan. He played violin in the first cinemas, and spoke French. When he was thirty-eight he swam around the whole island of Ireland. He'd started out like any of us, he hadn't shoes even when he was small, but he couldn't help making money or giving it away and whatever he knew or could do he'd taught himself. I couldn't get enough of him. He was the great figure of my childhood. My family treated me like an heirloom, but he brought me close. He made demands on me. I passed the summers with him and cycled over on Saturday mornings during the school year. We sat on the floor of his library with our backs to the shelves. He'd tip a drop of whiskey into my tea. He showed me the excitements of the mind and how they could be given form.

When he was eighty-six and I was fifteen he had a heart attack.

When I look ahead of me now, the view is short, he said.

We were in his parlour. There was a tartan rug on his lap. He spoke in the whisper of the suddenly enfeebled. I was sitting across from him with my Uncle Sean. I call him 'uncle' and he was that, he was my mother's youngest brother, but he was just three years older than me. I thought of him as a cousin and spent more time with him than others because he taught me how to get more leverage into a strike with the *cumán*. He could be aggravatingly competitive. His face had just three obdurate settings. What would you have made of him? He might have made you laugh. He could be good at that. He made someone else laugh a few years later, though he didn't mean to. It's why I am here and you are there.

Let's liven up the old lad, Sean had said, and we went over to the big house.

He did his best. He went around the room in a duck walk imitating a neighbour. Generous watched with a wintry smile. He seemed too tired to laugh. His cheeks were hollow beneath his beard. A tooth had gone to black. His eyes were watery and dim.

Sean kept trying.

Tell us, Uncle, he said, how was it to run with the boys back in the day?

How was it, you say?

That's it. Tell us a tale, said Sean.

He looked at us long and slow.

I will, so . . ., he said.

There were three of us in it. We were sent over to Keady to get guns off an Englishman. Ex-soldier. I was young and green and a little frightened. I'd only ever shot at milk bottles. We were to take the guns, leave a receipt and get out. October 1919. All very clean . . .

He squinted a little, as if to get a better view.

We waited in a hedge. We saw him weaving up his path. He was a giant – bald, red in the face, fearsome-looking. Well jarred that night. As he comes up to the door we put our guns in his back and push him through.

Generous lifted the tartan rug and stood up. His knees shook and he fell back. It took him two tries. He pointed left, right and ahead to show the layout of the Englishman's house and where the two others went to look for the guns and then at us to show where he had him tied up and under guard. The blue came up in his eyes. He dipped at the knees and spread his arms.

And wasn't there a bang in the yard that made me look out? he said. Eh? And didn't he slip the rope and come up behind me? And didn't he get his arms around me and squeeze the life out of me with the power of a bull and roar that he'd kill the lot of us? Wasn't that it?

He stalled and looked out the window. Then he reset himself. He wheeled around the room as he became himself, aged nineteen, on an arms raid in Keady. His arm shot out and a lamp went over. He paid no attention. He moved like a boy. He showed how he got the Englishman over to a step, hooked him around the ankle and brought the two of them down. Generous went down with them. He writhed and twisted. The gun fell from his hand and flew across the floor. He scrambled after it. He got his hands on it before the Englishman could. He jumped up. His glasses dangled from an ear. He spread his feet and his arm went out like a plank. He saw the gun in his hand. His finger was on the trigger. His hand began to shake. He saw the Englishman try to rise. He saw the look of fear and hatred and wish to kill in his eyes.

BANG! he shouted, and we jumped. BANG! BANG! BANG!

The shake went up along his arm and convulsed the whole of his body as he told us how he emptied his gun into the Englishman.

He fell back into his chair then. His head dropped. We thought we might have lost him. We ran to him but he waved us away to where we'd been.

What do you think it takes to kill a man? he said.

He looked hard at us. We couldn't speak.

A second? An hour? . . .

Eh? What do you think?

. . . It's very slow, he said. I'd put six bullets into him and he was still on all fours coughing up blood and trying to speak . . .

We picked up all his guns and went out. I looked back in at him through the window. One hand slipped in his blood and he went down into it on his face. He was sprawled out and still breathing, still moving. He was trying to get somewhere. One of the others went back in and shot him just above the ear. That was the end of it.

He poured himself a glass of whiskey.

That's how it was, he said, back in the day.

He drank off the whiskey. He tapped the side of his head and scowled.

It was bestial, he said. The lot of it. War of liberation or no. Don't let anyone tell you otherwise. The romance comes into it afterwards and it's all a lie.

Again he looked at us, long and with rebuke and maybe some pity.

And it's all for nothing unless you make something from it. You. Both of you.

You don't know this place or these people or what a *feisanna* is. You wouldn't have a great-uncle who went into someone's house and shot him. Does it shock you? Well it might. I never took you there, I said little, I dissembled. Up to some point I lived with and through them. Then I turned away, made them into ghosts. They embarrassed me. It seemed expedient to shape, edit, make harmless.

Sometimes now I think I should introduce myself to you again. Ronan Treanor, aged forty-two, provisionally single, former holder of the McIvor Chair in Architectural Theory at Columbia University, presently resident in New York City, born and raised in Bough townland. It seems I couldn't escape. It pulled me back. Generous killed a man nearly a century ago on another continent and it reaches down to me now, in this moment, writing to you. Event became story,

story was told, one who heard it laughed in a way that haunted a boy, boy became man, man married woman . . .

Two years later we lost Generous. An embolism travelled up into his brain and took him from us as surely as a bullet.

The day of the funeral was cold and wet, the black sky touching down on the rooftops. People came from all over the county and beyond, above a thousand it was said. They were in farmhouses, out in the road under umbrellas or already in the church, waiting. We went over that morning to his house to say goodbye. There were forty or so scattered around the parlour, drinking tea and eating sandwiches. His wife was long dead, his children in distant countries. Only his youngest daughter Eimear was left at home. She suffered from alopecia and kept Kerry blues and wolfhounds. She was in a corner, half-bald, fretting with her hands like she was knitting something.

Generous was laid out in a black suit, one of the wolfhounds on guard below. There was a tricolour over the coffin and beyond was his portrait on an easel. Eimear had shrouded it in black. No one other than Eimear and me ever found out who'd painted it, though they'd asked. He was in a striped robe in the picture, like he'd just risen from bed, a stained-glass window behind him, his face as bright as the morning sun and his eyes drilling into you over the rims of his glasses. Just as they did when he asked us how long it takes for a man to die.

I held back in the shadows of an alcove, looking at the dead man. I wanted to say something to him, I'd been thinking about it since the news came of his death, a last thing before he was taken away for all time, a goodbye or thanks or prayer or message that I'd miss him and that he'd never be replaced and that I'd try to live up to what he'd asked of me. I stepped a little closer. His nails had been lacquered, his skin was like wax, there was a faint aura of chemicals. He looked like he'd been shrunk, like a dried fruit. I didn't kneel as the others had. I feared that my father would tell me to kiss the head or touch the hands. They were a jaundiced, bloodless colour, like prostheses, and were wrapped around a fiddle he'd played in championships when he was a boy. I looked at his face in the painting so intelligent and formidable and scrutinising. It came up on me slowly, how still and final and empty is a corpse. I'd never met death before. Soon the signal would come, the nails would go in, the coffin would be lowered into the ground and the men would take turns shovelling the earth onto him. But what was he now? Was he somewhere?

I turned away. I wished I had no longer to be in this place, but to be instead out walking in the hills. I went back to the alcove. Before me was a little group facing each other on sofas, my Uncle Sean among them. They were telling stories about Generous. They smiled, shook their heads. A small boy ran red-faced towards the kitchen. Eimear watched her dead father. The big front door creaked open. Cold air crept towards us along the floor.

Then a stranger came in.

My Uncle Sean paid him no heed. He tapped a spoon brightly on a tabletop. It rang through the room.

I have something for you, he said.

The man walked towards us across the long room. No one but me looked at him. He drew steadily into focus, as if through a camera lens. His head was down, his expression intent. He had a clod of mud on his boot. He wore jeans and a brown suede jacket. I recognised the clothes first, then the way he moved and finally the face. It landed on me then. I nearly called out.

It was the stranger I'd seen with my brother Dermot from the top of the apple tree.

The people turned to face Sean.

It's a story about how Generous killed a man in Keady in 1919, he announced.

The stranger bowed before the coffin and moved to Eimear. He took her hands in his. He whispered to her. Her eyes looked into his, she nodded. She waved a hand vaguely towards the portrait of her father. How is it he could know Eimear and I not know about it? He moved away then and took a chair by the window. He turned to look out. Dim light fell on his face. His eyes were a Pacific Ocean blue and a small triangular piece was missing from a front tooth.

It was like this . . ., said Sean, and he began to tell the story Generous had entrusted to us. There'd been something terrible and intimate in the telling, something privileged in the hearing. Now Sean, so needful of attention and so fearful that I or someone else would tell the story first, was defiling Generous's corpse so he'd be remembered on the day of his funeral.

I fled the room. I walked past stuffed owls and herons. I passed the death mask of Fintan Lalor in a mount on a wall. Wolfhounds loped like giraffes through doorways and along corridors. I was thinking about my uncle and I was thinking about the stranger but most of all I was thinking of how I might be alone with Generous this one last time. He'd lived in this house for fifty-five years after buying it on a fortune made young from violins and the importing of champagne and cognac along routes he'd run guns for the IRA. He lived large and recklessly. Even as a boy I could see that.

I went up the stairs and passed the library. Empty bottles of whiskey were among the books. Old republican rifles were stacked in corners. Generous conducted his tutorials with me here by the week – the making of treaties, the acoustics of Roman amphitheatres, the history of dance. He told me about Cuchulainn and Ferdia, who battled by day and tended each other's wounds by night, and Étaín, a great beauty and a rider of horses. No one else could do it as he did not before or after or no matter what celebrated institute of higher learning I attended. I went along the corridor. Abandoned children's rooms, stacks of theatre programmes, a broken easel. In his bedroom was a massive baronial bed and in the corner the cot where he'd slept since his wife died, a worn spot on the wall above it where he'd rested his head. I saw his coats on a rack, the dresser with his combs and cologne and spectacles. I sat on the cot and looked at the books beside it. He'd marked places in them with the silver lining of cigarette packets. He'd written little notes on them. The hand was unsteady. I was all right until I saw that, but then I felt my breath get short and the brine rise up into the back of my eyes. I began to weep. It was all over now. By noon he'd be in the ground. I'd not be with him ever again.

I walked back out into the corridor. At the end was the ballroom. Here were pale blue curtains half-eaten by moths and a sunken floor filled with gramophones and lacquered tortoiseshells and harps and flags and violins, all covered in dust. Generous. I called out my last goodbye in a faint voice.

When I came back down I could see that Sean had finished the story of how Generous had lived through the killing in the telling of it and how we'd thought we'd lost him. I saw too he had them where he wanted them. Eimear's face was in her hands. They were all shaking their heads. An old woman named Sheila Dean who'd arrived on crutches seemed to be saying a prayer. The stranger was looking out. There was no sign he was listening. Sean began to speak again, about the curious case of the television interview Generous had given in the last year of his life about his time in the IRA. Sean pretended that he didn't have an idea how they heard about the killing Generous told us about that night, but I knew it was him.

Sure we all watched it when it came out on the television, he said. He was sat over there at that table with his hair combed and all buttoned up and calm. He told about going on the raid to Keady, how a terrible fight happened there and how to defend themselves they'd shot a man.

Did he die? asked the interviewer.

He did.

Was it you who shot him?

Two of us did. I shot him with a 6.3 millimetre Webley automatic.

Then they brought the camera right up into his face as the interviewer asked, Does that event haunt you, sir?

They thought he might crack, Sean said. But he looked your man right in the eye.

Not at all, he said.

What about that? asked Sean of the people. 'Not at all.' Can you credit it?

No one answered him. They all leaned back into their sofas as one. A sigh like a dying wind went round.

God love him, said Sheila Dean.

Queer, said my father.

Aye, queer all right, said another.

He didn't flinch, said Sean. Men like that . . .

He shook his head in wonder.

I heard a sound then away to my left. I knew it was the stranger by the window. I turned towards him. There was nothing you could read on his face. He was just quietly laughing. It was a shocking thing to do on a funeral day, after a story like that, the dead man a few yards away in his coffin and his daughter weeping in the corner, even if it was meant for no one but himself. He must have earned the right to it somewhere, I reckoned. I only knew I'd never heard a sound like it, strange, sad, chilling laughter, soft as the beating of wings. It weighed more than it could carry. It had been released but could not expire. There was knowledge in it beyond my own, beyond anyone's there I'd say, bar the dead man's. From it I could tell that he knew Generous in a way I never could. It was the loneliest laughter I'd ever heard. And yet there was a privilege in it I almost envied. It cut right into me. If I'd never heard it I'd not be writing these words to you in this lunatic room.

We got to our feet. Eimear walked over to where the stranger sat by the window, held his face in her two hands and kissed the top of his head, then moved out behind her father's coffin. She knew something I didn't. He'd danced in the trees and now he was laughing with the dead. We all followed, him away on his own to the rear. It was as if a judgement had been passed. Then we buried Generous.

I left home to study architecture not long after that. Edinburgh was first. I'd feared the city but found I took to it right away. It was the click of heels on the pavement, the whoosh of revolving doors, all the turning wheels and people with preoccupied expressions moving fast amid slate and glass and stone. It seemed a mistake had been made when I was born on a farm and was now being corrected. I grew my hair. Different kinds of clothes came off racks and onto my back. I adjusted my accent. I met a girl, Arpita Bhose from Uttar Pradesh, who'd come there to study classical dance. I won an essay contest. Professors invited me to their homes for dinner.

I didn't look back. I was too busy. And anyway no one asked me to. They stopped expecting me to come home for the holidays. They didn't chide me if I didn't answer their letters. I was out in the wide world pursuing my destiny . . .

Bough had begun to fade, like a photograph left out in light. But then it came back, as it has been wont to do of late. In the summer before my final year at Edinburgh I cycled on my own to France. When I got back I found telegram notices stuffed under the door of my room. They reported the death of my brother Dermot. Run down by a lorry on a country road on the border, said Paddy down the phone line. Already in his grave. Nothing to be done about it now.

I never told you about Dermot. All the others were accounted for, but not him. Omissions are as good as lies, are they not? I wonder now what I feared. You gave me no reason. There were seventeen years between him and me. I can't get his face so well. I remember being in a car with him. He was wearing a GAA jersey with a ribbon still pinned on it, singing snatches of songs that came on the radio. He left me down at school. He stood watching me a long while, hands on hips, elbows out. He got smaller and smaller as I walked away. That was the last I ever saw of him. I close my eyes now and try to get him. I see his gangly arms, the loping stride. He used to do a song-and-dance shuffle, wrinkle his nose, throw me a wink and head out. I see his back. Sharp bones beneath a long white neck. The Ostrich, Paddy used to call him.

Was it true what that girl I knew from school, met by chance on a London street, told me about a volley being fired over his grave? There were times when I wondered was he really dead. He's an incomplete sentence, a tap on the shoulder and no one there.

At least he was until last spring.

It's deep in the night now, Erica. Very quiet. No light yet in the east. I turned abruptly around there just beyond Gramercy Park and headed home. I took a cab. I had to catch the words before they fled. I can't say what time I arrived. I've been writing them for you since, all about my brother and Generous and the man with no name. I'm at my table made of oak on the twenty-fifth floor of our building just to the north of Hell's Kitchen. Pages and images on strings hang over my head like bats. The house has never felt like this before. Vacated, like Generous's corpse. It's difficult to imagine how this might change. I'm not tired. Well, I'm tired but not sleepy. I'll go on while I can. I'll lie on the sofa there if I must. I'll not go into our room. I'd smell your perfume. I'd sense your skin. You and Lydia are changing planes in some European hub, moving ever further away. You'll be met in a while in Turku by your father. He'll have his ironical smile and his Volvo. He'll open his arms to Lydia. She'll run towards him.

I am not well, there can be no doubt, but still my hand moves over the page. It soothes me. I hope to go on until the story is told. There's nothing in my way. When I look up I see through the window the pulse of the city and the darkness of the rivers around it.

Life was so very different last early spring. It was melodious, it was sweet. The house was full. Two adults and a child gave life to the walls and air and each other. I'd start to feel it from blocks away as I walked home. The senses would lift, the pulse quicken. This was one of the gifts you gave to me. It seems near enough to touch, even now.

There arrived an evening last April before all began to change when I put tickets and my passport into a bag and stood up from the table where I am sitting now. I was to pass four nights in Spain on an academic mission. I'd be back by the weekend. I see it now as I saw it then, soft light spilling from the rooms, Lydia working out algebra problems with Judy Garland songs as background, you doing stretches in your bare feet on the living-room carpet. Onion soup bubbled on the stove. I felt lucky. I hadn't gone and already wanted to be back. It was home in a way nothing else had ever been. I picked up my bag and stepped forward. Kisses at the door. Lydia gave me a drawing she'd made of her own winking eye.

I flew to Madrid that night and then on to San Sebastián in the north to look at the Plaza de la Constitución, an ovoid in the city's old part with tiers of numbered doors rising from a floor that had at different times been the site of bullfights, a food market and open-air masses. I was to write about it in a special number of a scholarly journal devoted to multi-use urban spaces. I made notes into a Dictaphone. I dined splendidly. On my last night I went from bar to bar with a group of the city's professors. Beaming epicurean men with hooked noses over their thin lips and aprons tied around their girths poured glasses of sparkling *txakoli* from green bottles and pushed plates of smoked cod and lamb brochettes at us with the fluency of casino dealers. We finished in a basement watching a woman with feathers in her hair singing Spanish pop songs from the 1960s. After that I went around the corner to my hotel. I called you on the way to say good night. It was nearly light. A newspaper had been pushed under the door of my room. I got into bed and almost fell asleep trying to read it, but just before I did my eye was drawn to the word 'MONAGHAN' in a little box in the city's events column. 'Pinturas Nuevas de Niall Dempsey', it said beneath it, and gave the address of a gallery. Some kind of fate, it seems now, took its first step.

The morning call I'd booked came three hours later. I'd been scalded dry by late gin and tonics with the professors. Rivets of pain were in my eyes. I'd had worse, but not before a transatlantic flight. I drank half a litre of orange juice and some sweet coffee in the hotel breakfast room. I'd take a look at Monaghan for half an hour. The coincidence was too great to ignore. What had Niall Dempsey, whoever he was, made of my home county? Then I'd get my plane. I'd sleep all the way back if I could. My phone said it was going to be a warm spring day in New York. At the end of it I'd lie in a cloud of Egyptian cotton sheets with you.

I checked out and took a cab to a little street off the Plaza Cataluña. The gallery was above an optometrist's, two white rooms and an entrance hall. Paintings were up on walls, others still leaned against a doorframe. A woman talked on a phone and blew plumes of smoke out of a window. A fair man hung paintings. Another sat in a chair beside a sleeping dog, running his fingers through his wiry beard. Black clouds rolled in over the Bay of Biscay and the air cooled. I wanted to get it over with. The closer I got to Monaghan, the more I yearned for New York.

I stepped in. No one paid me any heed. Three paintings were on a wall under beams of light. They were dark mostly, in reds and blues of night. Holy men and women had come from far away in time and space and been placed in the canvases on hard American streets, Saint Jerome with his begging sign and his hand propping up his chin, Saint Lucy being cuffed by the police, Saint Teresa of Ávila living rough in a plastic shroud over a vent. Her fingers were long and brown and worn by supplication. All were in duress. Police grimaced, animals and angels looked on. The faces of the saints were radiant and pained. What had it to do with Monaghan? I had to be in the wrong place. If not, they were taking the name of my county in vain. But then the paintings were too decisive to be vain.

I walked back and forth before them. I had time. I passed Saint Jerome but then stepped back. Something had caught me. Weren't the lower lip and the wide spacing of the eyes familiar? In fact the whole construction of the head? More familiar in fact than nearly anyone living or dead. I looked a little closer and knew for certain that the man in the painting was our Generous McCabe. It was striking, and unsettling. Time seemed to slip a little. Fragments from Bough came towards me like spores. The smallest thing can throw you after a night of drink. But then there was a tiny scar in the eyebrow. I would have overlooked that if I'd been asked to describe him, but could see it now as if he were with me in the room. I caught the accusatory power of his sharp eyes.

I turned back to the man in the chair. I was going to ask him what this was all about. Then I saw something more familiar, green fields on a hillside, a lake. They could have been from the homeplace in Bough. But hedges separating the fields were like haemorrhaging veins, and the sky seemed a wound trailing blood. The canvas had been ripped open in the foreground and stitched together. The stitches were crude, like a soldier untrained in medicine might administer to a comrade on a battlefield. I stood before the man with the dog.

Are they yours? I asked him.

He took me in with brown, amused eyes.

The gallery is mine. The paintings are by an Irishman.

23

Thunder like military drums sounded over the bay. The dog woke and shuffled closer to the man's feet.

I am from that place, I said.

What place?

Monaghan.

Interesting, he said. Interesting that you should be the first to see this work. We open tonight.

But why does it have this title?

The man shrugged, smiled.

A caprice, perhaps. I don't know. You'd have to ask the *pintor*.

Is he here?

He's the person you will see if you look over your left shoulder . . . Niall? he said to the fair man.

The painter and I each turned fully around as if in a courtly dance until we were face to face across the gallery floor. He took a step towards me. My heart was like a bird plunging to earth. It was him. The turquoise eyes and the gap in his tooth.

I know you, I said.

I knew more than I would wish. I learned it years ago on the night of Generous's funeral walking on a dark road with my cousin Paul T. It was just the two of us. We'd been in the pub with the others and were just coming up to his house. He asked did I see the one with the brown jacket and the mud on his boot and then when I quickened because of what I'd seen from the tree and said that I did he said it was really something that a man like that with half the country after him would take the risk of coming to Carrachor to help us bury Generous.

What do you say? I asked.

He looked at me, tipped his head.

You don't know about him? he said.

I know nothing of that man, I said.

He walked on twenty paces, then stopped.

Everybody knows about him, he said. Best shot in South Armagh, said my uncle, and he would know. No one like him, he said. He took on a foot patrol on the street on his own, closed two barracks with mortars. He's a one-man regiment. Works alone mostly. Has about fifteen names. Do you see? No one can understand it. How do they not catch him? How is he still alive?

You mean he's *killed* people? I said.

He stopped in the road.

You think they shoot at rabbits?

He turned in at his gate then.

How is it you don't know this, he said, with your family?

I watched him pass into his house. The night was black and I walked into what seemed a cave. I was alone, and felt it. It had been a rare day and was rarer now. You have to imagine how protected I'd been, Erica, how careful they'd been to keep me in ignorance. And so when Paul T said those things the war so previously unreal came up on me fast, incarnate, too strong to resist, like a boar or wolf come into a room. How could anyone bear it, day after day? Generous couldn't. What did he mean about my family? What else didn't I know? My brother had brought that man things. Eimear had kissed the top of his head. How many had he killed? I felt the corpses piled up behind his bleak laughter.

Now he was before me, Niall Dempsey, painter of saints, slayer of soldiers, a hammer and nail in his hand.

Flecks of grey ran through his hair from the temples, hatching struck out from the corners of his eyes. The eyes were blue quartz. I saw his body stiffen when I said that I knew him. He'd never been caught and held, never charged. He had to live with an unrelieved wariness. I looked down at his hands. I'd read that snipers pamper their trigger fingers with oils and gauze wrappings. They're like the fingers of court ladies or small children. His nails were cracked, there were crescents of paint in the cuticles. He'd killed with them, he'd made these paintings.

You know me? he asked.

Well I don't know you. I saw you at the funeral of Generous McCabe.

You have a long memory.

It was an unusual day.

Yes.

My uncle embarrassed us.

How did he do that?

Telling yarns. Showing off . . . I'm Ronan Treanor, I said. From Bough in County Monaghan.

Son of Eamon and Ann.

Yes . . . and brother of Dermot.

I watched his eyes at this, but he showed no sign.

That would make you great-grand-nephew of Generous, he said.

Yes. You know a lot.

There was no one like Generous.

No.

He came forward with eyes softening. He had a light step and a gentleness so intense it seemed an intrusion.

You're an artist, I said.

That's a big word.

Can I take you to lunch?

I can't have lunch, he said. I can't leave here until tonight.

I see.

Can you wait until then?

I have a plane in three hours.

Oh well, he said.

I picked up my bag. I was ready to leave, wish him good luck, say I hoped we'd meet again sometime. But I knew it would never happen. I had this one chance to learn what only he could tell me. So I asked,

Did you know my brother Dermot?

Yes.

He's no longer with us, you know that.

I do.

The last time you saw him, do you remember that?

I was with him the night before he died.

He stood full-square facing me. He'd offered this for free, knowing, I think, what it must mean. I looked around the walls at his saints.

I could change my flight, I said.

Do that. I'll make a meal. I'll put you up.

I see. Thank you.

In the Labourd.

That's where you live?

It's like Monaghan, he said.

That soft word, like a sigh in sleep.

I will, I said.

I left him in the gallery and went out through the streets and onto the esplanade. I wouldn't go to his opening. I had to be alone, I had to think. The sky was black and turbulent. Gun-metal waves rolled in and birds pecked at the wrack. I walked up and down between the hills on the esplanade and then found the bar where I was to meet him. It was down two steps, brightly lit, the light a dirty white, hams hanging from the ceiling. There was a room at the back with waiters wearing waistcoats and ties. I entered, I sat. I ordered rabbit stew and a small glass of Rioja. I closed my eyes. Monaghan came walking in – gnarled trees covered in vines, chocolate flake, football pennants on the electric lines, Packie Geoghan staggering on the steps with a pan loaf under his arm. The pictures came up like bubbles in a spring. Then other pictures – checkpoints, gun barrels with squaddies at the end, dynamited border crossings. I didn't want them but they came in too. Then I saw a monument I passed once on my bicycle, built to a lad from Knockacullion just down the road from us who'd been shot dead on the ground by the SAS. No one can accuse me of running away, he'd said. He was young, he had skin and blood and a girlfriend, maybe he liked to dance and kiss and think and would like to go on doing it. Maybe he'd like to have children. Why wouldn't he run away? I would. I did.

He came in, face freshened by rain. We had two shots and went out to the street. He had a *deux chevaux* at the kerb, cream, a headlamp held on by tape. I got in beside him. There were daubs of paint on the upholstery and a dog – the gallery dog, caramel-coloured – stretched out on the back seat. We set off, out of the city the back way through a long river valley and then up through oaks towards France, woodland and hawks and wild goats, black water crashing over rocks. Clouds hugged the high land. We passed in and out of them, the land whitening and then coming back fiercely green. It seemed we had left the known world. He didn't speak and nor did I. He looked at it, eyes wide, receptive, nothing in the way. I'd seen such a look before, in Lydia when she was small, the gaze clear, liquid, alive, nothing to weary or circumscribe it out of fear or habit. I might once have looked out at the world that way myself. I think I did, long ago. You're born with it, or it's bestowed on you. But you can fritter it away.

We came down from Spain through switchbacks into the Labourd.

He lived in an old schoolhouse. Lavender lined the path. All was quiet, dark. He opened a bottle of wine. He cooked white beans and *boudin*. I told him about Generous playing the violin for his hens and he laughed. Then I told him how he got a terrible whack in the testicles from the swing of the tail of one of Eimear's wolfhounds. You got any more? he asked. A few, I said. He set out the plates. The dog lay down in his basket. Night was closing in. He ate the food, pushed his plate away. He reached for a notebook and put his feet on the table. Then he began to draw my eyes.

What should I do? I asked.

Stay still.

Can I speak?

His eyes moved from the page to me, back and forth.

Yes.

How did you do at the gallery?

I sold four.

Not bad.

Some people say art shouldn't be sold, he said. That it's like selling prayers.

I can't imagine thinking like that, I said.

I see.

When did it start?

What?

You and art.

He held up the drawing to the light and watched it with a scowl.

It started with a cat, he said.

A cat?

A cat on a wall.

You drew it?

No. I didn't draw it. I was six . . . no, seven. I couldn't draw. There was sun and shadow. The cat moved. Sometimes it was in sun, sometimes shadow, sometimes both. I watched it for a long time. All afternoon. Colours flashed up, spectrum colours. Its edges blurred. It kept changing. It wasn't just a cat. It was a sequence of distinct things. I'd have watched it until it got dark but it got up onto a roof and ran away.

He made a gesture of helplessness.

Do you get me? he asked.

No.

I can't talk and draw at the same time.

All right, I said.

He made harsh lines on the drawing.

That saint in your painting . . .

Which?

Jerome.

Yes. With the cardboard sign.

That was Generous, wasn't it?

His hand paused in the air.

Aren't you cute? he said.

It was that little scar cutting through his eyebrow. And the feel of him. But I don't think I consciously realised he had that scar. The painting made me see it.

I looked at Generous for a very long time, he said.

Just tell me one thing.

Yes.

Why did you call it Monaghan?

Monaghan is *painting*, he said. No, it's a *pause* . . . between two things . . . In the pause was painting.

It was like talking with an oracle.

He reached for the bottle but there was nothing in it. He crossed the room to a cabinet for another and set it before us. He looked at the drawing. He held it out at arm's length. Then he threw it away and started another one. He said nothing. His silence was a wall, difficult to breach or circumvent. He looked at me with his wide blue eyes. He shaded and hatched. Sometimes he looked amused, the way musicians do at an improbable note. Finally he stopped. He looked at the drawing under the light, lay it on the table again to make a change, checked it and handed it to me. I put it in my pocket. He walked to the window.

The sky's cleared, he said.

We went out in one mind it seemed with our bottle and glasses and looked up. The firmament glittered and pulsed. It was as if a silver dust had been strewn across it. I opened my mouth to ask him about my late enigma of a brother, then stopped. I needed more time. I needed a way in. It had to be right. It was my only chance. Distant houses were silhouettes. All was quiet. We drank the wine. Everything and nothing were important under the sky.

Do you ever sleep out? I said at last.

Yes.

I haven't done it since I was twenty. I cycled from Edinburgh to Ronchamp in the Haute-Saône and slept out every night. I saw skies like this.

He kept his eyes on the stars.

It took three weeks, I said. Eight hundred miles. When I got back to Edinburgh I learned my brother Dermot was dead.

It was a big funeral, he said.

Like Generous's?

Not quite.

What was he like?

He was your brother.

I never knew him, I said. I wish I had. He was very good to me, but he was so much older, like from another world.

He loved riddles, he said. Who buys me doesn't want me, who builds me doesn't need me, who uses me can't appreciate me. I got that one. A coffin.

He used to run around flapping his arms like a seagull.

That's right.

I saw you with him once, I said. From the top of a tree.

That stilled him. He looked at me once, then away.

That could be, he said.

He walked on.

Art wasn't your profession back then, I said.

No.

War was your profession.

Who told you that?

A cousin. It seemed everyone knew but me. They said you were special. That you were the best.

War was the profession of the British, he said. We were amateurs.

He left the road and turned down a path towards a stream that flowed over rocks. I followed him. On the way I switched on the Dictaphone in my pocket. It was dark here, total blackness amid the bushes and trees. I could sense his presence, his breath, but could see nothing of either him or myself. It was as if we were in a tomb. Perhaps he could only speak of these things in the dark. I heard the rocks click like ice cubes, I felt the cool air rising from the water. We sat on the bank of the stream with a flat stone like a table between us. We set the bottle and glasses on it.

Was my brother in the war? I asked.

He was.

I was in an apple tree in Generous's orchard, I said. Dermot drove up in a white van and handed over boxes and things wrapped in blankets. What were they?

I met him in Generous's orchard more than once, he said.

This would have been 1984. Autumn. The time of ripe apples.

An M60 and three Armalites, he said.

What did you do with them?

We opened up across the border on three Brits who thought they couldn't be seen.

Did you get them?

Yes.

Where did he get the guns from?

They were on your land. We kept a dump in a field there.

Were there other things in this field?

Yes. Rocket launchers, Semtex, handguns, timers.

What did Dermot do?

He was the quartermaster.

Was he active in England?

Yes.

Did he ever kill anybody?

He placed a bomb that blew up some Guardsmen in a park in London.

How many?

Seven.

He waited a moment, then said,

And a boy.

What boy?

A boy who was watching.

Did he know about the boy?

It would be impossible not to know. The boy's face, the way he died, they were everywhere.

Jesus Christ, I said.

I stopped. The sky came down and lay on me like a body. He waited for me.

How was he about it? I asked.

He talked about the boy for years. He wondered about the life he'd have lived if he hadn't killed him.

He poured us out two half-glasses. He waited again for me to speak, but I didn't. I couldn't.

I heard about a soldier from the First World War, he said, who'd been guard on a German prisoner. They became friends. They used to play cards. Someone asked him when he was an old man if he could remember what the German looked like. He said no, he couldn't, but he remembered very well the one whose head he'd cut off with his trenching spade.

The glade was an echo chamber. I'd lost track of where he was.

When I went home that day from the orchard, I said, I told my family what I'd seen from the top of the tree. That can't be, they said.

Dermot's away in Birmingham. I insisted it was him. But they wouldn't have it. It made me wonder was my head right.

I see, he said.

Did my father know about those things on our land? I asked.

He did.

And about Dermot?

Yes.

My mother?

Yes. But not everything.

Paddy and my sisters?

The same with them.

I didn't.

That would mean they didn't want you to know. That it would implicate you and be a burden to you. Or that you could be a risk.

We leaned back in the grass. It was wet, but I didn't pay attention. Dermot's face passed by like a carnival mask, watching matches at home on the television with his mouth hanging open in wonderment. His mask of gormlessness. What did it cost him to wear it? He'd killed an innocent boy. My past broke up as I lay there. It surprises me now how fast it was. It was a flimsy thing I'd made up of bicycle rides through the oaks and snow on the barn roof and my family acting like I was the beginning and end of everything. There was an evening when I was very small. I couldn't yet speak. My first memory. I'd got away when they were getting ready to give me a bath and climbed up on a chair. All I had on was my little vest. I was like a small piece of fruit in this big armchair. They laughed. They pointed. Dermot was there. He ran to get a camera. I watched them. They looked like I was the funniest and best thing that had ever happened to them. I can do anything I want with these people, I thought. They are clay in my hands. But it wasn't true. They were all part of the killing machine and I knew nothing about it.

I stood up. I walked to the stream. I breathed in its air. Then I went back and sat down.

What's it like to kill someone? I asked.

What makes you think you can ask? he said.

My brother. All that gear on our land.

I heard him shift in the grass. I wondered would he walk away. But he didn't. Finally he spoke.

I killed Corporal James Nealey of the Staffordshire Regiment on a summer afternoon. I was eighteen, he was twenty-four. He was from a small place called Hixon. His father was a vicar. He was to marry Alice Paulson the following spring. That was the first man I killed. There was haze in the air. I had a scope and an AR-18. I didn't always have a scope. It would have been better for me if I hadn't. I was in an upstairs bedroom window with a clear line on the gate to a barracks where we'd disabled a Saracen with a mine. No wind, eight-degree drop, three hundred yards. Corporal Nealey came and went twice. He was bringing tools to a mechanic who was lying below the undercarriage. I could see him very well. He had red hair and big teeth. Sweat ran down from his hairline. He was dead still, talking with the mechanic. It was a clean, simple shot. But I couldn't do it. My head had decided on the moment but my finger wouldn't move. I ordered it again. I was paralysed. He was so near, like I was in a room in his house, like he was about to turn and say something to me. I didn't know him but I saw him so well it seemed I must. One of us had got too close. It was so intimate it seemed obscene. I was there to take his life. He turned around. He went back to the barracks. I stayed at the window. The gun was on my shoulder, I was braced on the window ledge. I thought I'd lost him. But he came back out. He waved away a cloud of midges. Something made him laugh. He looked up, towards me. If he could see me as I saw him, our eyes would meet. I'd learned the procedure – check angle, distance, wind, breathe in, hold, pull, move out, dump the weapon, change clothes. I took the breath and pulled. He flew back when the round hit him, his jaw came away. He landed with his arms out. A jet of blood came out of the artery in his neck.

I fade the recording. His voice grows smaller, then seems to run down a hole. I click the stop button. It's still dark. I hear a New York siren. I get up from the table and go to the bathroom, look into the mirror. I haven't cut my hair in three months. Would I have startled Lydia? Would she even have recognised me? I go back to the room. There, like an entanglement of strings and wires, is all the detritus I've collected from his life. How to sift and order it so you will understand why I blew everything up between us when it was so rosy and bright? But what else would I be doing if not this? Writing essays that no one would read, or should. I click on the machine. I turn up the volume.

After he killed Corporal Nealey he broke down the gun, got it to a woman waiting with a pram in the back lanes, went over walls and into a house where he washed the evidence off his clothes. Then he sat. That night he watched on the television news his victim's mother weep, his father pray for peace, his fiancée describe her loss and the police speak of the turning of the wheels of justice which would inevitably arrive to crush him. But he'd known anyway as soon as the round hit that like Generous he'd been marked, that all had changed and that he could never go back to who he was.

We talked that night until light came into the valley. I asked him did he wish he hadn't killed Corporal Nealey.

No, he said. I don't wish that. But I wish he could have married Alice Paulson.

You can't have both, I said.

It's like that, he said.

You will read the rest of what he said. When he felt he'd said enough we went up the bank to his house where he led me along a corridor to an army cot in the corner of his studio and said good night. I looked at my phone. 5.53 a.m. They're in bed in Bough and

36

New York and here in the Labourd. But I was disturbed and alert in a way I had no precedent for. A stranger was rewriting my life. I hung my jacket on the back of a chair. I checked the Dictaphone to see that it had recorded. I walked around his room, a room more extreme than this one where I am now, he'd written and drawn right onto walls, quotes, faces, exhortations. There were stacks of canvases, clots of paint, photographs of street scenes and demonstrations, postcards, notes, drawings and bills all over the floor and desk and hanging out of drawers. It was like a mind turned inside out. I poked and inspected. I took photographs. I felt entitled because he knew more about my own family than I did.

I lay down on the cot. Light spilled in through the windows. Sleep was distant. On a shelf beside my head was a row of books and papers and magazines set at odd angles. One was a gun magazine. I saw through a gap that there were more things behind – piles of photographs, a mug filled with nails and three envelopes bound with twine. I lifted out the envelopes. They were coated with dust. A web trailed from a corner. Across the top was written 'San Francisco'. I untied the twine. They weren't sealed. Inside were relics from his life. I began to read . . .

There was a moment just after I met him in the gallery when I arrived at what seemed a fork in a road, something I could not see but sensed, a high road to the left, smooth and gleaming and climate-controlled like a great marble transit hall in an airport leading back to you and Lydia and my tenured, award-strewn career, and to the right a way down, a darkness, a portal at the end. I was ready for the high road, I had the ticket, my bag was on my shoulder, my hand about to extend in fare-well. But I stayed. I felt a pull, a command to go down before I could rise, back before forward.

He was the catalyst. It didn't have to be him, but it happened that it was. He had no intent, or even awareness of what he had set in motion. The more I learned about him the more precipitous became my descent. At times it was exhilarating.

But it came at a price, to you above all, who did nothing to bring it about. I am sorry for this, Erica. I have been following something. I've followed him into the truths and fictions of my past because I thought he would show them to me, but I found something else, something I didn't expect – his struggle against greater odds to do something I might have done had I not thrown it away. He made things, he risked. He didn't flinch, even when he might have wished to.

It played out in San Francisco in the summer of 2009, with and through the people around him there – his friend Alexis, the girl Nicky and an investment banker named Paul Crane. I went looking for them, I met them, the story came up before my eyes. These people were like none we've ever met. I followed the story. It was all I could see. It seemed there was something at its heart I must discover. I will try to bring it to you. Maybe it's too late. Maybe I've lost you. I don't know. That's for you.

I will leave you now. I've written through the night. Taxi horns far below blare like a flock of geese. You know how these sounds arrive to the twenty-fifth floor. I can't think any more. I'll lie down and then start again later. All that you read from now will have already happened. I'll go on until I finish and send it to you in the hope . . .

I woke in his studio being licked by the caramel dog. A woman came in, black hair tumbling down, the red of apples in her cheeks. She wore baker's whites. There was a dusting of flour in her hair. *Désolée*, she said, then, *Moi, c'est Juliette*, as she led the dog away.

How like him never to have mentioned her, I thought.

I rose, I dressed. I could hear them in the kitchen. A radio, soft murmuring. The clink of delft. I walked along the corridor and stepped to the door. I saw a table laid out with pots of jam, wild flowers, a baguette. They were by the window. Her face was lifted to his and he was taking something out of her eye.

We sat down to have breakfast. We spoke in French, the conversation innocuous. He put in a call for a car to take me to San Sebastián for my flight. I could see that there was more of him now, he was more present, his eyes alive to a higher degree. It was as if during the night with me he had been playing within his range and the stakes were greater now that she was there. She went to a counter to pour coffee for herself at one point. I happened to look up. I'd been too shot to really notice her before, but now suddenly I did. I saw the light in her eyes, her self-possession. She seemed almost too much for the room. You know, you've seen it in yourself, how an idea, or a piece of art, or a person, can move out from where they have been misplaced and in a moment be realised. I saw her, as she walked back towards us, becoming herself, right there in front of us, waking to it, feeling the pleasure of being a woman and the effect she could produce just by being herself. He would have to rise with her to hold her there. The baker Juliette.

The taxi arrived. I went to the studio to get my bag. I rolled up my suit, stuffed it in and closed the latch. Then I saw the three envelopes on the floor beside the cot. I heard the taxi's engine running. I leaned down to pick them up, but instead of putting them back behind the books as I intended to do I opened my bag and buried them under my clothes. Then I saw on his desk a disc marked 'Drawings and paintings'. I put that in my bag too, and left the room.

He was waiting outside in the drive. We shook hands and I got into the car. As it pulled away he tapped on the roof, smiled and said, Good luck. I watched him through the rising dust, his hands in the pockets of his jeans. That was the last I ever saw of him.

We headed up into the hills towards Spain. I leaned back into the seat and watched the spectacle. The theft was for me a salient act, grossly transgressive, unforgivable, like broad-daylight plagiarism conducted in the Academy. It made me intensely uneasy. But there was something bracing in it too, like a blast of sea spray taken on the prow of a boat. The exhilarating taste of lawlessness. A portent of things to come . . .

I kept it at bay, as I had schooled myself to do. I could think of it later, if think of it I must. Somewhere over the Atlantic, with a business-class upgrade and a nice nap, it began to ease. It was springtime in New York. Lydia threw her arms around my neck. I put the envelopes and disc into a drawer and went to bed with you. Summer was on the way.

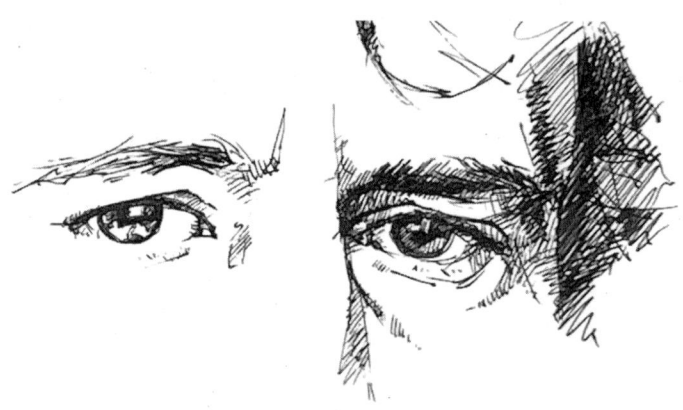

PART I

War

CHAPTER ONE

The Russian Priest

Belfast, 1971–82

The boy opened his eyes. He didn't know how long he'd been asleep, seconds, minutes, maybe even an hour. He was too young to have an accurate sense of the passage of time. But he knew, nevertheless, that he had this lack. He was in the back yard of his house on a hot July afternoon, his back to the wall and his legs stretched out before him. The air over the ground rippled in the heat.

The street door had slammed. That was what had awakened him, he now realised. He had dreamed something, but what? He tried to chase an image but couldn't get it. He heard the footsteps of his father move through the house. What a scorcher! said his father through the kitchen window, then pulled his head back in again.

The boy looked along the yard to the end wall. He saw a white cat stretched out there on the ledge, his hind quarters in the sun and his head in the shade made by the shed. The boy rose to move away, but a heaviness in his legs kept him there. He slumped back against the wall. There was no wind. The boy heard the woman in the house next door singing along to the radio. He watched the cat. He watched the way the light came off its fur in a different way as it breathed. After a while the cat got up, stretched, turned around and lay down again, its head resting on its paws, the line of the shadow bisecting its face. The sun bothered it and it closed its eyes. The boy narrowed his eyes too and when he did the lines that defined the cat became indistinct, the light splintering into bands of colour. He opened them and closed them. He leaned a little to his right, then to his left. He could, he believed, go on doing this through the whole of the afternoon.

Each time it was a different cat.

When he was nine his father's hair began to fall. It came out in clumps, like grass in a drought. He was forty-one years old when the illness came to him. In his time he'd boxed for Belfast. He'd been to Berlin and Paris. A boxer moving down stairs would be like water flowing over rocks, he'd told his sons. A trainer had showed him how to stand, watch, move. The father let the boys pound the solid plane of his torso. He could catch their punches in his fist as if they were slow-moving flies. Now the boy heard him vomiting in the night. He watched him sit in a chair growing yellow and weak.

They lived in the Ballymurphy Road in West Belfast in a small house at the end of a terrace. There were nine of them there, with his parents and his grandmother. He was the fourth of the children, and slept in an upstairs room with his three brothers. At times the house seemed like the weaving machines he'd seen in the linen mills – all moving parts and noise, his brothers practising football moves, his sisters fighting over the radio, his grandmother saying prayers under a blanket on the sofa, his mother pulling her coat on as she ran out the door to her cleaning job. All the doors of the house were forever emptying and filling, like the gaps through which the needles of the machines passed as they weaved. The others wondered about the boy's stillness and his silence.

Are you depressed? his sisters asked, then smirked.

He didn't understand the reason for the question. He was never depressed.

Each morning he collected Ambrose McGuigan, who was a year younger than him, from the house next door, and walked with him to school. Ambrose bounced a golf ball out in front of him all the way and told stories from comic books that had been sent to him from a pen pal in America. Above them they could hear the fluttering of military helicopters like the panting of a dog after running. The first drawings the boy made were of the heroes in these books, faces at the beginning, then of figures rappelling down skyscrapers, flipping over cars, flying over buildings with girls in their arms.

Christ! said his father one time as he passed behind him. He looks like he's about to fly into the house!

When he finished them he pushed them in through Ambrose's letterbox and Ambrose taped them in a line to the wall of his room.

The boy drew as naturally as he walked. Drawing had a rhythm to it. He had no objective. He drew what he saw or remembered and didn't think, at least not at first. He drew over his mistakes when he was small, then erased them and tried again when he was a little older. In time he came to doubt what he did, to make harsh judgements, but he survived this and kept drawing. He drew spaceships at war, Egyptian gods, insects. When he finished a drawing he didn't look at it again. He didn't want to think of what he had made. To think was to question, and he didn't like the feeling this gave him, at least not then. He only liked to do it.

At night he sat on the window ledge of his room and looked out while his brothers slept. The walls of his room were full of posters, schoolbooks, pegs with coats on them. Nearly everything there belonged to his brothers. The window, though, was his space, and the night his time. He looked out over walls and chimney pots. Beyond them, the dark silhouettes of the mills, the observation towers of the British and the rolls of barbed wire on the barracks walls. He saw the weak yellow glow of the lights from the centre of the city where none of them ever went. He listened to the sounds of the night. They each came to him singly, as if framed in their own moment – a breaking bottle, the howl of a cat, running feet, a rifle shot, songs of men going home from the pub. When he sat in the window in the night he felt the world outside and also the way it arrived to him, the way his senses took it in and the way his thoughts moved. Nothing like this ever happened in daylight. It was as though he was meeting himself for the first time.

His father went to the hospital for his treatments, then came back home and lay in the shadows. They all moved around him as if he were no longer there. As a boxer he had won thirty-eight fights and lost four. He never turned pro because he married at nineteen and found a job driving a bread van. In time as the disease progressed and he lost more hair and his body shrank the boy thought he looked more like a baby than a man. But that was later. One time when his father could still walk, when he could still feel anger and pain, the boy looked down from his room into the yard, where he saw his father drive his head over and over into the wall. Blood ran down the bricks.

In the days of his life the streets could fill suddenly with people and chaos spread like a flame touched to paper. When it was over there would be broken glass and burning buses and people walking with handkerchiefs to their brows to staunch the flow of blood. Clouds of yellow smoke, angry faces, single shoes left behind. The boy watched from his window or as he moved through the streets. He saw more barracks and watchtowers go up, slogans about the dead appear on walls, men with masks run in the shadows. Sometimes the tension was so concentrated that it seemed the whole of the city was being squeezed in a vice. These things had been there for as long as he could remember. They were like rain or his father's anger. He did not question them. Only one thing made him wonder – when boys with rocks in their hands ran at armoured cars or when a man refused to move for a soldier who was screaming at him, why were they without fear?

The boy heard a melody in the night. He was sitting in the window of his room after midnight watching snow fall. The melody was slow, the playing soft, the sound like nothing he'd heard before, long, long notes like those made by a singer, some cries, some whispers. But the sound was not made by a singer.

The boy opened the window and felt the cold air move over him and into the room. The snow fell as feathers do on this night without wind, then sparkled in the spheres of light made by the streetlamps. The colours of the city – beige, slate, rust – and the lines which separated things were vanquished by the snow. Everything now was white, indefinite. It was as if clouds had come down and lay on the city. There was no sound but the melody. It seemed to slip through the falling snow. It was more like speech than music.

The boy closed the window and put his clothes on over his pyjamas. He took his coat from a peg downstairs and went out the back door into the yard. Everyone in the house, it seemed, was asleep. He stood still in the yard and let the snow fall over him. He realised that he'd never before been out so late at night. It was as if midnight were a frontier he had crossed for the first time. The music which he had heard faintly from his room now filled all the space he could sense around him. There was nothing else there, just darkness, silence. It was as if the people were not asleep, but rather absent. There was only him and the music and the falling snow in this place that was no longer Ballymurphy, or Ireland, or anywhere else known to him.

He climbed over the wall into the McGuigans' yard and then over fences and around hedges, moving towards the music. As he grew nearer to it he could hear that in it there were two sounds, one like a long, groaning breath or rolling thunder, dying away and then finding life again, the other made of notes that dived and slithered and flew over the first sound. Sometimes the notes trembled before they faded. The night was cold and fresh and alive, the snow soft and light, the sky dark and vast. He felt he could go anywhere he wanted, out beyond the limits of the city to places unknown to him. He felt also the strangeness and the freedom of this. All this, he found, was in the music. It was as if the music described this rare night and him moving through it.

He went over walls, hedges, sheds and along alleyways, the snow falling down under his collar. Years later he would do this again, blood dropping onto the snow from a wound in his leg. When he did he would remember this night when he went looking for the music. He came finally to the last wall. On the other side was the sound he had been following. It was tremendous now, like an organ in a church. He felt it moving through the ground. He put his foot on a bucket and lifted himself up onto the wall.

He seemed to be looking then into an abandoned place, missing panes in the windows of the dark house patched with cardboard, in the yard the shapes of tyres, washing machines, engines, lengths of wood under the snow. An old man in an overcoat sat on a stool, playing the uilleann pipes. The boy watched his long fingers slide over the chanter. The man's feet were covered with snow, his body rocked back and forth and his head dived like a swooping bird as he brought out the notes of his music. No one but the boy was there to hear him. Sometimes the man made a sound as if he were trying to lift a weight. The music rumbled in the ground, pierced and shook in the air. To the boy, it seemed that it was made inside the man, passed out through his hands and then moved towards and into him. It seemed to be explaining something to him.

Finally the man ended the tune with a bow of his head and leaned back and lit a cigarette. He saw the boy propped on the wall and looking at him.

Hello, lad, he said.

Hello, said the boy.

Do you like music?

The boy thought, then said, I don't know.

Do you like my music?

The boy thought some more, then smiled.

Yeah.

Well, good. I'm glad. What do you like about it?

It's like this night, said the boy.

He surprised himself when he said this.

That's it! said the man. That's it!

He got up from his stool and ran over to the wall where the boy was. The boy could see his face now, his uncombed hair, his liver spots, the patches of white bristle where his razor had missed. His skin sagged and it looked like no one cared for him, but his blue eyes were bright and young. He put his hands on the wall and looked up at the boy.

What about this night, lad? he said softly.

The boy wanted to tell him for he could see that the man needed something from him, but he didn't know how to explain it.

I don't know, he said.

The man laughed and went back through the snow and the objects of the yard to the stool where he had been sitting.

Don't worry about it, lad, he said. It's all right. I get you. I caught that tune out there in the night air and brought it here into the yard and played it. Just like that. You came to listen. So now you'll want to be going home for you'd be tired, and I'll stay here and play you something for company on the road.

The man put the pipes around him and began again to play. This was a different kind of tune, as light and easy as birdsong. The man's cigarette was burning in the corner of his mouth and he had to tilt his head to keep the smoke from going up into his eye. Sometimes he laughed, as though he was finding jokes as he played the notes.

The boy got down off the wall and began to walk towards home. He listened to the tune as he made his way back over the walls, the notes seeming to sparkle and float like bubbles rising through water. He laughed sometimes too, but it was about the man he'd met rather than his music. Maybe not even the man, but the idea of the man, the way he'd picked that music out of the air and brought it out of himself as he moved his fingers over the instrument. The boy felt light and clear and alive and as though he were moving towards some new place where he wanted to be, this place where such things could happen. What he might do if ever he got there, though, he could not say.

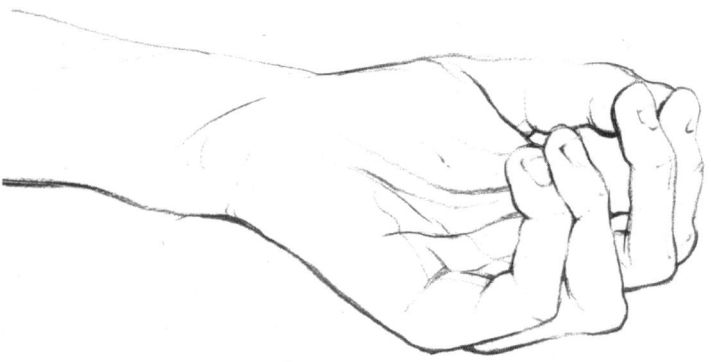

That same winter the boy's mother brought from a house where she cleaned a pile of history of art magazines and left them for him. He had drawn for years but did not know what art was. He sat by his window and looked at the reproductions in the magazines. He saw elongated necks, blue faces, whirling skies, flying brides and a donkey dressed as a priest. He saw light made of pinks and greens, he saw wars, typhoons, saintly ascents and faces that showed defeat, defiance, serenity or desire, sometimes more than one of these at once. The faces seemed more present to him than those he saw in the city, the pictures together arrived as a chorus speaking directly to him. They intrigued and invited him as the piper's music had done. He tried to make copies on sheets of paper with coloured pencils. He changed sizes and positions to see the effect. How did the painters see what others couldn't? How could they show him things about himself that he did not yet know?

In a shoebox in their attic the boy found a photograph of his father in the ring. In it his father's left hand was up around his eye and his right was swinging towards the side of the head of the other fighter. This was a punch that was about to connect, for the boy could see that there was nothing that could stop it. Lines of muscle ran up the right side of his father's body like braided hair, as leg, hip and shoulder turned with the punch towards its target. His eyes were open, his expression calm but alert, as though he were reading a note left on a door. Men sat in chairs around the ring, their faces lit. They looked worried or expectant or distracted, their hair slicked and parted, some in suits and others in shirtsleeves and all from a time unreachable by the boy. A flashgun on a camera braced on the ring floor blazed. On the back of the photograph was written 'Liverpool, 1948'.

The boy took the photograph down to his room and put it in a pocket of his jacket. In the next days he watched his father cross the room, stare at the television, lift food to his mouth, and tried to see what remained of the boxer in his face. He wanted to see more than he found, but still he saw something.

He took the photograph, some paper and a pencil and brought them to the Falls Road library. He wanted to make a drawing for him, but he didn't want anyone to know he was doing it. He would not include the ring, the crowd around it, the referee or even the lower halves of the two fighters' bodies. He would make the drawing as if it were a close-up photograph, just the taut swinging arm and shoulder, his father's clear and focused eyes, the helplessness of his opponent.

All day he worked at it. Some of it was there – muscles, hair, ear, the gleam of the glove, the feeling of movement. But not his father. And the neck was bad. He couldn't get it right. Finally he gave up and threw it away. When he went to put the box of photographs back in the attic a chair gave way beneath him and he tumbled down, knocking a piece from his front tooth.

The boy turned into the Ballymurphy Road carrying the bag of sugar his mother had sent him for. The street was quiet, as a flock of birds are before taking flight. The boy, though, sensed nothing of what was about to happen. He was thinking about a song, bobbing a little to its rhythm as he walked. He was watching the shapes made by the white clouds being blown by the wind high above Cave Hill away in the distance.

Six Saracens entered the street just as he arrived at his house. He stepped through the door and closed it. He heard the soldiers come out of their vehicles. He heard their radios and shouts and boots on the pavement as they ran. A door was kicked in. A woman screamed.

He ran upstairs to his sisters' room. He sat on the floor and looked out into the street through the legs of the row of dolls they had put in the window. He saw the soldiers push two men into the back of a Saracen. He saw them kneeling on the ground with their rifles up, looking through their telescopic sights. He saw four of them run through the door of the Doherty house just across the street from where he was. He could see the soldiers but none of them could see him. If they looked up they would just see the smiling dolls in their miniskirts lined up like girls in front of a stage at a pop concert. Later he would remember the cover they gave him, the dolls' look of innocence.

A soldier had been shot in Ardmonagh Gardens the day before. It was a single shot from a roof or window – they couldn't tell for sure, the radio had said. Just afterwards a dark green Ford Escort had come out of Norglen Parade at speed and disappeared down the Spring-field Road. Mr Doherty had a green Ford Escort. It was parked there in front of his house. He worked nights as a porter in the Royal Victoria Hospital. Everyone in Ballymurphy knew him because he could do tricks with cards.

The boy saw two soldiers pull Mr Doherty out through the door by his arms and into the street. He was barefoot and was naked to the waist. They brought him around to where their vehicles were parked. One soldier let go of Mr Doherty's arm, moved over to the side of the road and spoke into his radio. The other walked Mr Doherty around to the back of the Saracen. He was doing something the boy couldn't see. He stood up in the window. He saw then that the second soldier had one hand on Mr Doherty's shoulder and with the other making a fist in his hair was smashing his face into the back of the Saracen. He saw the pulped nose, the mess of red and white like a skinned animal and heard the dull, heavy sound of each impact. The soldier's helmet was obscuring his face so that the boy couldn't see his expression, but his right foot was braced behind him like his father's was in the photograph of the punch he threw in Liverpool. The boy dropped to the floor and sat back against the wall. He had to breathe fast because he thought he might get sick. He kept hearing the sound, like a melon breaking on stone, or his father's forehead hitting the wall of their house, or a punch that connected, bone on bone.

When the ten men were dying of hunger in the prison blocks the noise of the city was like a hurricane. Bin lids banged in the road in the night, shouts rose up, shots went off and bombs exploding in the distance shook the windows of the boy's house. Armoured vehicles moved through the city like parade floats with soldiers firing at cars, people, windows with their lights on.

His father held on until the boy was seventeen. He was brought into the hospital weighing six stone and stayed there in silence for the last three months of his life. He was without hair, his eyes glassy and untroubled, laid out on the bed like a strip of gauze. They buried him in Milltown Cemetery on a morning when sirens wailed and boys in masks ran down the Falls Road ahead of soldiers firing plastic bullets and carrying shields. They couldn't hear the priest. In the city then the people could think of nothing other than the city itself.

There is no place here, he thought, that is not a jail.

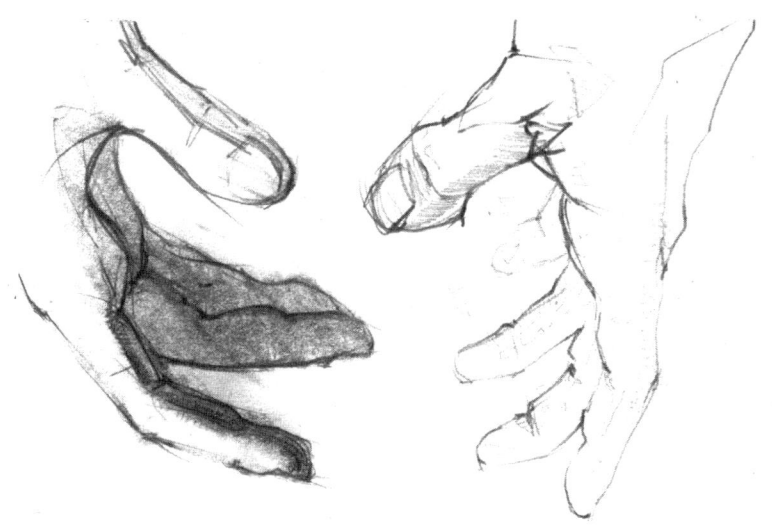

This was the time when the walls of his part of the city began to be covered with paint. Rifles, testimonials from the dead, women with fists upraised, the smiling poet with long hair who had died in the blocks. There were colours and faces from Africa, greens and deep browns, ochres and reds from the tribes of the American plains. He walked among the pictures, wondering who had made them.

One morning early then, in a cul-de-sac in Springhill, he saw a small man on a ladder painting a phoenix onto a gable wall. In the upper right white paint had exploded over the tip of a wing and then dribbled in streams down the length of the wall.

Who did that? he asked the man.

Brits, he said. They threw a milk bottle full of paint at it.

Don't you mind?

Mind? That's what I do it for. Annoys the fuck out of them.

The man leaned back and looked at the wall.

It's part of the picture now, he said. Don't you think?

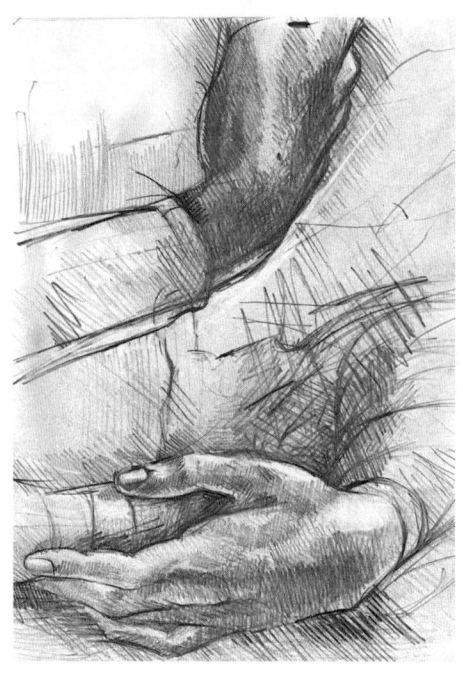

In the photograph an Orthodox priest from a village on the Black Sea looked up from a book and into the camera lens. Of all the photographs in the magazine that his mother brought home that week, this was the one that drew his attention. The priest wore a beard and a clerical hat of a life ancient and far from his own. But there was something in his eyes that was vivid and present and familiar to him in a way he couldn't place. Was the priest annoyed at the photographer's interruption, taken by surprise, still mournful or held by what he had just read? He didn't know. He knew only that he felt an intimacy with this picture, that he must enter it somehow, and that in this moment it was more real to him than the doors and walls of his house or the streets outside or even the people moving through them. Perhaps this was not about the priest, but rather about his way of looking at him. He saw dimensions he had not seen before, complexity, shadows, structure.

The priest had a look of intelligence but also of otherworldliness that was not alien to him, though he didn't know the distinguishing features of intelligence or otherworldliness. The photograph and the thinking of making a drawing of it were showing him what they were. He saw the drawing, and the way it could be done.

He tore off the page the photograph was on and brought it, the magazine, paper and a pencil out through the front door and into the light. He sat down then with his back to the wall, the magazine and the blank paper on top of it braced against his legs. Everything in this picture he imagined he would make spun around and faded from the eyes, and he began with them, turning them down in the corners, letting the irises float up under the priest's lids, smudging the pencil markings with a finger for depth. He drew brows, crossed lashes, shaded the cornea for the effect of roundness. He watched the eyes come alive under his hand. The work was quick, rhythmical, unceasing. He knew where he was going. He had no awareness of time or place.

Then he heard the bouncing golf ball of Ambrose. Ambrose on a diet of sausages and chocolate bars now rolled more than walked, the fat of his torso packed into his T-shirt like sand in a sack, his breathing in the heat already laboured. He had black curly hair, pink cheeks, glasses inclined to fog and nearly always a wide, wet, toothy smile that seemed pleased by a joke that he believed would have to please anyone who heard it. Ambrose waved at him and he waved back. He was carrying a cake his mother had made over to his aunt on the other side of the street, bouncing the ball as he walked.

When he looked beyond Ambrose he could see that while he was drawing the eyes of the priest three Saracens had dropped foot patrols at different positions along the street. He looked through the window of his house at the clock on the living-room wall. 2.35, it said. The soldiers walked with slow, silent steps, crouched a little, rifles up. No one else was there, bar Ambrose and a man in his vest clipping a hedge. The sky and the things of the street were indistinct in the hazy air. There was no wind, no sound. He looked at the page with the priest's eyes and then back at the street. The soldiers were vague and distant but somehow gigantic next to the cars and houses, which seemed to have shrunk since he looked at them last. He felt as if he were watching a puppet show.

When Ambrose stepped off the pavement into the street a soldier stopped him. Ambrose put his golf ball in his pocket and the cake on the ground. He watched as the soldier spoke and Ambrose answered. Ambrose pointed back at his house and then again across the street to the house of his aunt. The soldier wrote things in his notebook, then pointed to the ground and said something. Ambrose sat on the pavement and took off his shoes and socks. The soldier gestured with his rifle for him to stand up again, and then for him to lift his shirt. His white fat fell out from his shirt and settled over his hips. The soldier walked slowly around him, then searched up the legs of his jeans. Finally he stepped away. Ambrose pulled his shirt down, put on his shoes.

He saw Ambrose's cousin look out through the curtains and into the street. The door opened and his aunt came out onto the step, holding her housecoat closed at the neck. The man down the street stopped clipping his hedge. The soldiers moved in lines and arcs and without destinations, silent, predatory, tense.

Ambrose stepped forward and began again to walk, but was stopped in the middle of the street by a second soldier. Again the questions, the notebook, the pointing at the houses, the removal of shoes. When Ambrose lifted his shirt up to his neck the soldier folded his arms and stared at him for a while. Then he held up the middle finger of his right hand and slowly buried it in the wide ring of fat hanging over Ambrose's jeans, as if giving him an injection. When he took it out again he said something to the soldiers on his patrol. There was a short burst of laughter, like radio static turned on, then off.

Ambrose put his shoes back on, picked up the cake, squeezed the golf ball in his pocket. He stepped forward, but when he got to the pavement at the other side of the street a third soldier came around from behind him and cut him off. His aunt had gone forward to meet him but then moved back into the shadows. The clock on the living-room wall said 3.10. The third soldier put his face close to Ambrose's and shouted rather than spoke. He pushed him to the pavement when he wanted him to take off his shoes, then pulled him up again by the hair. When Ambrose lifted his shirt everyone in the street could see red blotches like islands in an atoll running up his chest to his neck. He was breathing as if he'd been running up a hill. The soldier went around behind him, put his hand around Ambrose's scrotum and squeezed, a kind of spasm moving up from the soldier's boots to his head, then hissed something into Ambrose's ear. Ambrose seemed to implode, his shoulders moving in, his body suddenly limp like a shot animal, then dropped to his hands and knees. When he finally got through the door of his aunt's house it was 3.24. It had taken him forty-nine minutes to cross the road.

The thought came to him that one day maybe he and Ambrose and Mr Doherty and others in the houses around them might become the ones who would be asking the questions. But it didn't stay at the time. He looked at what he had so far made of the drawing of the priest. Then he packed everything up and went inside.

Later, in the evening, he saw Ambrose in the kitchen of his house and called him to the wall.

Are you all right? he asked.

Yeah. Hurt like fuck though.

What did he say to you?

He said the streets were theirs.

Anything else?

Just 'Fenian cunt'. I couldn't get it at first. It was like that accent they have on *Coronation Street*, only worse.

In the dark, he put the drawing through Ambrose's letterbox.

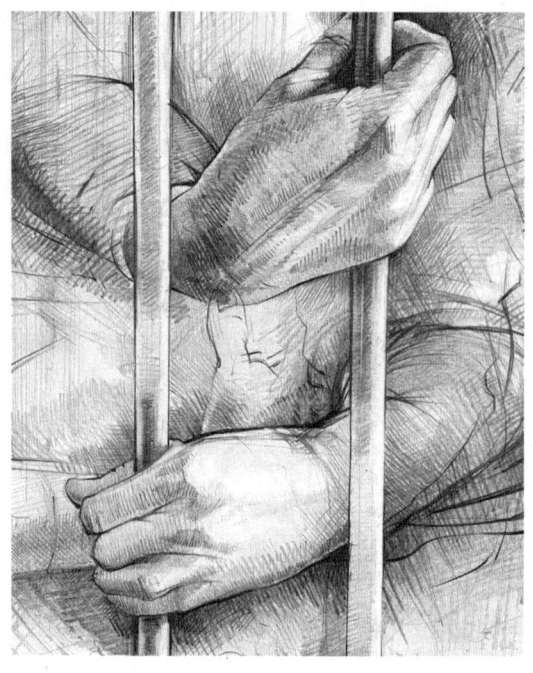

He drew his picture of the Russian priest that night on the kitchen table after everyone had gone to bed. His hand moved over the eyes, drawing them again in the air as if to catch the rhythm that had made them. Then he let his hand fall to the page. He put some tone on the lids, some texture in the irises. When he thought the eyes were finished he watched them for a while. He saw that the two halves of each eye were not symmetrical. They hadn't the almond shape he'd always used in the past. He hadn't tried to do it that way this time, but it pleased him nevertheless. Then as he watched a little more the idea came to him from somewhere he was not looking to let a shadow fall over the priest's left eye, to soften and deepen it. He put it there, light as breath. He'd never done that before. When he saw the effect he felt something move within him, a passing adrenaline wave like leaves stirred by a sudden wind. It was the recognition that he'd done something just beyond his reach. But he didn't stop to think about it. He dropped down the page and made a nose, a half-circle for a lower lip, a beard, a hat. He made a glimmer of light play on the moustache. These things were arriving from somewhere. He wondered would they continue. Then he could see that there was nothing more to do. This too was new. He looked at the drawing. It was awkward in places, he could see that, the eyes a little too closely set, the brow too brief, the features floating free of one another. But it was not borrowed, nor was it a thing merely of an adept child. It was his. And it was a man, or on the way to being a man.

The drawing of the priest stayed on Ambrose's wall until he took a job in Southampton in England serving drinks on a ferry. Ambrose's mother cleared out his room and put it in a box along with other drawings he had collected and stored it in her hot press. There was a time when she and others in the street thought that he who had made the drawings was dead, and they became solemn about them. But Ambrose knew otherwise and let her know. When her husband died and she moved to Athlone to be with her sister the drawings came back to Ambrose. He kept them until news he received twenty-five years later led him to post them to a schoolhouse in the Labourd.

By then the boy artist had become Niall Dempsey. He was surprised when he opened the package and saw the drawings, particularly the drawing of the priest. He knew more about drawing now, about how a face is not an oval line but rather a structure made from a skull, and about how features are not individual things to be made one by one but are rather part of an inter-relating system of shade and light. The drawing was a declaration of his ignorance of this. But it surprised him, nevertheless. He was surprised by the drawing's ambition and authority, however frail, but even more by what he saw in its lines, its occasional messiness, the smears, the scribbled cross-hatching in beard and hair, for this was how he still did it. These things had been found then and stayed, in the way that a gesture or expression or manner of making a stride of a small child can move forward through time and on into old age.

I found the drawing of the priest leaning against a blue ceramic bowl in his studio. I photographed it there. For now, it is here with me, on a window ledge overlooking Hell's Kitchen.

He'd gone up to the City Cemetery at noon. A hole had been blown through a wall there by a rocket, and twelve of them sat in the rubble under the trees. Eight lads, four girls. They talked of dance moves, the cities of Europe, haunted rooms, country accents, rioting, memorable kisses. He told them the story of the forty-nine minutes it had taken Ambrose to cross their road. They walked along the Whiterock Road after in a straggling line, diminishing as they turned into their streets. The sky broke open and the city flooded with light. Deirdre

Blaney was one of the last to go. He watched her talk to a neighbour's child in the shadow of a van, then walk on into a radiant pool of yellow-orange, her long stride like the swing of a pendulum in a clock.

He'd have an alertness later about the emptiness of rooms and buildings, something acute and instinctive like another sense, and he felt it for the first time on this Saturday afternoon just five days after he turned eighteen when he went through the door of his house. Always before he'd met noise. Radios, shrieks, hairdryers, disputes, whistling kettles. Now there was silence. He stepped lightly through the door. He saw a magazine left open on the sofa, a cardigan hanging from a door handle, a half-eaten sandwich. It was as if they'd all left at once, on command.

There'd been a time when everyone knew where everyone was, the house a hub to which they were all attached by strings. Now they were older, more disparate, the house beginning to break up. Of the nine who had been there through the years, four were gone, his father and grandmother dead, a brother away on an oil rig and his sister Maire training to be a nurse in Newry. Still, he wasn't used to this. Had he ever been alone here? He thought not. At least he had no memory that he had. He looked around. Pink nylon hydrangeas in a lacquered vase, a plaster bull with straw hat from Torremolinos, a photograph of his brother Martin, solemn and pious in altar boy robes but with a lick of hair standing up at the back stiff as a playing card. It was as if he'd been let into a museum after hours.

He went up the stairs. At the top, one platform shoe on its side and a string of beads on a banister. He saw the faint impress of his mother's form on her bedspread, the wall his sister had painted black. Why did what he saw each day suddenly look so strange, so inert and prominent as if framed and put on display by the silence? They were becoming stark and fossilised in his memory as he looked at them. He heard the calls of children in the street outside, a television voice conducting a quiz rising like a plume of smoke into the atmosphere. The things of the house seemed to pass from his eyes and fingertips into his memory as if through a fold in the air. He looked into his room at clothes, banners, postcards that seemed old and redundant, at the window he'd sat by in the night. He hadn't done that for years. He remembered a little of how he'd felt, but it was vague, far away.

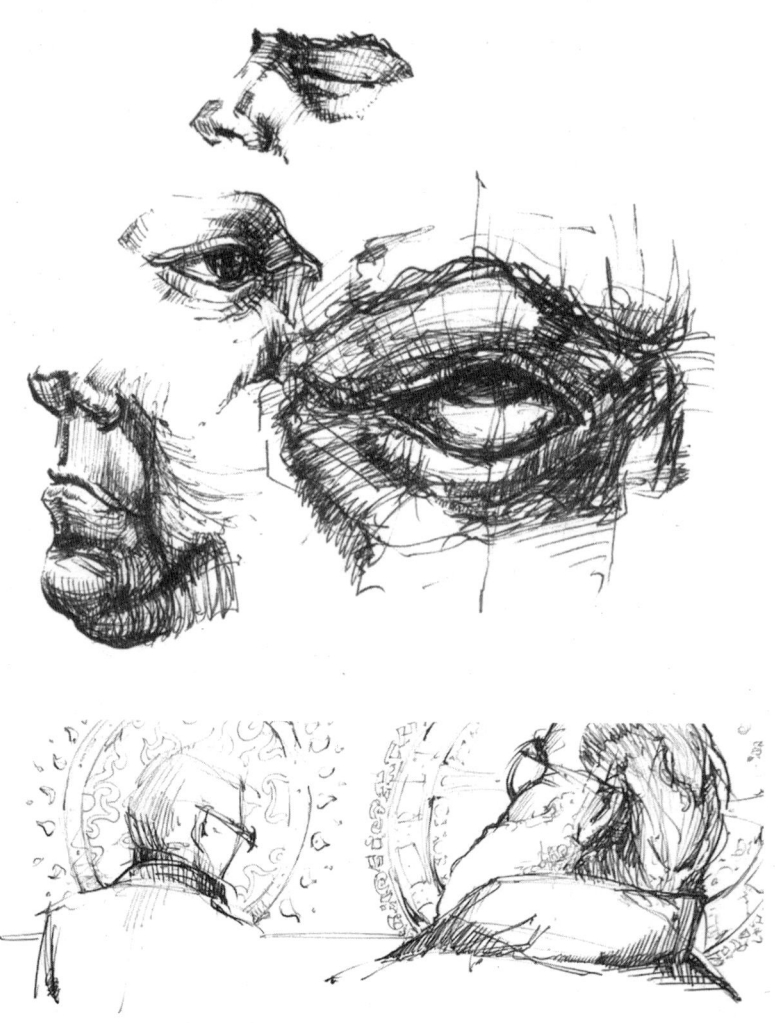

He sat in the grass of the Hatchet Field with his sister Maire. She'd called him from Newry during the week and made him promise her the time.

Just the two of us, she'd said.

Right, he'd said.

I've already turned down Jimmy Crowley for you, she'd said.

Who's that?

Disco prince of Turf Lodge, she'd said.

Oh, he'd said.

Plus he's got a car.

Right, he'd said.

When she'd got to Belfast that morning they'd made sandwiches and a flask of tea and went up the Whiterock lonan to the Black Mountain without telling anyone where they were headed.

From the Hatchet Field you can see from Slieve Donard over to Carrickfergus and in the east over the water all the way to the Mull of Kintyre, if the day is clear. Stormont ghostly amid the trees of the Castlereagh Hills, the city itself on its plain like a single coin set down on a plate. On this day it throbbed a little under a summer haze.

What's it look like to you? he asked her.

Small. Grubby.

Come on.

I don't miss it, she said.

And Newry's like Tokyo.

I know what size Newry is, you big eejit.

She threw a clump of grass at him.

But it doesn't *pretend* to be anything else. That's the difference. It's just a wee country town, with country people. There's this nurse I work with. Patsy she's called. Grew up with cows until they moved into the town. She's got a little brother named Jackie. Can't get the country out of him, she says. Not that they try. Anyway, we saw him go out the road with a fishing rod from a window in the ward. Then we saw him come back five hours later. Patsy called out to him, 'Did'ya catch anythin', Jackie?' 'Eight!' he yelled back. You'd think it was a wonder of the world, his eyes popping out, jaw hanging loose, fingers up to show the number. His teeth are the size of stamps, I swear. 'Aren't you hungry, Jackie?' I said to him. He set down his rod and bag, put his hands on his hips and said, 'I could ate the road to Belfast, and it twistin' and turnin'!'

Right before his eyes she became an old farmer, or a boy imitating one. He laughed freely, and she was pleased.

You're sound, Maire, he said. I don't know when it happened. I remember you sitting on the sofa with Granny, looking as cross as her. You had the mumps. You were around four years old. Now here you are all of a sudden. I was in the Green Briar for a pint last weekend and saw you dancing. It was really something. You were faster than the beams from the glitter ball. Where did you get that from?

I love dancing, she said. I'd do it all day if I was let.

Do they let you in Newry?

Newry's hopping, I tell you.

Right, he said.

Snob. Anyway, makes West Belfast look like a funeral home.

They looked down the hill.

Aye, he said.

They lay down in the grass, watching the clouds blow over them. She sang 'A Bunch of Thyme', then they ate the last of the sandwiches.

What are you going to do? he asked.

With my life?

With your weekend.

I'm going to hang around you.

There won't be much dancing, he said.

I'll manage.

And your life?

Nursing's good, she said. Except for changing bandages. But you can do it anywhere, almost. That's why I went into it.

She sat up and leaned over him.

I just want to take off and keep going, see it all, she said. Don't you? I'm like that wee Jackie, I look at a map and I just want to eat it all up.

He got up onto his elbows and looked at her for a while. He saw the breeze blow through the loose waves of her long blonde hair, the readiness in her eyes. He kept looking at her until he got it.

Let's go down, he said then.

They went through heather and grass, around hedges and over gates, past fields with cows and goats. Around them the smells of silage and tractor diesel, the sounds of birdsong and the light wind. The tinkling of the bells around the goats' necks seemed to him like devotions in a monastery. Maire stepped around the stones and clumps of heather with her hands up at shoulder height for balance. They gained the path then and she took his arm. They went down easily, in silence, then 'A Bunch of Thyme' came back and he whistled it. She liked that and squeezed his arm. Somewhere they crossed an invisible frontier of sound. There were the distant radios, the calls of children in narrow yards, a humming bassline of engines and tyres moving over the roads. Behind them in the barracks beside Dermot Hill a landing helicopter caused a gale in the trees and threw up clouds of dust.

They stepped from the path onto the Springfield Road and were again in the tarmac and concrete and brick of the city, resolute, impenetrable, the shadows hard-edged, the low sun catching fragments of broken glass in the wastelands. A foot patrol moved towards them in the silent crouch of formal wariness. One by one the soldiers stopped and tracked them through their telescopic sights. They walked along and through them as if they weren't there. They crossed onto the Whiterock Road. He felt they were smaller here than up on the hill. Strange that, with so much space there, the sky so vast above them.

Somewhere here he told her he wanted to show her a book of the drawings of Auguste Rodin he'd got from the library.

I want you to tell me what you see in them.

OK, she said. Then you'll take me dancing.

She slid forward on one foot, her whole torso rippling like a flag in a slow wind, as if to get him in the mood.

How do you do that? he said.

That's nothing, she said.

They turned into the Ballymurphy Road and moved towards home. He saw Declan White get out of a car. They'd called him Steeple at school because of his slenderness and height, but they didn't call him that any more. He'd acquired a look that was no longer suited to a nickname.

What about yez, said Declan. Maire, long while since I've seen you.

I'm in Newry all the week, she said. Look, we're out hours and I'm burstin'. I'll see you back at the house. Slán, Dec.

Slán, said Declan.

I'll be there in a minute, he said to his sister. He watched her move through the shafts of light that came out from between the houses. She walked fast, then ran, her hair lifting and falling behind her.

Beautiful day, said Declan.

It is. We were up the Black Mountain.

Only trouble is, everywhere you put your eye there's a Brit.

There's that.

Saw that drawing you did.

What drawing?

Hands on bars.

Oh, that.

Yeah. I was in talking to Francie McGuigan. It was up on a wall.

That was just something I did for Ambrose.

How come?

He shrugged his shoulders.

Just, he said.

Here, remember Jimmy Burns? asked Declan.

He thought a minute, but couldn't find him.

No, he said.

Bones Burns we called him.

Oh aye. Of course.

They broke a breeze block over his head.

Who?

Brits.

What for?

What for? Hard to say. Green Howards. Their tour was up. It was their last night. A parting shot, maybe.

How is he?

He's fucked. Permanent brain damage. Doesn't recognise anybody.

He winced at this.

Know what else happened? asked Declan.

Do I have to?

Your call.

All right. Go on.

They killed an eleven-year-old boy in Derry. Shot him in the head with a plastic bullet.

He looked away, took a breath.

What do you think about that? asked Declan.

What can I think? What would anyone think?

Some think, some do.

I know that.

So why don't you do something?

Everything in him stilled. He raised his eyes slowly to Declan White's.

What do you mean? he asked.

Declan tipped his head in the direction of Glenalina Crescent. Come on, he said, and stepped forward. They walked along the pavements, through passageways between houses and back alleys. He had nothing to say to Declan White as they walked, nor he to him. He understood everything about each place they passed. He knew it all as well as he knew his own house. But after today, he already sensed, it would all look different.

They went over a wall and into a rear garden. An old woman named Magee lived there. He could see her back through the kitchen window as she sat at a table in her housecoat. In a corner on a patch of grass was her dead husband's pigeon coop, set up on short struts. It needed paint.

Who minds it? he asked.

I do, said Declan.

They went up the steps, in through a door and crouched in the shadows. Pigeons paced, flapped their wings, cooed. He could see feathers float and twist in the beams of light that came in through the gaps, the mineral blues and greens in the pigeons' necks. Declan hauled away sacks of feed from the top of a wooden box and opened the lid. He felt the beating of his own heart as he watched. Inside was a yellow blanket, unravelling a little by the trim, smudged with dirt and grease. Declan lifted the corners and let it fall open. He saw then what he had been brought there to see – pairs of gloves, binoculars, balaclavas tied together with string, an old, pewter-coloured revolver like from a cowboy movie and two AK-47s. He stood in the shadows amid the murmurs of the pigeons and looked down at the guns.

That's it, said Declan. That's what I mean.

I was twenty when I cycled to Ronchamp. I was in Edinburgh studying to be an architect, and still innocent. I had Lewis Mumford and Keats in my rucksack. I would look at Le Corbusier's Notre-Dame du Haut chapel there, then turn around and cycle back. Generous had told me about it. If you see it, you will understand, he said.

It was summer. I slept out all the way. When I arrived I put my tent up in the forest below the chapel so I could walk towards it in first light. It appeared and disappeared as I climbed the hill, a forest mushroom on a bare summit. I walked all round it when I got there. I moved my hands over the rough walls, the imprints of shells and wood, the bright paintings he'd made there. An old man sweeping a path was the only one present. He unlocked the door. I hadn't expected the fortune of being alone with this building. I stepped in. Le Corbusier had made the floor slope gently down towards the altar so it would feel effortless to arrive there. The altar is made of white stone from Bourgogne. When diocese officials considered who would make the replacement for the church that had stood there before being flattened by bombs during the war they took a great risk in choosing him, an agnostic. But Le Corbusier's acts are devotional. There is no vanity in them. He has taken himself out of the way of the building's purpose, even if it is a purpose he was equivocal about himself. He placed scores of windows of varying shapes and angles, some just tiny squares or slits, in the walls. The walls are up to twelve feet thick. They swell like waves and are filled with shattered stone from the bombed church. The walls are massive, the roof seems to float, the light is like liquefied jewels, red, green and yellow as well as white. It arrives through tunnels made in the thick walls and floods the space. The chapel is out of time. It is both primitive and complex. Soft currents of air move over you, you hear birdsong, see branches wave through the windows, arrive at details you didn't expect, a wooden Virgin and Child set in the wall between panes of glass, a violet wall, paintings of hands, the name *marie* written on a blue pane. Something begins to happen. The shapes and textures he made move towards you. It's intensely intimate and very gentle. You feel a lifting of fear and of small bothersome things. And something more. Grace? Love? He said he did not know the miracle of faith, but did know the miracle of ineffable space. It asks for nothing in return. You are not awed so much as moved. You know things where before you didn't.

A building did that.

At the end he lived in a hut by the sea, having renounced architecture. It was said of Le Corbusier that he had hands such as he himself might have drawn, that appeared to hesitate but from which precision came, hands where could be read his anxiety, his disappointments and his hopes.

I wanted to grow into those hands. And unaccountably, later that day, and for the first time, I felt that I could. Nothing I had ever done justified this, but the feeling was clear. I stayed four hours in the chapel that morning. I saw what I told you. I thought I had taken everything. I was ready to start back to Edinburgh. But instead I decided to see what the chapel would look like in a later light. I went to my tent, ate, slept a little, and then walked back up the hill in the evening. This time I didn't look at the building, at its techniques and puzzles and effects, as the professors had trained me to do. I looked instead at Le Corbusier. Or listened to him, for it seemed that he was speaking. He was speaking at all times, in darkness or in light, whether anyone was there or not. There was tentativeness and brilliance and a holy aspiration in his voice. And though what he had done was perfect there was also a strange and even twisted self-abnegation in it, like a martyrdom. The building was this speech. I felt myself rise to hear it. It was exciting. It was privileged. It was almost shameful.

You will see what I did with it.

It was Generous who had led me to architecture. We sat between the shelves of his library. Ideas are no use unless you can touch them, he said. He'd blown up barracks and burned big houses like his own to the ground, but now we looked at pictures of pyramids and temples and skyscrapers and read about how they were made, so that, I understood, I might go out into the world and learn and then come back to Ireland and make beautiful and meaningful things. It's our own state now, he said. We've no one else to blame. Let's not make fools of ourselves. He told me the stories of Gaudí, Nash, Bellini, Wright, Callicrates and Gropius as though they were heroes in a fable. I'd dream about taking my place among these people one day. Later I collected things – leaves, tide-worn stones, cross-sections of trees, magnified fragments of illuminated manuscripts. I set them up on mounts in my room and drew them into my projects. I studied light, texture, density, sound. Frozen music, architecture is called. I wanted to make a building that would survive everything, fashion, my death, even its own destruction. I believed I could do it.

CHAPTER TWO

Monochrome

Belfast, South Armagh, 1982–93

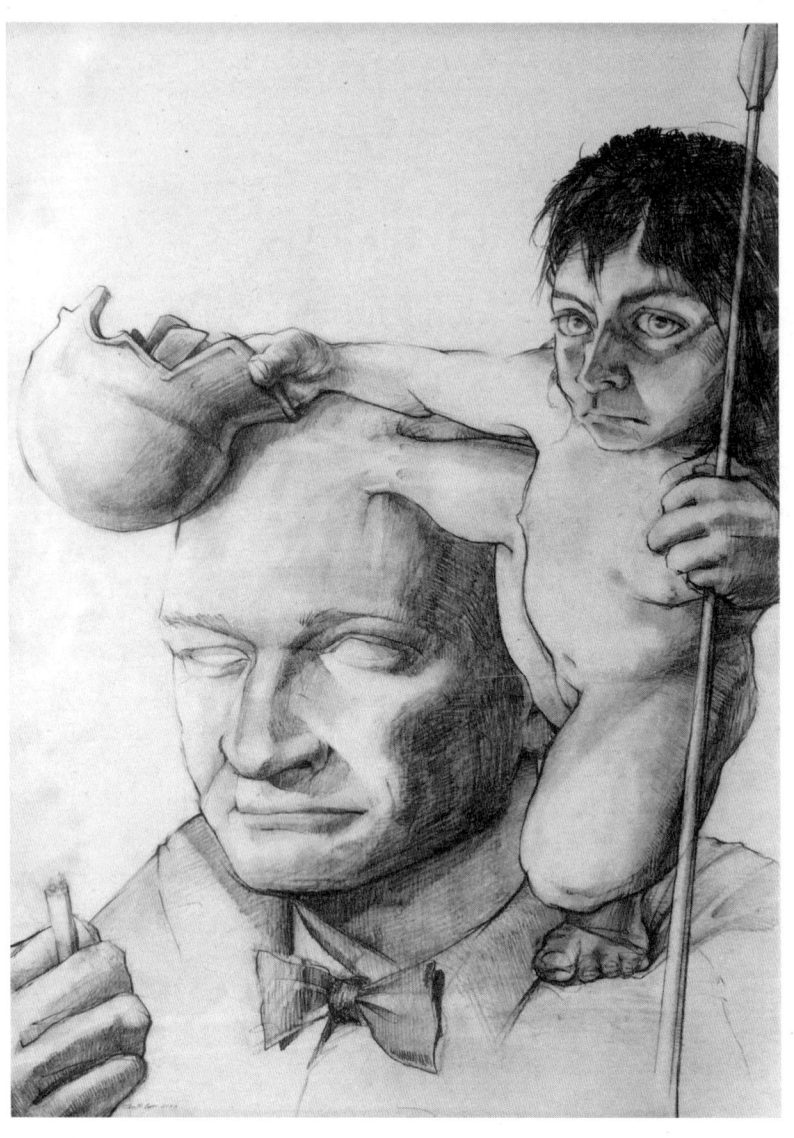

H e entered the time when he had many names. Some lasted only for an hour. His own became an oddity to him, as if it were a species of fruit of which he had once heard. Let's call him Francis, for now.

His first shot of the war was with an AR-18 from a cinema roof at a foot patrol in Clonard. Two hundred yards, light wind. It missed. He watched through the scope as a column of powder rose from the pointing on a wall. One soldier scratched his ear, others crouched and pointed their weapons in all directions except his. He pulled again and hit one of them below the knee.

One month before he took this shot and six weeks after he'd gone into the pigeon coop with Declan White he waited on a low wall over the border in Muff. Two men in rubber boots and with muck on their trousers drove him west through Donegal on a July day. Down the shore of Lough Swilly to Letterkenny and back up. When they spoke it sounded to him as if they were whistling. Ellistrin, Kilmacrennan, Creeslough and up past the Ards Forest to Dunfanaghy, rivers, men on bicycles, dogs chasing cars, bog cutters, hay gatherers, children with ice cream cones, water rushing everywhere, the sun on leaf, bog, stone, eye, cheek. The recruiting officer Declan White sent Francis to told him he'd likely go to jail, be beaten and maybe shot, never get a job, his house would be raided and his family harassed and he'd probably never hold a gun or shoot a Brit. I've already decided, he said. He had eighteen years, two months. On through Falcarragh and Gortahork, then straight west to Meenacladdy and there it was, the water shimmering gold, brown wrack and cream beaches, the pale grey islands like discs of smoke. He'd never seen the ocean before.

He slept in a shed behind a school and the next day a grandmother drove him into the mountains. Keep your eyes on your shoes now, she said. When he looked up they were in a deep bowl where masses were held when they were against the law and where six men and two women with no names were gathered around short arms and timing devices. They ate Galtee cheese and sausages and pan loaf with butter, slept in sacks in shepherds' huts and learned how to break down a gun, take over a house, withstand interrogation and understand the reasons for their war. When they fired at targets the recoil sent most rounds skyward. Francis hit a cigarette pack six times out of ten at a hundred yards with a bolt-action rifle. How do you do that? they asked. He didn't know.

On the last night they ate in the grass. The sense of where they would go from here carried an ominousness, but it was also as yet abstract. They did not know what being in the war would do to them. Someone sang. Someone laughed. They were all poised at a point between two lives, their own and another in front of them that had to do with history. Would there be a way back? some of them, Francis included, asked themselves.

They broke up then to gather what they had brought. There had been a brief squall but it had cleared. Just before midnight with the light not entirely gone Francis sat with his back to the stone wall of his hut. He saw one of the women recruits come over a low rise. It would be more than three years before he learned that her name was Annaleena Brennan. She sat beside him. She'd been walking in the rain. Drops that shone like mercury were in her hair and on her lips. A silver chain ran in the hollows of her neck like a stream over rocks. She began to speak as if taking up from where she'd left off. She spoke not of war but of the land – golden chalices and tubs of butter that came up out of the bog, the pyramid orchids in the dunes of Cruit. Why did she want to tell him this? He'd like to know but didn't know how to ask. He felt the warmth of her shoulder against his, her hip. She was fresh and clean like the rain. He saw her hands, the bones around her neck, pale light on her silver chain. He didn't know anything about being with a woman and all this came to him from a place he couldn't see and he wanted to stay in it. But that was all for him this night and then in the morning everyone went away.

By the end of a training camp conducted a week later by a former British Army sniper his distances had increased, the target had shrunk and his miss rate was down to seven per cent.

The policeman's experience: If I shout at a man at the edge of a protesting crowd and raise my truncheon, he will first go numb with terror and then take to his heels. The experience of the man at the edge of the crowd: At the sight of an approaching policeman I am seized by fear and start running. But this time everything turns out differently. The policeman shouts, but the man doesn't run. So that's the way it is! There is a moment of silence. We don't know whether the policeman and the man at the edge of the crowd already realise what has happened. The man has stopped being afraid . . .

Let's analyse it: every profound political protest is an appeal to a justice that is absent, and is accompanied by a hope that in the future this justice will be established. This hope, however, is not the first reason for the protest being made. One protests because not to protest would be too humiliating . . .

A rebel is a person who says No, but whose refusal does not imply a renunciation. He refuses to let anyone touch what he is, and from the moment that he finds his voice, he begins to consider things in the particular . . .

Guns move when brought close to the body. Through a high-powered scope the features of a target's face cannot usually be distinguished because of tremors in the gunman's hand, chest, head.

The gunman does not have to be nervous for this to happen. Breath, heartbeat, muscle and nerve all produce movement. But there can be moments of stillness where all can be seen clearly, strands of hair, the colour of an eye. Each gun has its own characteristics and each person will sight it differently. The difficulties of sighting a gun in a clandestine war are high. The fewer people who touch your gun and the fewer who know what you do, the better your chances of being effective, and of surviving. Francis became his own operations officer, his own QM. He brought his weapons in and out of operations himself. He arranged his own dumps. He had the .45 automatic known as the 1911 and an AR-18 that had been brought in on the *QE2*, where Ambrose McGuigan was a steward. He shot from hedges, the backs of trucks, bedroom windows. He shot soldiers at checkpoints, prison wardens getting out of cars, policemen on the street. He tried to select vantage points where only his victim had the chance to see him. Everyone knew what he did, but no one knew where he was.

The imperialist infantilises, domesticates, cartoons, tortures, repudiates, kills, bestialises and demonises the colonised. The imperialist uses the colonised in order to take what he has and to see himself in an enhanced light. The colonised puts forward the demand to be regarded as fully human. He reasons, wheedles, lies low, strikes, marches, vandalises, votes and appeals to the world at large to understand his predicament. The imperialist goes on with his project.

He built himself a false wall that he could fit behind at the gable end of an attic in a safe house in the Kashmir. Sometimes he slept there. He had others as well, some for just a night. His sleeps were fitful. He moved from place to place of which none were his home. He could be taken at any time. Armoured cars pulled up in West Belfast streets in the night and revved their engines to declare a presence. The war was in part a war on nerves.

He used the house in the Kashmir sparingly, but over a period that lasted ten years. He watched children grow and their father lose his hair. The space behind the false wall was just three feet wide. He had a sleeping bag, a bucket, a jug of water and a mirror. He added pencils and a notebook. There was a small window at the tip of the gable. Sometimes if there was moonlight he copied images he brought in with him or looked in the mirror and made drawings of himself.

The time came then that when he looked at his face he saw light and shade instead of lines.

Anything I can get ya? the man called up to him one morning. Biscuits? Fags? *Penthouse*?

Charcoal, he called back.

*He of whom they never stopped saying that the only language he under-
stands is that of force decides to give utterance to force. The imperialist
has shown him the way he must take if he is to become free. The imperialist is the bringer of violence into the mind and into the home of the
native and by an ironic turning of the tables it is the native who now
affirms that the imperialist understands nothing but force.*

Pacifism is a comfort to the powerful.

The barber studied the head before him and then went to work. All
was silent except for the swish of his blades. Hair fell as gently as snow.
There were seven men and boys in chairs along a wall, five with their
hair already cut. Another, in a mask and gloves, watched them from a
doorway. A handgun lay on his shoulder, his finger on the trigger. It
was a Saturday and as people came in the man in the mask directed
them to the wall. One by one the barber cut their hair.

Francis waited by a window that looked directly at a barracks set in
the fork of a road. There was a collection of stuffed bears the barber
kept to entertain children. Francis had stacked them against the window's glass. He did it because he remembered how his sisters' dolls
disguised him when he watched the soldier smash the face of Mr
Doherty against the side of the Saracen. Two boys had a magazine
open between them but kept looking over at Francis. The men seemed
not to want to look. They were like patients in a hospital room await-
ing a critical diagnosis. One whispered prayers quietly to himself.
Information had arrived that, unaccountably, soldiers arriving back at
the barracks from patrols exited the Saracens outside the gate instead
of within the barracks yard. Francis had been waiting for two and a
half hours to kill them. He would shoot from a prone position, braced
on the window ledge, the barrel of his gun hidden by the bears.

When a Saracen arrived the man in the mask gave a sign and the
barber and everyone waiting hit the floor, their arms covering their

heads. The soldiers had been full of tension on their patrol around West Belfast, but now believed they were safe. They were covered by the watchtowers. No attack had yet been made at a barracks entrance. One lit the cigarette of another. Francis began to fire. They were the shortest and easiest shots of his war. He hit all three soldiers that came out of his side of the Saracen. Tremendous waves of fire were returned from the barracks watchtowers and the soldiers on the ground. The street filled with smoke and the smell of cordite and hundreds of rounds came in over the heads of the barber and his customers. Every window in the building shattered under the fire. Francis rolled towards the door. The man in the mask waited at the edge of a window. The room filled with spent bullets. When two soldiers ran towards the barber's firing their guns and not hearing the warning shouts of their colleagues, the man in the mask hit a button on a device and a mined car that had been left waiting for them the night before went up in their faces and killed them.

The way out the back was clear. Francis washed his clothes and body in a safe house. Soldiers, in grief and rage over the attack, took the barber into their barracks and beat him to the point of death.

Numerical weakness comes from having to prepare against possible attacks; numerical strength, from compelling our adversary to make these preparations against us.

Rouse him, and learn the principle of his activity or inactivity. If your opponent is of choleric temper, seek to irritate him. Force him to reveal himself, so as to find out his vulnerable spots.

He wins his battles by making no mistakes.

It was after making a mistake that Francis saw his blood fall onto the snow.

He'd waited at an attic window on the Falls Road to kill soldiers coming out of the barracks in Ballymurphy and then making their way down the Whiterock Road. The fall of the hill was such that if he hit the first in a patrol the others following wouldn't know where the bullets had come from. It was winter. He had a long coat. The AR-18 folds down to a size where he could get the barrel up his sleeve and the butt into a plastic bag stuffed with newspapers. He had no cover or car or assistant for this attack. When it was over he'd walk out with his gun in the bag looking as if he'd just come from a shop.

The day was overcast, the window darkened with cobwebs and dust. The snow was grey in the street, white in the City Cemetery. He didn't obscure the gun's barrel because there was no line of sight from which it could be discovered. The tip of the gun came out from beneath the window frame. He'd been waiting since eight in the morning with the butt to his shoulder and his eye on the sight. He had one chance to fire and it would pass within three seconds. It was now 2 p.m. Sometimes, in these circumstances, the most difficult thing was to stay awake.

The sun broke for a moment through an aperture in the clouds. The light hit his face and a point on the tip of his gun. The metal flared like a match being struck. Then he saw an army helicopter hovering over the Falls. He realised that neglecting to consider the sun was a mistake. He could not know if those in the helicopter had seen him or when or if his target would appear. He made two decisions, the first of which he would be unlikely to make later. It was to wait and see if he could get a shot off. Less than three minutes later an armoured vehicle came along the Falls Road at speed and pulled up in front of him. Soldiers inside opened fire at his window through apertures. Far below he heard the garden door at the back being smashed down. Those in the helicopter, he knew, were directing this operation. He also knew that his gun could be traced to three years of near-daily attacks. Many had resulted in death. If they didn't kill him he would never get out of jail.

There was no way to the roof other than through his window and if he came out of it he'd be shot from the road. The second decision he faced was to surrender or somehow get out the back. He chose the latter.

Below, the soldiers broke through the door. He felt the stark change in atmosphere, an alien, dark, anonymous presence. It had its own smell. He'd never been in the same enclosed space with it before. He dumped his gun down through a hole in a disused chimney shaft. He dropped from the attic through a hatch. They were up to the hall on the ground floor. There was a bicycle on the landing. He threw it down the stairwell at the soldiers and went through the glass of a second-floor window onto an extension roof. He jumped from there to the garden next door, landing on snow and wet earth but nevertheless opening lesions in the cartilages of his ankle and foot. He tried to run. Bullets flew around him. When he went over another wall he was hit in the thigh.

He ran past the houses of people he had grown up around. Mac-Curtain, Kelly, Quinlan, O'Rourke. He was running and bullets were around him but everything seemed to move slowly. He saw his blood fall onto the snow. He saw scenes from a life which he may have been about to lose and among them was the night of the piper whose music he'd followed through the snow when he was a child.

In the last garden of the terrace he faced an officer from the High-landers Regiment. The officer knelt with a blackened face half-hidden by a wall and had a strip of tartan on his beret. Francis went for the wall but the officer dropped him with a shot from his handgun to the already wounded leg. Soldiers coming over the wall in pursuit screamed abuse at him and would, he believed, have killed him had the officer not stopped them.

It's over, he said to Francis, close to his ear.

Francis lay on a bed with starched white sheets in a medical unit in a British Army barracks at the edge of Belfast. His leg was bandaged and he was on an antibiotic drip. All five of the other beds in the unit were occupied by men who said they were republicans. He wasn't sure of any of them, save one. He let on to no one that he could walk.

The atmosphere was eerily light. There were no cells and the prisoners, the soldiers believed, had been immobilised by their injuries. Music came in from a radio. Nurses played cards. Prisoners traded insults with soldiers. One of them, a gun boffin from Wales, sat beside Francis's bed listing the wonders of the Armalite.

The man in the ward of whom he felt sure was Tommy McClennan, who'd been interned three times since the 1940s. He now faced jail for keeping Semtex under his floorboards. A soldier in the raiding party had hit him so hard in the chest that he'd collapsed a lung.

They still didn't know who Francis was. The gun hadn't been found and the only charge so far was evading arrest. But that wouldn't last.

From the time he came on the ward he looked for a way to escape.

In the nights he spoke with Tommy McClennan. He was told that guns could be got in for them, but it would be fruitless. They'd have to shoot six soldiers before they got out of the ward and after that there was the whole barracks. Tunnels, roof space and vents were all impossible. The only chance was a rear barred window close to an exterior wall. Strangely, an officer, speculating idly it seemed, had pointed it out.

That has to be a set-up, said Francis.

Maybe, maybe not.

What about these ones? Francis asked, pointing to the other beds.

You have no choice but to trust them.

Files came in in the nappy of a child visiting a prisoner with her mother. Francis sat at the rear window in his wheelchair, playing chess with one hand and filing the bars with another. Sometimes the prisoners sang to hide the noise. After three nights' work, he and Tommy McClennan and the only other patient who could walk got out the window and over the outer wall into the unknown like otters into a river.

For three days he lay under the floorboards of a house, the undersides inches from his nose. There was a throb in his leg and heat where the upper wound was. A hematoma had developed. A doctor brought to him there gave him a new supply of antibiotics and told him he'd need two months to be fully mobile. They brought him then from house to house under cover of night by car and boat and on foot over the border to the house of Generous McCabe at Carrachor. They treated him as if he were a newborn or a quantity of high-volatility explosive.

Generous's wife by then was already dead and he was living with Eimear, who raised her dogs and cooked for the two of them. The vacated rooms of his scattered other children had filled with the detritus of his and their enthusiasms. He cleared a room for Francis and made up a bed.

The snow melted, the crocuses came up and faded and winter moved to spring. Days opened into wide spaces, the war ebbed away. He drew doors, scythes, mice, dogs. He tried with charcoal to get the play of light through trees on water. He walked the land. If he found Generous they walked together. They tended to his bees and to his cattle and horses. At night they played chess. Wolfhounds moved like grey ghosts through the windows and around the rooms. He had come from the war and would return to it. Sometimes he missed it, more often he wanted to hold it off. In Carrachor he had entered a parenthesis.

He slept by a window facing east and let the light wake him. Then he lay, looking out at stands of oaks and maples, trimmed lawns, small ringforts of flowers, lines of magnolias, vines on walls, the water of the lake, a world of blues and greens that cooled and eased him. A drawing is a report, he thought, but colour makes you feel. *I know I can't paint a flower, but maybe with paint I can convey to you my experience of a flower.* One day Generous had seen him drawing by the lake. Wait here, he said. He came back an hour later with a box of brushes, rolled canvas, tubes of paint, all that was left of a middle daughter's brief engagement with painting. Take the greenhouse for the light, he said.

It was a long structure of iron and glass that came out from the house like a hawk's wing. Inside were ferns and orchids, candelabra-like aloes, lime and banana trees, night-blooming cactus, the atmosphere humid and rank with decay. Francis took a space by a small fountain. He squirted out domes of colour onto a square of plywood. He mixed and layered them, changed their densities with turpentine and linseed oil, learned their hues and qualities of brightness, which were transparent and which opaque. The opaque permanent green lay like a mossy stone beneath the watery ultramarine. Alizarin crimson spoke softly, phthalo blue was a stain. Colours turned to mud when he mixed them and sometimes stayed there, but at other times he could push them through to a new colour that had beauty on a brush moving over canvas. He learned to tune them as you would a guitar. For days he made nothing that resembled a shape. Then he tried a cucumber and after that a farmer on a coffee tin. The smell of the turps in the greenhouse came to him when he arrived like incense in a church. Somewhere a clock was counting the time he had left. He couldn't quite hear it.

Every rebellion contains a demand for unity, the impossibility of attaining it and the construction of a substitute universe. So it is in art.

The message came and they brought him to Dundalk. In a room there he found four men and a woman. The woman was Annaleena Brennan. He had known nothing of her since the camp. That she was in this room meant that she had been in the war as he had and was now among those who made decisions. The men nodded to him as he sat. Over their heads he saw her smile and raise her brow as if to say, So this is the boy who could shoot straight in West Donegal . . .

They began to speak. He watched her when he could. She was different now, more economical, more contained. All that moved was a finger over her lower lip. She had spoken of the wonders that came up out of bogs and the colours in the dunes of Cruit the way others spoke of boyfriends and girlfriends and football teams and pop songs. He couldn't imagine that now. She was lean, taut, assessing. What would draw her attention? Still, the fine silver chain lay among the bones of her neck. Her hair fell thickly around her face. He remembered the way it held the rain.

Materiel had arrived in large quantities, he heard one of the men say. He had a high voice like a cartoon bird and an earnestness that seemed to amuse her. Heavy machine guns, RPGs, enough Semtex to last five years. They were close to possessing the technology to bring down helicopters. They had the wish and the capacity to take the war to a new level. He struggled to listen. Pulling back to the war from Carrachor, from his study of her, had the feeling of lifting a large stone. He turned to look at the speaker.

There's an aura of prestige about a snipe— he was saying.

Prestige? said Francis.

The man looked at him, briefly perplexed.

OK. Wrong term, he said then. The point is snipes hit morale but not manoeuvrability. At least not significantly. We want to extend the territory where the Brits can't go, starting from South Armagh. We think you could be useful. Are you fit?

Would she be there? he wondered.

Yes, he told them.

Will you come? the man asked.

The decision was easy when it seemed to him he was making it on behalf of someone else, a person he'd provisionally agreed to be when he'd gone with Declan White.

Can you give me three days?

They assented. They had what they came for now. A scout came in after a while to say that the way was clear and cars were outside. He walked over to her. She seemed to be waiting.

We heard about you, she said. I just didn't know it was you – the one with a tongue in knots when I came back from a walk.

I think I can speak now.

Good for you.

Any chance of a drink?

They're waiting for me, she said.

He'd been watching her for an hour. She was a kind of milepost from which he could sense how much the war had changed him. The war came to him as something fated. He moved as it moved. It had made him practical. Equivocation had of necessity been eliminated. Everything except maybe those daubs of colour were determined by the exigencies of the war. There had to be someone for him, sometime. He had to know what it was like. Better her, he thought, than another, better her who had been in the war and would expect nothing that would extend forward into a future that was so unlikely to exist, who would set her sights no higher than respite.

Last time you got away, he said to her. I wished you hadn't.

Again she looked amused. This would become familiar to him. Her blue eyes were like craters, fathomless. She squeezed his hand and went out.

He came back to Carrachor by bus. Generous played a slow air on the violin and Eimear served them roasted hare under a silver dome. There was no ambiguity now about the clock. He had this night and two more. They drank cognac. At some point he put forward the idea that the first painting of his life would be a portrait of Generous. They all raised their glasses.

At 6 a.m. Generous came into a sitting room with tall windows, wearing a white T-shirt and pasha's robe, his pale hairless legs like dried cornstalks below the hem. The night before Francis had toned the canvas with phthalo green and raw umber. Some of the green can still be seen in the neck. He was waiting for Generous with an easel and two chairs.

What about you, Generous?

Too old to sin was the reply.

They were at this time eighty-three and twenty. Francis mixed alizarin crimson, raw umber and ultramarine blue into a kind of near-black and sketched the features of the face, all but the eyes. If he'd left the eyes to last in the drawing of the Russian priest he'd have found a more believable place for them. The brush slithered in the oil like a fish in a current. Where there was intricacy – earlobe, ribbed flesh, gleam on the lip – he looked along the length of his arm, his raised thumb at the end like a sight post on an Armalite. He painted spectacles on the bridge of the nose to give him an alignment in case Generous moved. He laid in the eyes above them. Generous, or some illusion of him, began to appear.

That night they went to a dance in the village hall. Generous wore a black suit and overcoat with velvet on the collar. When there was a waltz he crossed the hall and asked women to dance.

Learn to dance, he said to Francis. It'll never let you down.

They drank whiskey from Generous's flask and kept going when they got home. They didn't part until first light.

Later, Generous got to the room first. Whiskey from the night gnawed at the foreground of Francis's skull. When he tried to move the painting into a greater brightness he thought he'd ruined it. Generous's gaze looked suddenly scrutinising and pitiless, while the face in the painting now looked like nothing at all. He could go nowhere, he thought, other than to break through to a further brightness, beyond what had sense. He needed brightness because he wanted the face to come towards him. In a while the painting began mildly to assemble itself again. The bite from the whiskey weakened.

This is what I'd be doing, maybe, if things had gone differently, he thought. Sometimes the painting sank, sometimes it came back up. He went on through the day, trough, crest, trough, crest. He'd end on a crest in case he lost the feeling. He stepped back. He saw the swirls and ridges in the centre of the face as if through a lens, while the neck and the outlines of the head were so unfinished as to seem abstract.

That was all right. He drew two green lines below the irises as shadows from the upper lids. He left a gap in the right brow where a small scar cut through it. He stepped back. He felt something faint and fading, like the vibrating wires in a piano after a note. Then he turned the painting towards Generous.

If you know the enemy and know yourself, you need not fear the result of a hundred battles. If you know yourself and not the enemy, for every victory gained you will also suffer a defeat. If you know neither the enemy nor yourself, you will succumb in every battle.

For the guerrilla, the populace acts as camouflage, quartermaster, recruiting office, communications network and intelligence service.

War is based on leverage and deception.

His war changed. The tight streets of West Belfast gave way to the lanes and open fields of South Armagh, single shots by his AR-18 to fusillades from the heavy machine guns that were like artillery. He was no longer alone. Units were deployed, dozens more were beyond, building switches, welding mortar tubes, driving, shifting weapons. It was a thing of many moving parts. Everyone had a part, but the part had to be found. A showband emcee was given the job of driving a car packed with ammonium nitrate over the border because his bonhomie could get him past checkpoints. He smoked a cigar to cover the smell. The soldiers laughed as he brought in the makings of bombs intended to kill them. The enemy too had moving parts – watchtowers, armoured vehicles, touts, jails, helicopters, limitless funds, control of the news and the courts, wave after wave of armed professionals trained to kill.

In the place where he was now trampled grass was noted, a spent match, a gate ajar, footprints, unfamiliar cars and faces, sounds in the night – all were collected by a forensically surveilling populace and passed on to the IRA. The flow was constant and if a pattern formed so did the need to act. The need to act was heavy, because to act was sometimes to die.

Francis's unit acted when they learned of three soldiers who had hidden themselves in a van in a scrapyard just yards to the north of the border. These soldiers formed one point in a total of four that had been deployed in the village. Often watched, often ambushed, now, the soldiers believed, it would be their turn. Sometimes they got out, stretched. They broke radio silence. Francis's unit saw all that they did. They tapped into their radio messages. The soldiers were wet and hungry and bored. They broke radio silence just for someone new to talk to. Francis then experienced the strange coincidence of being driven in the early morning to a spot by a stream at the edge of Generous's land where willows grew and where he collected an M60 and three Armalites from a tall, loose-limbed local Volunteer named Dermot Treanor who had a fondness for riddles and who kept weapons in his family's fields across the river in Bough. Late that afternoon Francis's unit opened up from a hillside at dusk, blind shots through a hedge at a hundred yards with a spotter on the far side giving the line to the van containing the soldiers. Two died, one was injured.

They acted again when multiple units of the Ayrshire Regiment hoping to kill them dug in in hillsides and outbuildings in sixteen positions. It had taken, farmers told them, more than a month to make the redoubts. The weakest was identified and hit from three angles with five hundred rounds at night, a mine blocking the line of pursuit and a helicopter watching as Francis and those with him made their escape. The officer running the operation was killed. And they acted against the SAS, Francis coming up through the sunroof of a car and firing at them from behind. The soldiers' car crashed and burned, a dead body falling from a door and another from the boot.

The war was louder now and more populous. It moved with a momentum which he had in part created but which seemed always to be about to move beyond his reach. It was of wits, technology, terrain and morale. Pictures were made in the mind, the obstacles to their realisation assessed. The war's acts were acts of the imagination. Aborted acts outpaced realised ones by a factor of fifteen. Mistakes were made. Equipment didn't arrive. People froze, or people died.

The war became for him like a sea, encompassing, heavy, ceaselessly moving. Its compass points were calculation and adrenaline, its tone monochrome.

Annaleena Brennan gave him colour. They had no courtship, just the key to a house at the edge of a wood and a box left inside the door with potatoes, carrots, a side of bacon and a chocolate cake. They wondered at who had composed the menu. This game filled the time for them as they moved around one another. They walked in the wood, they ate. In the evening he took a step towards her and she to him. The colours were pinks, beiges, creams, the colours of her body, pale blue from her eyes, black from her hair, greens and greys and nut colours from the shadows on her skin. In the morning they found another box with pan loaf, eggs and cornflakes. Time seemed barely to move. There was a presumption through all of this that love would not be spoken of, not here by the wood, or the other times in Louth or Generous's stable or the caravan in the dunes in Donegal, and he couldn't say anyway if he loved her, he had nothing to compare it to. Could love exist in these small pockets of time surrounded by war?

The guerrilla fights the war of the flea and his enemy suffers the dog's disadvantages: too much to defend; too small, ubiquitous and agile an enemy to come to grips with. If the war continues – this is the theory – the dog succumbs to exhaustion and anaemia without having found anything on which to close his jaws or to rake with his claws.

He brought the war he had learned in Armagh back into Belfast. Drogue bombs, grenade attacks, rockets, open gun battles from multiple positions. In the tightened landscape he felt the velocity increase.

One June morning in a mass operation involving thirty people he came in from an Antrim scrapyard on the back of a hijacked flat-bed truck with ten mortars bolted onto it, covered with carpet. The target was a barracks embedded in a Ballymurphy neighbourhood. The soldiers who had beaten Mr Doherty and humiliated Ambrose had been based there. But this was not the principal reason he wanted to destroy the barracks. Four were in the truck, two up in the cabin and Francis with another on the flat bed who was to take the carpet off the mortars and prime them. Others had been assigned to keep the people in their houses until the operation was over. Cars with British undercover operatives at this point merely curious buzzed past. Francis, the man with him and the one in the cabin with the driver fired on them with Armalites and handguns. A helicopter came in low. They got the truck into position in a small street with two-storey houses. They had thirty seconds, at best. He looked to his comrade. He saw a figure frozen in the midst of heaving off the carpet. Francis looked into his eyes. The man wasn't there. There seemed to be no mind for the body to obey. He pushed him from the truck, set off the detonators and in a sequence of ten tremendous blasts that would later affect his hearing the 150-pound bombs were lifted over the rooftops and into the barracks on the other side. They got away on bicycles.

For the first time he wondered how long his luck would hold.

She picked him up in Dundalk. They drove west through the late summer heat. The land whirled and eddied in the west. Limestone slabs the size of whales broke the surface. Fuchsias and thatch blazed under the sun. He felt high and free in a way he didn't recognise. When they got to Belmullet the land was blue and red from a bleeding sunset. In a house there the implicit vows to have no names and no pasts were slowly broken. He sensed with some fear that the only route to that high and free feeling was through her. They had time. He didn't know how much. Word was to arrive from someone who would drive up on a bicycle and direct them back to the war. He drew, she spoke. She was older than him, he learned. She once taught music to children. She had a child herself, a boy aged ten, being looked after by her mother in Derry.

There was a piano there. She played 'Begin the Beguine', then put her hands over his to show him how it was done. Over and over through the days she walked her fingers over his until he had the tune memorised.

He almost told her he loved her, but stopped short. It may not have been true.

He had a clear shot from a child's bedroom window at a checkpoint in Divis Street. Three hundred yards. A block-built Para in a beret stepped forward to take a licence from a driver. It was a sunny day. The Para dropped into shadow by the car. Francis breathed in and held. He would wait until the Para lifted his head away from the woman in the car. As he stood up the yellow autumn sunlight hit the Para's face and, just behind him, a mural of Cuchulainn, sword in hand, rising from a lake. Francis saw the purples, blues, reds and golds and the way they threw forward the illuminated face of the Para. It seemed he was looking into Francis's eyes and walking towards him through his scope. This is what he had been looking for, this is the way to bring a face forward. His finger weakened on the trigger while he watched. When he stopped, he saw that the Para had got into a Land Rover and was being driven away. He raged at himself. It seemed he'd committed a kind of treason. That a man would live another day or that he had found the solution to his painting did not at the time console him.

It took him the whole of a night to paint in a round stained-glass window behind Generous's head. Generous stayed up with him, making coffees and telling him about the windows in Chartres and Rouen. Francis heightened the face with whites. It wasn't enough. He tried to pour light into it. The face must advance as the Para's had. He stepped back, Generous stepping with him, his hand on his shoulder as they peered into the painting. Still it wasn't enough, but it was something.

Two weeks after Annaleena Brennan came back from Belmullet a monumental sculptor working on an angel for a grave in the studio in the back of his house in East Tyrone was interrupted by a cousin of his who lived on the far side of the village. The sculptor's wife saw them talking, saw the sculptor leave down his tools and drive away alone. She thought he must have intended to be back soon because he had left wet plaster in a tray.

The sculptor picked Annaleena up from a house and they drove west. They were headed for a shed beside a farmhouse. At a bend in a road lined with poplars just a hundred yards from the shed a car following them and two SAS units hidden behind walls opened fire on them with Uzi submachine guns, Ruger semi-automatic rifles and a pump-action shotgun. Both were immediately killed. The remains of some 180 rounds were found, among them six spent cartridges from a handgun. A soldier had walked to the car after the attack and put three bullets into the head of each.

The shed was an IRA arms dump and the sculptor's cousin had told him that a man had used a gun from the dump to commit a series of robberies. The sculptor and Annaleena were thus lured along the road to the shed to check the condition of the dump. The theft of the gun and the subsequent robbery were in fact things the cousin himself had done. He was also an informer, one of three working for the police in the same village. For leading Annaleena and the sculptor to their execution they were granted immunity for the robbery.

Both Annaleena and the sculptor, to the surprise of his wife who had not known of his involvement, were given funerals with military honours by the IRA.

A grenade attack, three lethal shootings of soldiers and a bomb in a culvert lifting an armoured car with two policemen in it seventy feet into the air were all traced to weapons and devices found in the shed. When the cousin's girlfriend threatened to expose him to the IRA after she saw him with another woman he asked his two fellow informers to deal with her. She was strangled and dumped in a forest. All three informers were nevertheless uncovered by the IRA and shot in the head. The sculptor's widow engaged a solicitor to press for an inquest into her husband's death and for charges to be brought against the soldiers. In this she was supported by a local woman politician. A case against three of the soldiers came to court. The judge dismissed it and commended the soldiers for their bravery and their service in bringing the terrorists to justice. The solicitor was shot dead in his home by loyalists led there by their handlers in British intelligence. The politician was blown up when she turned on the ignition in her car. One of the soldiers involved in the ambush hanged himself in a barracks in Germany. The judge and his wife, returning from a holiday in Spain, were blown up by a roadside bomb. Francis planned and executed the operation. By this point in the story of the shed a death toll of sixteen had been reached.

I said to you back there that I am not well. It would be true to say that I have not been well for a long while, not truly, not deep in the grain. I don't think you noticed. I barely noticed it myself. It was mild, as has been my manner, a pale grey cloud, held at bay and nearly out of sight.

I contracted the disease twenty years ago, in London, long before we met.

I was high in Ronchamp. It was the most beautiful thing I'd seen. Pure devotional music made from stone and light. It did not refer. It just was. When I looked at it I had desire, that unmanufacturable thing. I knew well the nature of this desire. I knew where I wanted to go. The chapel had shown these things to me. I and others like me wanted to scrawl our imaginations across the skyscape in timeless buildings the way others wanted to score goals or make fortunes. Desire keeps you moving. It can be a companion. Look after it and you have it for life. Some of us actually did.

Ideas are no use unless you can touch them, Generous had said. What might have happened if I had left off studying when my belief in that was still alive?

They gave me a first in Edinburgh. I was passed from benevolent mentor to mentor onto internships in Lisbon and Berlin and thence to the Architectural Institute in London. It was there that I first met Theory.

I'd heard of Theory, but hadn't paid much attention to it. At the Architectural Institute you couldn't miss it. You couldn't even get around it. The Theorists were stars. The teachers of draughtsmanship wore cardigans, the historians were pedants, the actual architects couldn't get work and taught, bitterly, instead. But the Theorists had style. Girls watched them from behind tranches of hair. They wore tight suits and handfuls of rings. They walked the edge. Iconoclasts, elegant punks. Even the most prominent among the architects were Theorists. Hard to understand why they would do such a thing to themselves, but many had. Aesthetics is for artists, a painter once said, what ornithology is for birds. But what happens if the bird becomes aware of the ornithologist and begins to listen, and listens so well that he ceases to sing and instead speaks in the language of his classifier? The new exciting buildings were not music but rather essays, witty pastiches, inside jokes directed at other Theorists. How did I fall for it? It was like this. I looked up some of those who had graduated in architecture before me in Edinburgh. They were drawing floor plans of malls or working in coffee bars. One was driving a bus. The Theorists gave talks in Jakarta and Tel Aviv. They had book contracts. American universities clamoured for their presence. Theory was measurable in cash and prestige. But it wasn't really that. I was young and credulous and it seduced me.

I saw that I needed to define for myself a personal style. The Architectural Institute was an excellent school for this. The hippest stars in the firmament were there – Tschumi, the Archigram people, Zaha Hadid and Rem Koolhaas. We had seminars on shopping and erotic gardens. We built models showing how IRA bombs were reconfiguring the cityscapes. It seemed the height of wit.

You needed a style to advance but also to make yourself believe that Theory is of any consequence. You needed to dress it up in something. My personal model was Jean Baudrillard. I became an actor. I played Jean Baudrillard in a white suit. Most people want to be somebody else when they're young, don't they?, because they don't yet know how to be themselves. You would have no reason to know who this Jean Baudrillard is. He was a French critic. Some called him a philosopher. I did. For us at the time the French were the incendiarists of the intellectual world, visionaries not lecturers, associated more with protest and sex and clouds of Gauloise smoke than with study carrels in libraries. I curated in myself Jean Baudrillard's absolutism and contempt. There is no art! he declared. There is no reality!

Your style was more important than your thinking. It gave you position by giving you a noticeable personality. We got our PhDs. If we were going to get jobs we had to be noticeable.

I went to America on my parents' money after they sold a couple of fields and took out a loan. I worked the conferences, cultivated editors and deans and intellectual eminences. My thesis was published. A couple of notorious essays brought me an offer from Cornell. The *New York Review of Books* asked me to write for them. I was going somewhere. I had the evidence.

I had told myself at first that Theory opened a second door for me. I thought I was walking through both, that I could theorise under the protection of tenure while still creating my timeless buildings. But I didn't do that. I had become a Theorist, first and last. I would never make a beautiful thing.

It didn't feel entirely right. Something seemed to slip away, like a coin through a hole in a pocket, or Arpita whom I lost to a guitar player because I neglected her when I was in Lisbon and Berlin. But I didn't want to think about the nature of the transaction. I couldn't afford to.

In the fictive world my family had made for me I was not only gifted but had been made the repository of their hopes. Their eyes and my eyes were forever on me. It seemed natural. But being excessively lauded and protected as a child does not necessarily lead to an inviolable confidence as an adult. You begin to suspect it. You see it hasn't a foundation.

You seem remarkably free of pale grey clouds, other than those I've blown your way. How do you do it?

PART II

The Biography of a Painting

CHAPTER THREE

She's Not There

San Francisco, 2009

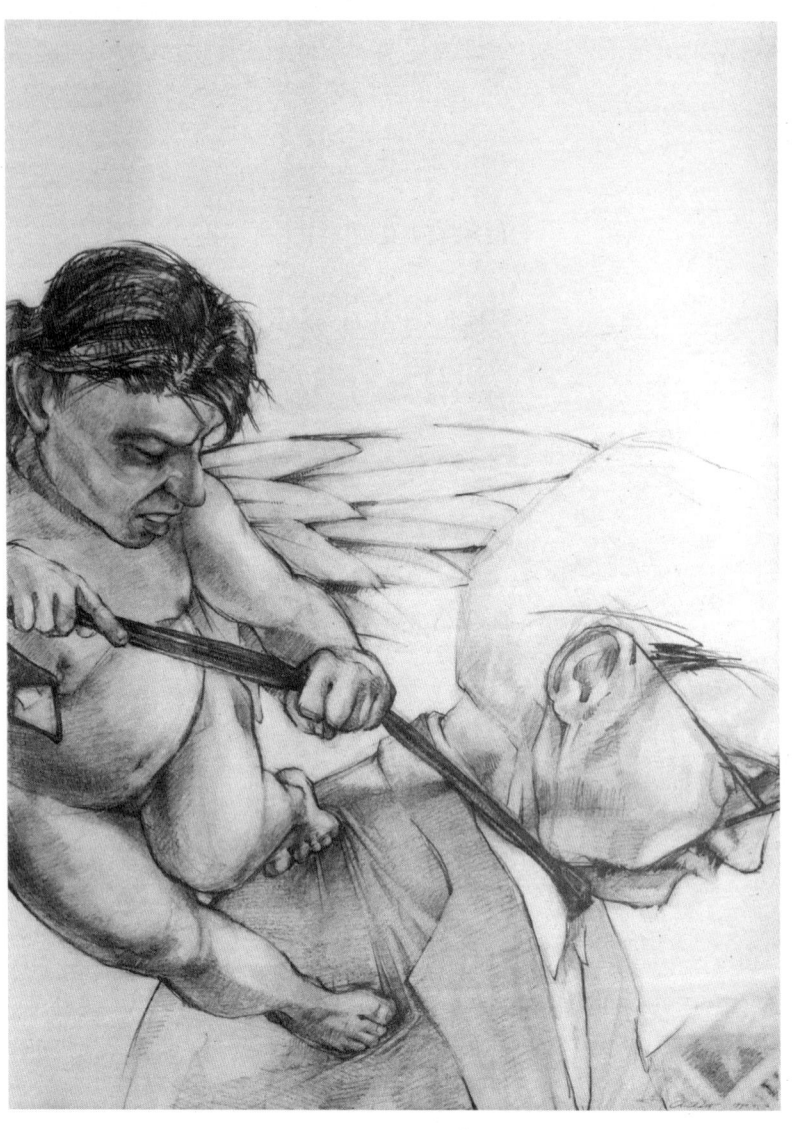

At the time, he was known as Ryan.

He was in a small hollow inside a city wall. A soft rain fell over the streets. There were other places he could have picked, a warehouse window, a bell tower. But the way out from the wall into the back alleys was clear and there was a gap further down where he could dump the gun. And it was dry. He had a Heckler & Koch MSG90 with a telescopic sight.

The light was dim. Cars with headlights on crossed his sightlines. A woman with a dog in a basket came out of a newsagent's, a boy went by on a skateboard. It was a street of buses and shoppers and the unremarkable, but with a sinister aura only he could sense.

He knew they were out there, one with skills such as he had, possibly two. They were stalking him and hoped to kill him. He'd set up a dummy arms dump and they'd fallen for it. Intercepted radio messages told him that. That was his story this night. But where were they, and how many? One missed shot and they would know where he was.

He went back and forth between naked eye and scope, trying to get the details and the whole all at once. He saw a girl at a window halfway up a block. She seemed to be scanning the streets, there was something in her hand. Could she be the one? He dropped the scope onto her and braced himself, then saw that the thing which she had in her hand was a plum. She took a bite, then looked back down at her book.

The scope played over the street, into shadowed doorways, over faces, along a gutter where a cat was running for cover, and up the brickwork of buildings. Then in the back seat of an abandoned car he saw a predator in a woollen hat and a leather jacket with a weapon in his hands. Light from a shop door fell on the man's face. He seemed unaware he was being watched. He was searching the street through the broken window of the car. How strong was he? Who had trained him? What had he done the night before?

Ryan steadied his gun, released his breath and felt pressure from the trigger on his finger. He used to go for chest shots, but the ballistics had improved. One round into the triangular area between nose and mouth would sever the spinal cord and disable any response. Should he pull now? Was it a trick? He was about to do it when he saw a sudden movement on a rooftop as a figure in black with night goggles and an assault rifle ran through the shadows towards a chimney stack. In the moment, just below his line of sight, a dim flare, like a match struck in fog. Then flashes of light from the barrel of the rifle of the man in the car. Tracer bullets hit the wall just beside where Ryan was lying. He had only seconds to make the two shots, but felt he had time. Time stretched when he asked for it. He dropped the crosshairs onto the man's upper lip and squeezed. One shot to the head for him and another for the figure on the roof just before he reached the chimney stack, each pull on the trigger featherlight. He watched through the scope as the two gunmen who had tried to kill him exploded into cartoon-like electronic fragments. The machine shuddered and the screen went blank. The words 'Balkan Assassins' came up, then his bonus tally in gold.

He let the gun fall and pulled back from the machine. Daylight seemed to walk into the arcade as the clouds rolled away, the sea air coming up from the bay to Broadway. He walked towards the light.

A Chinese man speared electronic fish and a boy in a virtual reality helmet fought with troglodytes. There was a clatter of curses and explosions. Ryan tapped the boy on the helmet, handed him a card with his points and stepped out into North Beach.

A squall had passed, followed by sunlight from which nothing could hide. Pools of water glistened and steamed. A woman untied her scarf from her head and shook out her hair. Shopkeepers rolled back awnings, windows opened, people stepped from doorways and looked to the sky. Ryan walked on. He was waiting for the night. He was always waiting for the night. Daylight was too dense, too specific. It left no room. He felt an easing as darkness fell, when the edges of things were indistinct. Day declares, night suggests. Laws made in the light don't hold so well. The night people come out. He moved among them.

He lived in a corner room of the Bostonian Hotel in the San Francisco Tenderloin. His war was twelve years behind him. For money he painted walls in houses for a designer named Ming. He cooked on a hotplate in his room. He slept fitfully. Dreams sprang him into wakefulness. At night he walked, he sat in bars. He painted or drew in his room after midnight with a bottle of wine.

He did this work to touch the pulse of a life of expression he'd once hoped to live but had left behind when he entered the war. Sometimes he came near. He could smell it, taste it. Among the things he had not lost was a good hand. He could make a likeness, he could shade, create depth with pencil or charcoal. But this was as nothing for him unless it bloomed into thought and feeling in colour on a canvas. Drawings were notes towards something, painting an efflorescence. A painting was speech. But he couldn't get there. His attempts were competent, but mute. He'd planned too much, been too fastidious, painted with his head. He didn't believe them. Perhaps he'd touched it when he'd painted Generous. He'd got close at least. But that was more than twenty years ago. Why was this? Why could it not be his?

It was springtime. Three weeks earlier, on a day that still bore the feeling of winter, he went out to buy a new canvas. The canvas was large, five foot by three, the size of a small wardrobe. That night he primed it and stood before it. It was 2 a.m. He was a little drunk. Music from a piper soared through his earphones. On a stool beside him he had a cafeteria tray with piles of Golden Acrylic raw umber and burnt umber he'd loosened with water. He had a four-inch housepainting brush in his right hand. The canvas was naked before him. He made big, sweeping passes down from the top, the paint spattering and dripping. He loaded the brush and threw a wide rooster-tail of paint at the canvas. The first marks of this painting described a wheel. The work was physical, thoughtless, fluid.

He went back to it the next night, and the nights after. The broad gestures gave way to intricate design with a white charcoal pencil. He drew in a lacy diamond pattern he'd seen on wallpaper in a synagogue. Then on a crossbeam he'd made upper right he drew white filmy circles like moons. He worked with acrylics and then with oils to soften the borderlines. *All paintings seem to me like prison windows in which the lines, precisely, are the bars.* He aimed for lines in the process of dissolution.

He made the red at the top with a still wet alizarin crimson and increasing amounts of cadmium red. Cadmium red could lift him like a drug. He placed it upper left and lower right. A dark rectangle lower left which he would later dislike was paired with the dark beam upper right. The lines between the darks and the lines between the reds were as cross-stitches pulling the painting in tight.

He wondered then if it might be finished, or nearly so. He set it against a wall in his room. It was midday. He shifted the curtains to keep direct light off it and sat on the floor. He tried to let the painting arrive to him, as if he were someone else. He let his eyes follow the painting's lines. They moved him around the painting's perimeter. He picked up the energy of the lines as his eyes moved. He stepped back, he unfocused his eyes, he tried to take in the whole. He hoped now for a good feeling, the feeling that he'd made a thing that could look back and speak to him at last, but something else happened, something he didn't expect or like, the sensation of a sudden blow or fall or sickness, the sensation coming before the sense as he saw that the painting was a gyre turning at the periphery around a centre that was a vacuum, a murky, inert, featureless plain in which one dark colour passed on to another. The area was vast, two-thirds of the canvas's territory. A small child could sit in it. The painting was decorative, but only of something that was absent. He didn't know what it was. It was like a ring whose mount lacked a stone.

He saw it plainly. He'd followed his instincts and produced a painting that was empty at its heart.

This had happened eight days earlier.

He walked on along Broadway, the crowd around him dense. They'd come out after the rain, bright expressions on their faces. He stepped around till receipts and lottery tickets with ink running from the rain. Meat turned on a spit, music boomed through the pavement, tourists consulted maps, strippers crossed their legs on bar stools under pink and blue neon light. A man in a hurry nearly knocked him down. The painting had haunted him through the days. The thought that he had made his own portrait came towards him like a foul thing on wings. He beat it off. Yet it hovered out of reach.

He couldn't make the rent. Ming had called to say that he was talking with a rich investment banker who'd bought the oldest house in San Francisco, up on Telegraph Hill below Coit Tower. Paul Crane, he was called. Four floors, everything to be done, unlimited money. A year's contract, Ming thought. It wasn't signed, but Ming was reeling the man in. Ryan knew he would have to bring life to the painting before he had to go to work, or else it would be lost.

He stopped walking and leaned against a wall. The hours of light were growing longer as the spring advanced. The sun hung over the bay, vast, orange, festering. He watched the people pass. He saw their forms and shadows. They seemed mechanised, and far away. The crossbeams and circles and cadmium red of his painting passed over them like a moving screen.

He pushed away from the wall and crossed the street. He didn't drink before six and it was nearly time. His appetite rose, he sensed the bar's imminence. He felt he knew bars as other people knew music, that there were bars for certain hours, certain moods or expectations. He chose one. It was an early-evening bar. It would be a short stop, for he had an appointment in his hotel at eight.

He arrived at his motorcycle, a 2001 Triumph America in Goodwood green and silver. He drove through the city, along the flatlands on the shore and back up into the heights. He saw the neon over bars he didn't know. Piano music, the gleam of a high-heeled shoe disappearing through a door, talk and laughter like waves in the sea, backs crouched over pool tables. Cross-streets terraced the hills. Fog lay in the troughs like soup left in a bowl. He plunged through and up again into the late light.

Later he sat with a beer and a shot of Jameson by the window of a quiet bar in the hills south of Castro. There was a chalkiness in his mouth, a taste he associated with dissatisfaction. He watched the sky go from red to sapphire. Lights from the houses flickered through the rolls of the land. People were just arriving home. He saw office workers in loosened ties, couples carrying bags with takeaway meals, holding hands, anticipating. He watched the street through the glass as it receded from him. It grew indifferent. He remembered walking under this same sapphire sky through dunes in Donegal with Annaleena Brennan to a clamorous bar with nets and seashells hanging on the walls, beer taps on the counter among chocolates and hams and balls of wool, a fiddler and an accordionist in a corner barely heard as the crowd passed pints over their shoulders, the beer spilling down necks and the froth catching in girls' hair. Then back with her to a caravan in the dunes. The colour of her skin, the smell of their hunger, the way the atmosphere stretched to a tautness as they sought one another. They were on the run and it seemed to them they were in love, even if they never said it. That he could never go back to that place or feel again what he had felt there had occurred to him many times, and never with diminished force.

One evening in May 1997 a sharp crack sounding like that of a judge's gavel being struck was heard in the courtyard of a block of flats off Curzon Street in Mayfair, London, glass shattered and a man reaching for a telephone fell from a gunshot wound that severed his carotid artery. His daughter, a university student, ran from her room when she heard the fall, but could do nothing to staunch the blood or prevent her father from losing consciousness. He died before emergency services reached him.

Within an hour news broadcasts in Britain and Ireland and, too, in other parts of the world transmitted images of whirling lights, sirens, police cordons and crowds of people looking up at the building where the man had been shot. The victim was named as Sir Matthew Hayford, chairman of the Joint Intelligence Committee for the Cabinet. The Prime Minister and Home Secretary spoke. The crime was denounced and vows were made that the terrorists responsible would be pursued and captured, no matter where they went or how long it took.

In recent years the IRA had bombed three London railway stations, the centre of Manchester, Heathrow airport and a flyover, mortared Downing Street and detonated massive explosions in Canary Wharf and the City of London, resulting in a call to make a walled fortress of the financial district. During peace negotiations then taking place British officials interpreted the IRA's willingness to talk as a sign of weakness. Demands to disarm were made of the

Irish delegates in order to publicly display that this was their view. Orders were in turn given by the IRA's Army Council to pursue the campaign. In all the years of the conflict the shot fired in Curzon Street had been the only sniper attack carried out in England.

At the time of the broadcast Ryan was in a house in Brixton, south of the river. He had shot Matthew Hayford with a Barrett M82. Intelligence about the occupant of the flat in Curzon Street had been received from a Scottish window cleaner. It included a telephone number. The M82 was moved from South Armagh, a vantage point selected and secured. Ryan travelled from Ireland by coal boat. He went into the building from which he would take the shot in a gas fitter's boilersuit, the call was placed, the shot made, and he went out into Chesterfield Gardens in street clothes afterwards. The gun was passed to a man and woman waiting in a car. In Park Lane Ryan got onto a southbound bus. He had by then been nearly fifteen years in the war.

In less than an hour after the attack he was picked up in Brixton by a furniture van and taken to Wales and back across the Irish Sea. The following day the van was loaded onto the Cork–Roscoff ferry and driven to Pau in the south of France, where he was let out of the crate in which he had travelled. Basques who would look after him again twelve years later when he fled the United States moved him from place to place until the spring of the following year when, with the peace agreement already signed in Belfast, a flight that originated in Nice brought him to Montreal. He was driven west to a small town on the Pacific Coast north of Vancouver and finally down over the border to San Francisco. All that had engaged him since he went into the pigeon coop with Declan White had come to an end.

The driver who picked him up on the Canadian coast was Pat Garrity, a Roscommon man who'd sold his cows in 1982 and bought a paint store in the suburbs between the city and the San Francisco airport. He was slow-moving and genial with a head of thick, black, unruly hair, lately going to grey. Not long after he arrived he joined a small group that laundered the identities of republican fugitives and integrated them into American life. He put Ryan into a room above the garage at the back of the store, dyed his hair and handed over to him sets of documents in different names that had been forged for him. In this room before him had lived Garrity's mother when she had been over from Ireland looking after her young grandchildren. It had a single bed with a candlewick cover, a stuffed chair with a lace doily where the old woman had rested her head, and paintings of Roscommon farms and a 1916 Proclamation on the walls. It seemed a stage set, eerily inert, caught in time.

His life in the war had been populous, adrenaline-injected, clamorous and at times deafeningly loud. Mind and body were stretched, movement was ceaseless. In his first weeks in the room above Garrity's garage his mind still moved along tracks created by the war. He half-slept with an awareness of the door, he assumed each moment would present a new task or threat. But all was silent and still. He was not called for. For company he had only Garrity and the Mexican woman who ran the taco stand at the end of the street. He laid low. Time moved slowly. And in the silence and stillness he discovered that he was different. Something had happened to him. As a boy or as Francis or under any of the other names he used he'd drawn, joked, planned, shot, grieved and, perhaps, loved. Now he watched but could not feel himself. He watched the interrupted sleeps that continued even as the habits of war dropped away, the distractions while reading, the empty wine bottles gathering along a wall. But he received no signal from what he saw. It was as though a nerve had been cut.

He tried to see what it was made of and from where it had come. There was nothing in it that was familiar. It seemed not to belong to his life. The light on it was dim. It slipped away when he looked. It was like a sea in which he must now swim. He understood that it was something different from remorse, or bitterness or the sense of having been betrayed such as he had heard that those who have been in wars suffer from. He wished that all those he had killed and those killed by others could be alive again. But he didn't wish that he hadn't fought. He understood why he had done so in the same way he had done when he had entered the war. What was it, then?

Garrity put him into a team painting the walls of offices and houses. He went out into the world. But it was a world of which he must be perpetually wary. Men and women he'd fought beside were walking out of jails since the agreement had been signed. Others on the run had been given letters of assurance that they weren't being investigated and were unlikely ever to be. They could go home without fear. He was different. No one knew who he was. He'd been caught once but had escaped before his identity had been established. No letter of assurance could be sought for him by republicans because it would only make the British interested in him. No one he knew from the war had caused so much death as he had. Among the dead was Sir Matthew Hayford. The intelligence services might overlook the soldiers he'd killed, but not one of their own. Their appetite for vengeance had no end. He'd seen it himself – a spy or special forces operative killed in action and someone from the IRA unit responsible found ten years later with a bullet in the head. They'd know of the high number of republicans planted by Garrity around the city. Loose talk could lead them to him. He felt their scrutinising eyes. He knew what a prize he would be even for a cop on the beat seeking advancement.

He moved from the room over the garage. He moved often, he changed names. He called on his capacity for opaqueness, for always seeming to be passing through even as he stood still. The condition he noticed in Garrity's garage stayed with him. He wondered if it would pass. He could be well, eyes bright, anticipation rising, and it would come like a desiccating wind blowing him to a place that had become familiar and where a voice asked, What does it matter? It was faint or loud but always there or at least potentially so. When he reached for the brush, he heard its deadening message. If he was in a room with people laughing or if a woman asked when they would meet again, it spoke then too. When warned by the recruiting officer of the sacrifices he would likely make to take part in the war, he had not anticipated this one.

He bought a motorcycle. At high speeds he didn't notice it. It was supplanted by an intensity that imitated that of the war. In certain stages of drink it was the same. But drink and speed were limited by time and then the thing would return, as if it had a home in him. He worked with men. Most were immigrants, some of them Irish. None got to know him, though they tried. He preferred the company of women. He met them in music clubs, bars and in the places where he painted walls. Sometimes he stayed with them for a time. Sometimes the voice was silenced. But there was a limit on how long this could last that he was not aware of imposing, like a device regulating the speed of a vehicle.

During a break while painting walls in a house in Carmel, Ryan made a drawing of a clay pot on a window ledge. Ming at the time was designing the homes of Silicon Valley executives one after the other and this was one of them. He was there frequently. He observed Ryan, he observed everybody. Ryan seemed to him distinct in the way he moved the brush. His colour mixes were subtle, surprising. He was self-sufficient, organised. He respected the material. Ming watched him make the drawing of the pot. He saw the acuteness with which Ryan perceived and replicated the play of light on the pot's surface and the loveliness of its slopes. He thought the drawing better than the pot.

Ming approached Ryan in a suit the colour of Curaçao, and with fingertips pressed together like a prince assessing a jewel said, I didn't know you could do that.

From the beginning of his time as a designer Ming had seen the nuances of his vision destroyed by the crudeness of the painters hired to execute them. He had been looking in vain for someone who would stand in relation to him as a studio assistant did to a Renaissance master. He decided to invest in Ryan. He hired a specialist in effects to show him how to produce the appearance of wood grain, stone and glass with paint. He learned the mix of marble dust and wax needed to make Venetian plaster and he watched the specialist put down seven layers of translucent paint to achieve a particular hue of peppermint. A muralist was brought to teach him perspective. Ryan acquiesced. He was getting the art classes he'd never had.

He moved into a trailer in Salinas to be nearer the work. He felt easier there. There was more room. The scrutinising eyes seemed to recede. In Salinas he began again to draw with purpose. He drew trees, tables, signs, the faces of the Salvadorian lettuce pickers who sat out in deckchairs in front of their trailers. He drew their children. He asked if he could photograph them and then drew from that. Drawing held out more promise of deliverance than alcohol or high-speed runs on his motorbike or love. Love, he had begun to conclude, was an illusion. In drawing was a feeling from an earlier time when he believed that all was before him. He drew in order to feel the desire to draw.

One evening when he was in the city he called into a Tenderloin bar called the 21 Club on Turk and Taylor. There was an altar-like display of tinned spam among bumper stickers and Venetian masks behind the counter. Three men with long grey beards sat on stools along the window and watched a car break-in. A woman in a leather dress did a louche dance. Everyone there looked as if they had seen more than they wished but were still hanging on for more. They seemed held together in some kind of surfeit of the seen. Ryan watched them, and drank.

At closing time he stepped out into the street and began to walk. Night people of the Tenderloin were out, night people of a kind and of a profusion such as he had never seen before, staggering, pushing trolleys, asleep against walls, pulling up their pants in alleys, holding bundles against their chests, nervous, drunk, wary, buying, selling, sniffing, cajoling, carrying blades, looking for a connection, reeling from light to shadow with dust on their backs like the powder on moths' wings. They were exiles, exiles from where they were from and from the city where they lived and from the people in the street and from themselves, as he was. You could hide among them and never be found, he thought. He passed missions for the hungry, pay-day loan shops, drug clinics, fortified, bunker-like bars that were like emplacements on a battlefield. He saw two monks on either side of a semi-conscious man helping him along the pavement, a family of four from South-East Asia stepping in single file around people laid out on the ground and then going through the door of a hotel.

A little further on he went into one himself. It was called the Bostonian. It was a Tenderloin SRO hotel, the residents in long- or short-term decline, their bills paid by social security cheques. He was given a corner room on the eighth floor, number 814, with two large windows, a hotplate, microwave, refrigerator, desk and single bed. He could taste the salt on the sea air as it blew in through the windows. In the morning he went south, paid off the rent on the trailer in Salinas and sent his belongings in a cab up to the Bostonian Hotel. He painted the walls white and the floorboards a nautical blue. On a wall were postcards held by drawing pins, the corrugated leaves of a severed cabbage, Miles Davis bent low, two bandaged figures by Goya bludgeoning each other with cudgels, Mount Errigal in the sun, the laudanum poet James Clarence Mangan, his pencil sketch of the Russian Orthodox priest. They changed often, all but the drawing of the priest, but this was how they were that day. There were brushes in a mug of spirit, gun magazines on a small table by the bed. The magazines and sniper games in arcades were the last remains of a nostalgia he had yet to get rid of. The bed had sheets coloured cornflower blue. A woman's orange scarf was wound round the lampshade. Standing alone on an easel in the centre of the room was the unfinished painting with the vacant centre to which he must return.

Ryan came into the Bostonian Hotel from the bar in the Castro with two bottles of wine and a pear. The lift door shuddered open. It rose in lurches like a bucket being drawn up a well. Its metal walls were covered in tags, pleas, curses, ruminations, warnings and prayers. There was a drawing in acrylic of an Indian goddess with six arms, whose lotus flowers were watered by elephants and from whose palms poured a fountain of gold coins.

In his room Ryan sat on the floor and looked at his painting. Its lines were like a frame that turned around the empty centre. He had tried in the nights past to fill it, but hated each image even as he made them. The centre now was a platform of murky white where he'd painted them out. The feeling came to him that the painting would be his last or his first. It actively threatened him. He closed his eyes. He stilled his mind. He left room for the saving image to arrive, like an alighting bird. He waited. Nothing happened.

He was late for his appointment. It was already 8.30. He left his room and ran down two flights of stairs with a bottle of wine and came out onto the sixth floor. People leaned against walls, sat in garden chairs in their doorways. It was like a village square on a summer night. He smelled Caribbean spices, ammonia, pot smoke. There were arguments and sighs, languid kisses, cackling at old TV shows. He saw an altar to Krishna, a bandaged foot on a bed.

He stopped in front of room 618. 'Miss Alexis Johnson, B.A.' the door announced on an embossed card. The painting spread like a stain inside him, but he hoped that Alexis Johnson would make him forget it for a while. He gave a single tap. He heard a step and the rustle of silk. The door opened onto a tall, slender and very beautiful woman in a kimono, still as an orchid in a pot, a faint uncertain smile on her lips. Her skin was a dark amber, like an Eritrean's. Her hair fell in loose dark curls around her shoulders.

They kissed, a brush of the lips across the cheek. She stepped back and let him pass. Her room throbbed with candlelight. There were prints of women at their baths in frames on the aubergine walls. 'Funny Valentine' came out low from a speaker.

The room was familiar to him. He took her corkscrew from a drawer, lifted two glasses from her cabinet. The wine bottle popped. He poured wine for himself, water for her. She sat as she always did in a heavy chair strewn with cushions and he sat across from her. Then she lifted a small blue bottle and pointed at it with a waving finger.

I was just going to . . .

Paint your nails, he said.

Yes.

Persian blue.

She shook the stones in her necklace to show they matched. The kimono split around her leg as she lifted her foot onto the chair. But the light was dim and her eyesight weak. She squinted, pulled a candle closer, squinted again, gave up, and then opened a drawer beside her, raking through it with her long fingers.

I left my glasses right here, she said. Her voice was soft.

Do you want me to do it? he asked.

Paint my nails?

Yes.

She laughed.

You look so earnest, she said.

She set her foot on his lap. He picked up the bottle.

How is it done?

You know how to paint, she said.

She lay her head back on the cushion. He took a long drink of wine, then tipped the brush in the varnish and bent to the work. She closed her eyes. The music was warm and liquid.

He'd met her in the fall in Jonell's Cocktail Lounge on Ellis. She was slumped alone and asleep in a corner all in black with a wide-brimmed fedora tipped to the side, blood-red nails and lips and her hair tied up like a ballerina's. He'd seen her before in the hotel lift. She dressed formally by day, like a downtown banker, long sober dresses or suits with a string of pearls. When she got to her floor she nodded 'good evening', and moved along the hallway to her room, her gait strangely rigid.

He'd wondered about her. She always seemed so radically alone, suspended in something viscous, like an embryo. He drank beer at the corner of the bar and watched her. She didn't stir. At closing time he gently shook her shoulder. She opened her eyes and looked at him from under the brim of her hat.

Hi, she said.

Her voice was hoarse. She closed her eyes and he thought she would sleep again, but she spoke.

The boy with paint on his nails, she said.

He got her back to the hotel, his arm around her waist and her head resting on his shoulder. In the lift he heard her crying, faintly.

Pay no attention, she said.

She tottered, looking in her bag for her keys.

A small romantic disappointment, she said. Microscopic.

She held up her forefinger and thumb to indicate how small was her disappointment.

But the heart explodes, she said, and went into her room, hands up around her shoulders as if entering the sea.

She left a note in his postbox and when the weekend came she took him for dinner at a Vietnamese café. They told each other redacted and largely false stories of their lives. He was from Ireland, she a

Californian by adoption. He drove furniture vans around Europe for fifteen years, then came to America. She left a brief and forgettable childhood in the South, crossed the country and landed in Santa Monica, an all-white world of beach musclemen and surfer boys and cocktail bars and drives in turquoise convertibles along the Malibu coast. His job was painting walls. She came up to San Francisco and after getting a degree there was now a case worker in a Tenderloin drop-in clinic. She lived in the hotel so her clients would trust her. He painted canvases by night. He'd yet to finish one, but lived in hope or perhaps foolishness. One would be enough, he said. I just want to know what it would feel like.

In the months that followed they went on. They went for evening walks. She took him to exhibitions and sometimes to clubs where they danced. She was fine like spun glass. Her vagueness was curiously eloquent.

They played Scrabble in her room, where she spelled out arcane words with whole racks of letters at a time. Slowly, demurely, she let herself be known by him through words she spelled out on the Scrabble board. MEANDER led to VAGABOND to DRIFTER, a name she said she used when she was a prostitute in Los Angeles. She spelled out the names of the drugs she used to take and the brands of wine coolers she'd drunk for breakfast. Slang which he at first did not understand led to the revelation that she had resolved the yearnings and contradictions that had tortured her since childhood by having an operation in a Mexican clinic that changed her from a boy to a girl.

If you'd like to leave now I'll understand, she said. He stayed.

She had been Alexis for six years when she met Ryan in Jonell's. It was strange, it was unforeseeable. Neither they nor anyone looking on would have placed them together. That they would not be lovers brought her peace. She preferred longing for something she could not have than longing for what she could. And she'd seen something in him she recognised. She'd seen it before they even spoke. It hung around him, a shadow. He'd lost something or something had happened to him or he'd done something or perhaps all of these combined, she could not know for sure because he could not or at least would not speak of what had been the genesis of it. They walked the neighbourhoods. She dressed for the catwalk.

I'll not have you seen with a sloven, she said.

He blew on the wet varnish. Her foot waved like grass in a breeze. When he set it down and looked at the other she unwound from her trance and looked at him through clouded eyes.

I saw you yesterday, she said, edging upwards in her chair. Her voice was syrupy. But you didn't see me.

There was a slight tilt to her smile, as if she was trying to understand something for the first time.

I was on Columbus by Broadway, she said. That little Italian place with outdoor tables?

With a small piece of cotton soaked in spirit he removed a dot of Persian blue that had leaked onto her skin.

I see.

You were with a gorgeous woman with hair the colour of an apricot and a pork-pie hat on the back of her head holding your little finger and looking into your eyes like you were the Sun King.

He whirled the wine around the inside of his glass and drank it down.

You exaggerate, he said.

Who is she?

She's Melinda McCourt.

Where is she now?

Denver, I think.

You don't know.

She's a pilot. She comes and goes.

That makes sense.

What do you mean?

They can't come into your life if they're not going to go out again.

She smiled so he wouldn't take offence.

She's really pretty, she said.

Yes, she is.

I heard her laugh. It's a great laugh.

She tipped the bottle towards his glass and the wine tumbled in, glinting, the colour of lemons.

I'd never wear a pork-pie hat, she said.

She lay back and watched through her lashes as he drew a perfect blue border along the line of her cuticle.

Would you like her to come back?

It might not be the best thing for her, he said.

She can decide that.

He placed the brush in the bottle and pressed out with his laced fingers until the veins rose in his arms. Then he returned to his work.

You don't like this line of enquiry, do you? she said.

I can manage.

It's that I don't like to see you alone. If you had somebody you'd sleep better.

You don't have anybody, he said, looking up.

I get too wrought. I can't handle it.

I noticed in Jonell's.

You see?

She saw him swallow what remained in the glass. He'd been drinking since he'd started painting her nails and was drinking faster now. His eyes moved to the bottle on the table and hers moved with them and together they saw that the wine was gone. He would leave when he finished her nails or soon after for the lack of a drink and her night would become empty and she would feel dissatisfied. She crossed the room to her cooler and took a bottle still half-full from his last visit and left it on the table. The room seemed to alter with his relief. She took her place across from him.

Why don't you give her a chance? she said.

You're very determined.

You said you can manage.

He raised his hands as if about to make a declaration, then let them fall.

It never works, he said.

He poured wine for himself. His fingers moved around the beads on the glass.

I go out into the night. I might meet someone. I might get that jolt, you know it well, there's desire, fascination, nothing else exists. We connect for a night, or two, or a month. And then . . .

He stopped for a moment. He looked at her, then away, as if trying to find something there.

Yes? she said.

. . . then she starts to lose suspicion. I feel her open. She shows me something of herself. You know how it happens. Everybody does. She waits for me to move, to act in kind, I know it's time, I reach . . .

He held out his hands. She leaned across the table to follow the line of his gaze.

. . . but less out of belief than of obligation. The laugh, the touch. Her signal becomes thin, she fades . . .

They both watched the middle distance.

. . . and then she's no longer . . .

He turned to Alexis.

She's not there.

She stared at him. She seemed not to have heard, or understood. But he was emphatic. He'd reached an inescapable conclusion.

She was there, she said. I saw her.

There'll be a time when she won't be.

What if she is?

She won't be there *to me*.

This startled her, as something otherworldly would. His eyes were empty deserts. She remembered seeing her own like that in a mirror in a hotel room in Los Angeles, a blurred man in a bed beyond, two Quaaludes in her palm. She clutched herself by the arms and shivered.

What happened to you? he said.

I don't know. Something cold passed through me.

When I said that?

Yes.

Are you all right?

Her eyes moved to where they had been looking and back to him.

It was like a ghost, she said.

He reached for his glass. He watched her slowly come back to herself. But he'd unsettled her. She had understood that by saying 'She's not there' he'd meant that he was not and it frightened her. It brought her back to a dark time. He'd got into her head with a phrase. This became interesting to him. They stayed silent. He took a drink. He thought about fear. He had lived with fear during the war. He feared getting caught or being shot. More than anything he feared killing. To survive he'd had to enter it and use it. Fear became like an arrow that told him where he must go to stay alive. Even to feel alive. Then the war stopped and everything that went with it left him. What he feared now was the emptiness left behind by the receding tide of the war and that the painting he had made depicted it. It was not unlike his fear of killing. Should he not, then, enter it too?

Her music system flipped to 'Gloomy Monday'. He took a drink of wine and dropped his head back. The thought became inchoate. He wanted to hold onto it. He made the half-born painting appear on the ceiling. Its lines turned around the emptiness. Isn't this what he knew, what he was, and what he should paint? It was his truth now. Something seemed to be trying to gain entrance to the void. It appeared and disappeared. He drank another glass. Strange how desolating this emptiness felt yet how exhilarating it would be to express it.

The blood thickened. The night went deeper. He and Alexis moved along the perimeter of a twilight world.

Later he walked the streets until he went into a small bar on Jones. Only a barman was there.

Do you have brandy?

Yes.

Crème de menthe?

Yes.

The barman poured from two bottles over ice and set the glass before Ryan. There were old beer and spirit advertisements on the walls, ladies in ballgowns, cowboys with glittering teeth, Caribbeans carrying sugar cane. One was an internally lit box in lurid greens and blues showing pines and a rippling lake. A hunter stood by his cabin door. The Land of Sky Blue Waters. The electric bulb in the box combined with some mechanism made the tall pines appear to sway and the lake water to move. The hunter was still. What would he need? Patience. Alertness. Readiness. Kill.

Ryan called for another drink. The barman poured. He looked up to the sign Ryan had been staring at, then away. He slipped a disc of slow piano pieces into the machine behind the bar. Time passed.

It's like fur, said Ryan.

The barman jumped.

The beer sign?

No.

The stinger?

The music.

The barman cocked an ear.

How can it be like fur? It's a piano.

Who wrote it?

Frédéric Chopin.

The barman moved his fingers as if playing the notes.

It's more like rain, he said.

Ryan drained the glass.

It's like fur, he said.

After he left the bar he walked through the Tenderloin past Van Ness to Lafayette Park and back. He went up in the lift and stood before his door. He felt the key in his pocket. He waited a while poised between two notions. He heard his own irregular breath. He stepped forwards then back. Finally he went back along the corridor and dropped down the stairs to the floor below.

He arrived at a door with twisting blue vines painted on silver under the legend 'Mavis Bogdanovich's Painted Door', and knocked. She answered, pulling the loose sleeve of her sweater up onto her shoulder, then stepped back to let him in.

She was twenty-four. Her skin had a soft copper glow. One whole arm was covered with tattoos, from her fingernails up to her shoulder.

Books were stacked along one wall of her room and drawings filled others. Some were by Ryan. His nights with her were long. She cut his hair. She cooked beans and rice and they drank wine. Usually they smoked opium. She flavoured it with cloves and cinnamon.

Sometime around one o'clock that night she took her pipe out from a drawer. It was bamboo and had a dragon painted along its length. A hundred-year-old San Francisco relic that came in on a boat from China. She put on a disc of Maria Callas singing the aria from *Gianni Schicchi*, spiced a ball of opium and heated it over her lamp. Smoke wafted around them as they passed the pipe.

He felt the glorious exhilaration slither towards him and then roar. All that he could be was in it, all vision and nobility and heightened sereneness. The orchestra, Mavis's voice, the arcing soprano notes, all within and without. He sensed her liquid warmth, the burning oil and cinnamon. He rode this floodtide until it left him down in an endless hall with jewelled walls, a scene of silence and magnificence that could have been painted by Titian and went on and on. She spoke, he drew. It seemed they were not in time.

At 4 a.m. he was sitting on the floor of his room looking at his painting. In the centre now was a phantom in diaphanous blue. He waited to see if there was more, but that was all, for now. He sat back down and looked. This wasn't it. The longer he waited the less possible it was to escape from this. Finally he fell asleep against the wall.

My father went when a tractor tipped onto him and burst his spleen. Later I told you it was a stroke. Those big muddy wheels, those bodily juices . . . I was always tidying up when I told you of my life.

They held back the funeral until I could get there. I'd not been home in four years. I'd grown used to big American cars, big closets, big paycheques. Everything looked small and tight. Their struggles too seemed small, and overfamiliar. The Sacred Heart. The GAA trophies. Old magazines with crossword puzzles in a rack. They'd made a grotto of my certificates and graduation photographs.

We sat around the old dining table the night before the funeral. My brother and sisters told me about their jobs and my various nephews and nieces. Paddy was in the Guards. Ellen was a landscape gardener in Longford. Margo was in Nottingham. I forget what her job was. My mother was silent. She fretted at the hem of her cardigan. She was going to sell the house, she told us. No one wanted to tend cows. And she did sell it, two years later, and went over to Margo in Nottingham. It had seen six generations of us. It's owned now by a Dane who gives tai chi classes in the barn.

It all seemed so far away.

I walked behind the coffin and then sat in the family pew next to it during the Mass. I saw Margo raising her hands helplessly and letting them drop onto her lap and weeping. It occurred to me that it might be right or even useful to me to grieve as she was, but that wasn't available to me that day. He'd erased himself and elevated me so assiduously that I'd barely been able to see him. He mended things. He rode tractors. He ate mostly in silence.

Of course I didn't know then that he was the keeper of an arsenal for the IRA.

The next day I borrowed a car and drove over to see Eimear. Weeds had overtaken the vineyard and orchard. Patches of rendering had fallen from the façade. I rapped and it took a long while for her to reach the door. I heard her feet scrape along the stone floor. She was in black lace with a skullcap over her bald head.

Well now, it's you, she said.

She gestured towards her clothes.

For your Da, God rest him.

I took her parchment hands and kissed them.

And where did you learn to do that? she said.

Lisbon.

She cackled a little lasciviously.

I followed her down the long hall. Heaps of rags and shoes and hats came out from the rooms like sand drifts. She stopped at the kitchen. I could see yellow plastic bags stuffed under counters, boxes of rusted wire and car parts and old radios.

You go into the drawing room and I'll make tea, she said.

Her wolfhounds still loped through the rooms, stepping gingerly over heaped newspapers and through the windows. Fintan Lalor, the old rifles. All that was here when Generous was alive seemed to have proliferated like a fungus. The line of aristocracy and the line of a failed revolution have their logical end in a hoarder drowning in the past, he'd once said to me. It went over my head at the time, but I hadn't forgotten it.

Eimear came in with the tea.

I know what you're thinking, she said. You think I'm cracked. But there's not a thing here I don't know where it is. Your Uncle Sean is always at me to get someone to clear it out, but I won't let them touch a scrap, sure as God I won't.

The portrait of Generous I'd last seen at his funeral was above the mantelpiece, dusted, bright, a museum lamp shining down on it.

He comes right out of the frame at you, don't you think? she said. You can feel him thinking.

Who was it made the painting, Eimear?

A young lad who passed some time with us here. He told us it was his first-ever painting. Isn't that something now?

She leaned towards me and whispered.

They say he's still about the hills somewhere.

Then she winked.

An otherworldly kind of fear rose in me.

What did he look like? I asked.

Well he was tall, fair. *Very* handsome, if I may say so. And then when he smiled – he didn't smile often, mind, he was quite serious – you could see a piece was missing from a front tooth. I found it quite appealing.

There he was again.

I flew back to Ithaca. I resumed my life. Up to then it had been a rink on which I'd glided like the skaters at Rockefeller Center, but I couldn't shake an uneasiness. Then about a year later the pale grey cloud hove down out of the sky.

I was twenty-six. I'd been invited to a conference at Princeton. We all went out to dinner before the event, a neuroscientist, a poet, a medical ethicist and some heads of department. I had on a white linen suit and a pair of canvas tennis shoes. It was a beautiful spring evening. I put a rose from the restaurant through my buttonhole. We came in through wide glass doors with the arriving crowd and into a marble foyer. I remember my shoes squeaking as I walked. There was a group of what looked like graduate students off to the side on low benches. I think one looked up at me as we passed, an owlish young woman with drab clothes and spectacles. I'm not altogether sure. But when I was just beyond them I heard laughter – solitary, loud, female and what I took to be derisory laughter. It echoed in the vast foyer. I thought, I completely *believed*, that it was directed at me, at my white suit and the red rose and what I imagined was my look of self-satisfaction as I made my way towards the theatre. It rattled on inside my head. I spun around. None of the group on the bench was looking at me. I tried to read their faces. Nothing.

As we took our places on the stage I felt nauseous. I wanted to burn my suit. I survived through an enormous act of will, then went drinking with the poet. When the barman put us out we emptied the little refrigerator in my room. It didn't do any good. I felt exposed before the world, that everyone could see that I had nothing.

I wondered how it happened. To be undone in an instant like that. Maybe she wasn't laughing at me. Maybe she was just dismissing something insipid said by one in her group. But did it matter? The results were the same. I'd seen how fragile was the construct I'd made of myself.

When I got back I put my white suit into the back of the closet. I had a bad year. I kept hearing that honking, inhuman laugh. I laid low. I ground out cautious essays, sat on committees, played *Myst* on my computer. I wondered where I'd gone.

Then I took the summer job in Helsinki. I felt a little better there. I found a group of fellow academics and stuck with them. At Midsummer five of us took off for the lakes at Hämeenlinna and stayed in an old lodge there. We drank of course, like everyone else. A Korean medievalist pushed it up to 104°C in the lodge sauna and came out with a birch garland on his head and nothing else, his skin the colour of a pomegranate. We sat in a rowboat with a bottle of schnapps and headed off for a circuit of the cabins on the lakeshore. That's when I found you, barefoot on the water's edge. It was the night of perpetual light, the colour pearl. I knew little then about how to sense a woman's gifts, but I could see your structure, your class, your ease with yourself. You had on a white dress with small red flowers. The hem was up over your knees. You were looking back over your shoulder laughing at something someone said. Everything I saw told me you were beyond my reach. We sat with our feet in the water. The bonfires burned. The Korean sang. We went around the lake in a rowboat. It was all so effortless and transfixing. Like Ronchamp.

We had our summer days and nights in your apartment. We went to Turku to meet your parents. There was that weekend in Krakow when the concert violinist sitting on his own in evening dress suddenly broke into Brahms in the underground bar. The crowded oppressive sky lifted, the scavenging laughter trailed into silence. When we told each other the stories of our lives I didn't speak of Baudrillard or Princeton or of how Generous killed the Englishman or what I saw my brother doing from the top of the tree. The road was opening ahead of us. I felt newly born, unfathomably lucky, saved from the brink. Everything was obvious. Why complicate it with stories of the past?

The light was crystalline the day we married in the forest. Lydia came the following year. We moved to the city after I got that offer from Columbia. I'd wake in the night in our little apartment in Brooklyn, euphoric. I'd gotten away with it. I took the harvest.

CHAPTER FOUR

The Empty Dress

San Francisco, 2009

He was still on the floor when he woke. Somehow he had got his shoes off. He looked at the painting with its coy blue figure in the centre and felt nauseous. There was nothing there. He saw a milky low light behind the clouds. He couldn't tell if it was morning or afternoon.

He drove his bike 150 miles north on 101, turning with a dry mouth and aching muscles and sensations of panic into the Mendocino National Forest at Upper Lake. The sun had cleared the clouds and he could see that it was still morning. He'd slept two, maybe three hours. He felt exhaustion radiating upwards through his body.

He left the bike under a tree and began to walk into the wilderness. He'd go in deep and wait. A riot of calls from ground animals and birds accompanied him. He listened to his footfalls, watched the sun rise towards the treetops, trying to stay ahead of the phantoms that stalked him. He followed a river into a narrow canyon where there were four steaming pools fed by mineral springs. He took off his clothes and stood in a beam of light. Then he lowered himself into the hottest of the pools and leaned his head against a rock. He smelled sulphur and iron. He slept there in the bubbling water.

Later when he began to walk the call of the animals came up again. Dust rose around him. The river flashed in the sun. He knelt and drank from it, then sat in the gravel by its shore. He put his feet in the water. He stayed still until everything in the forest ceased to notice that he was there. He waited. He was looking for the respite the forest could grant him. The sun moved across the gap in the trees above him. Then it came. The silence rose. He felt an inner click. The extra sense came alive again. The alertness, the sense of now and nothing else he'd lived by in the war. He held it until it passed.

The days when he could do as he wished were about to end. Ming had been calling. He'd already written the contract for the house on Telegraph Hill. He was constructing the palette. The work would be detailed, taxing and long. They were to meet that night on the slopes of the hill above North Beach. I will introduce you to the house, said Ming.

At a roadside restaurant he ate an omelette and drank coffee with a shot of rum in it.

He made a decision that he would either complete the painting that was in his room within seventy-two hours or he would slash it with a box cutter.

Ahead of him Ryan saw Ming waiting at the foot of the Vallejo Steps. He was smoking a thin cigarette and carrying two English shooting sticks and for this evening had selected a sapphire blue cashmere suit, pink socks and snakeskin Chelsea boots. Ryan joined him and together they ascended the lanes beneath Coit Tower through low sunlight until Ming came to a stop.

There, he said, pointing.

They planted the shooting sticks beneath a tree a little way along from the house of Paul Crane, and sat. It was the tallest on this short street, rising four storeys from a brick base, and was set in its own land. A path on the left led to a garden behind. The houses beside it were made to seem deferential by its height and the scale of its windows. The bricks were a red that was almost black and the wood that made up the rest of the house had been painted violet. A colonnaded balcony ringed the top floor.

Ming pressed his palms downward in a request for silence and they watched the house. The late sun lit it from behind. Nothing moved in the street.

Very special house, said Ming at last. Original glass. Bricks laid by gold miners. The red cedar in the walls saved it from fires that came with earthquake. From up there on that balcony, you walk around, it's all there before you, whole wonder of this city – bridges, bay, hills, Alcatraz, boats on the way to China. You see plaque by door?

Ryan did. It read: '1852'.

Before baseball, Ryan, before presidency of Lincoln.

A yellow car of Swedish make pulled up in front of the house and a striking woman with a large head of black hair and wearing a track-suit got out.

Charlotte Crane, said Ming. Back from dance class.

She moved around to the back of the car to take her bag from the trunk.

Very vivid person. You think she might turn to fire in a moment. Then she's indoors for two weeks. Shade down. Deliveries from drugstore. A little strange . . .

How do you know this?

I invest. I put city historian on house and detective on family. This is important. Different strata. We get this, life changes.

He turned to Ryan and smiled coolly.

I know you don't care, he said.

The noise of the closing trunk brought the silhouette of a boy to a third-floor window. Ming raised an index finger to alert Ryan.

Oliver, son to Charlotte and Paul, said Ming. Chess player. Eleven years old and deeply loved.

The boy watched his mother walk up the short path to their door and then ran from the window to meet her.

143

And the husband? asked Ryan.

Inside. Almost always inside making money. Very strong mathematician. He invents devices. Investors beg him to take their money. He made his own bank and sold it for $4.6 billion. Bought house with cash from suitcase. It's a legend. You see that yellow car? Twenty-three years old. Dent on wing. It's the only one they have. He's from Midwest and has accent from England. You look at him and you see very strong and very weak. Same moment. Also like wife a little strange, but differently so. He plays me. I don't know why. Not necessary for him. A lot of designers lining up . . . But he's not important for now. She'll make the decision. He looks at her like dog waiting for master outside shop.

Ming rose from his seat but then stood still and looked at the house.

A sea captain from England made it, Ryan, he said. Tom Merriweather. Sailed out of Liverpool in 1817 as a cabin boy, landed here in San Francisco as a captain in 1849. Decides to settle. Marries American woman. I got documents. Picks spot for new house and they start to dig. Has warehouse full of things brought from all over the word he's going to put in it. Then dies, just like that, heart failure, no children. This happens in 1852. Year on plaque. Year they put roof on and hand wife the key.

You get tragedy just from the number of the years, he said. But that's all I know. Name. Numbers. Things on papers.

He took Ryan's arm.

Come on, Ryan. I'll take you to Tommy Toy's. You look a little rough. Need nourishment.

They began their descent into the city.

Ming had been born Duong Than Bao in the Central Highlands of Vietnam just before the American war and had arrived in San Francisco on a freighter out of Manila after years of a feral life around South-East Asia. He remembers parrots flying low through the bush and blue smoke rising from the hooches. He lost everyone in his family apart from his mother, who was in Saigon at the time, to a grenade thrown by a Korean into the bunker in which they were hiding.

He was twenty-seven when the freighter touched shore. He lived at first in a box in Golden Gate State Park. He fenced watches and bicycles. But he had a desire for standing and money that was ravening. He presented himself as Chinese because of bad associations with the war. He made purchases at vintage clothes shops and costumiers', stored them in a bus station locker, changed in a public toilet and travelled to gallery openings and first nights he read about in newspapers. No one refused him. In time they sent him invitations.

He believed that his greatest strength as a designer was the thoroughness of his preparation as an actor. He studied his clients and became what he believed he needed to be according to their susceptibilities. He watched films, wrote down phrases and practised in front of a mirror. He could play baseball fan, gay or mystic, be scolding or obsequious. Sometimes he spoke a level of English some steps below his own. But in spite of himself he had exquisite taste and could not prevent himself from exercising it. It brought him trouble sometimes. It came from his mother, whom he'd assisted in her work as a designer of stage sets for travelling players. When his ploys worked, as they nearly always did, he felt a satisfaction that was like revenge.

He was forty-six years old and lived in an apartment in the Mission with his Laotian wife and their four children.

They sat under a silk tapestry at a corner table in Tommy Toy's Chinese restaurant on Montgomery Street. Ming had ordered eight courses for them, a lucky number in China. The room was full. Candlelight flickered on the bare arms of women and the faces of men who leaned towards them in their suits. There were soft waves of speech and the sounds of moving cutlery and glass. Ming kept a small bottle of maotai at his side.

A waitress in a pencil skirt and starched white shirt arrived with bowls of jasmine rice and a plate with an ivory mollusc the size of a child's fist in the centre.

Treasure in the Snow, she said softly, and withdrew.

Ming was full of the house on Telegraph Hill. He saw it with a particularity that was unusual for him. He hadn't a need to reach for the generic for any of its parts. He understood how rare this was for a designer. He could taste the work. He'd offer to do it for nothing if that wouldn't make him seem mad, or an apprentice.

Got to have this house, Ryan, he said. I see it whole, like Mozart see concerto.

Ryan only partly listened. He watched the light. Chromatic, oil-spill colours pooled over Ming's face. Ryan squinted, turned his head from side to side. Gossamer filaments from the tablecloth flamed. Candles and lamps and particles of steam had spectrum hues. It was like the day he'd looked through the haze at the cat on the wall behind his house in Ballymurphy. He'd been in short trousers and had scuffed knees. The call of his father. Scorcher! He hadn't killed anyone yet. The voice of Ming came through. He heard him say the words *grisaille*, *chinoiserie* and *trompe l'oeil*. He heard the pretentious names suggestive of luxurious living given to paints. They were the common currency of his everyday exchanges. He knew exactly what they meant. Yet in this moment they faintly disgusted him. He'd fought a revolution and was making illustrations on the walls of the rich. The illustrations had no meaning. They were mute. If only his comrades in D Company could see him now. The painting in his room was likewise mute. He kept taking aim at it and missing. He must paint himself into life. Or what?

How much time do I have before this job, Ming? he asked.

You got something to do?

Yes.

What is it, if you don't mind?

I'm trying to make a painting.

Ming considered this, nodded.

Good luck with that, Ryan.

Thank you.

Paul Crane's not signed yet.

Oh, yes. I'd forgotten.

I have appointment with them next week. I humbly request that you attend.

All right.

The waitress came with the final course, bird's nest with papaya and almonds. Ming inhaled the aromas of the dessert and smiled at Ryan.

I'll get it for us, Ryan. I'll pick the lock. I've got you down for fifty-five an hour. I told them you worked in Geneva and Milan.

He lifted a forkful of the dessert to his mouth.

Plus you did the faux finishes at Keith Richards' house.

Ming left a hundred-dollar bill for the waitress and they went out into the street. The cool air stopped them. Small eddies of wind stirred around Ming's cuffs. He looked to the sky, then back to Ryan.

Strange. Like winter suddenly, he said.

He hailed a taxi and stepped in. You want a lift? he asked through the window. Ryan waved him off and Ming was driven away.

He walked towards home through the towers of money along Montgomery Street. The district was empty and the air loaded. It stirred like an animal waking from sleep. He felt it move along his skin.

He turned right and walked along the perimeter of the Tenderloin. Dark clouds of a purple hue moved in from the bay. There were distant flashes and rumblings. A store awning cracked in a sudden gust like a pistol shot. He had not seen such weather before in the city. He looked down the length of Leavenworth. His alertness rose. He was always looking for that. He would see what came of the storm. He walked on. The rain began to fall, light at first, then it gathered into a stampede, water and ice exploding on the pavements and the roofs of cars. The noise and sense of release were tremendous. It was as if the city were being sculpted by what drove down from the sky. He ran along walls, the streets primordial, the storm rising.

He stopped under a tin roof overhanging the window of a shop. It was backed with black velvet drapes and lit with cool greens and blues like a reptile house. He couldn't immediately tell what it was. It seemed a kind of installation. Then he saw it was for weddings. Women's shoes with ribbons and jewelled heels were mounted on glass daises, there were hats and guitars on strings and wedding dresses strung up on hooks to look as if they were flying. The rain and hail beat down on the roof. The sound was like a train roaring through a tunnel. He set himself for a dash through the storm, but saw something out of place in a corner of the window, a bridesmaid's dress in coral pink from another age on a headless mannequin, thick at the waist and shoulders, plain, stolid, a wallflower among the flying brides. A bouquet of synthetic carnations lay in the crook of her arm. He watched her. He wondered who had thought to place her there, out of her time, out of her style. He imagined her with dirty blonde hair and hazel eyes looking out onto the dancefloor. Her dress and form were there but she was not. No one would take her out onto the moonlit lawn to dance. She'd been made to grow used to being overlooked. Water from the roof ran down his neck. *She's not there, I'm not there. She's not there, I'm not there.* He took a notebook from his pocket and drew the bridesmaid's dress.

He ran out into the rain and hail. The painting came alive, viridian green, diamond pattern, moons, cadmium red, the empty dress. Broad wings tinted purple he saw there, something black and coiled lower right, the dress like a manifesto in the centre.

He got onto Market and turned towards the Tenderloin, running at full pace. He wanted to get there before the feeling left him. The sound was of a thousand pounding drums.

At Fell Street he stopped on an island because he couldn't see. He was as wet as if he'd walked in a lake. He cleared the water from his eyes.

He saw then through the sheets of grey rain a figure moving towards him, a woman in white. Her hands were in the pockets of her coat. She walked steadily, heedless of the rain. He watched her. The sight was as strange as if a gazelle rather than a woman were walking in the vacated streets. As she got closer he could see her face. Her mouth was open, her brow was set in concentration. But she seemed to be looking into some other world. Water poured over them both as if emptied from buckets. She stepped into Fell Street, seeing nothing, it seemed, and walked directly at him. Then she was so close to him he could feel the warmth of her body.

She moved past. White light hit them like a photographer's flash. There was a high whine of tyres moving over water. It was a car trying to beat the light. The woman stepped off the island directly into its path. There was no chance it could stop in time. The car's horn blared and Ryan reached back and held her by the arm.

Wait, he said.

She shook her head, still looking down.

Don't, she said.

You'd have died.

What?

Or worse.

She saw the car speed across Market.

Let me go, she said.

He released her arm, but she didn't move.

Are you all right? he asked.

She said something, but he couldn't hear it through the rain.

What did you say?

He leaned closer to her.

She looked up at him then, like someone just waking. Traces of mascara led down from her eyes. The rainwater shone like chrome on her skin.

I asked if you were all right, he said.

Yes.

She looked away again.

I've been walking a long time, she said.

Let's get out of the rain.

She didn't answer him but followed when he crossed the road. They went in under an awning. She stood a little distance from him, jaws tight, hands balled into fists, bisected by light from the streetlamp. Her hair dripped. Shadows of the falling rain moved over her face.

You're cold, he said.

Yes.

Do you have far to go?

No. Yes.

She shivered.

I wasn't going anywhere, she said.

Let me buy you a brandy.

She faced him, then turned away. She didn't reply.

To warm you.

Where would you take me?

There, he said.

He pointed over the border into the Tenderloin.

They watched the rain. It reached a plateau, and settled there.

In her trance she did again what he suggested. They moved along walls and into a low bar with hurling sticks and photographs of boxers on the walls. People of the Tenderloin trapped by the storm were there. Two Asian women sitting by the door looked up from their cocktail straws as Ryan and the woman entered.

He called for two brandies and brought them to a table under an aquarium where she waited. Electric hula dancers gyrated to either side of the tank. He took off his wet coat and hung it over the back of his chair. She kept hers on, still belted at the waist. It was white like the spume of a wave. They sipped their drinks. Green watery light passed over her face. He hadn't clearly seen her before. She looked intently into her glass. She was young, perhaps not yet thirty. She seemed to be thinking through a sequence. Her hair was white gold, her eyebrows dark. There were two blue stones hanging by silver chains from each ear, a flame tattooed on her wrist, orange baseball boots and bare legs.

Are you better? he asked.

Than?

I mean warmer.

The brandy is good, she said.

She smiled briefly.

What was it? he asked.

What?

That had you walking in the rain.

I have to answer?

You don't, he said.

You were there too.

I felt the storm coming, he said. I wanted to see it.

She tipped what was left in her glass into her mouth.

Do you think I can have another? she asked.

You can.

I didn't bring money.

He passed an absolving hand through the air.

At the bar he turned around and looked at her as he waited for the drinks to be poured. She was staring at the wall as though she could see something happening there. Her face tightened and flinched.

He placed the glasses on the table. They sat in silence. She moved a little in her chair. She opened her mouth to speak, stopped, took a drink of brandy.

I saw somebody die tonight, she said then. He was . . .

She breathed in but her voice caught. A kind of agony seemed to enter her. She began to weep.

I can't stop since . . .

She moved her eyes to his, unguarded, pleading.

Did you ever see somebody die? she asked.

Yes.

You did? Where?

There was a war happening where I grew up.

Were you in this war?

No.

What was it like, to see somebody die?

I understand you.

But no, tell me, she said.

It was very slow. There was struggle, then helplessness. Then nothing.

Yes, she said. That's it.

She saw it again, whatever it was. A shudder passed through her.

Can you tell me? he asked.

She looked around his face. She wondered if she could or would. She drank her brandy.

It was an accident. Someone fell from very high. A man, Srećko . . .

Her voice caught again. She had to stop.

Sorry. I'm in a circus. Not a regular one. We're little, just six of us . . . now five. We travel around, we make up plays, do things we're not supposed to do, disrespectful things, we think they're funny things. Sometimes we do dangerous things, but nothing ever happened. Then tonight . . . Srećko was one of us. We met him in Belgrade. He's from over there. Talented, innocent, crazy. Big bear. We had a thing for a little while. And sometimes . . . He was very lovely. Ingenious. He had a trick where he juggled with live chainsaws . . .

She laughed a little.

He was up on the wire. He'd been with Russian circuses and he didn't believe in harnesses or nets. I was on the stage in a chair. He was doing his things up there, in his top hat, splits and somersaults. And then he missed. He came down. I watched him all the way. His mouth was open. He spun like a seed pod. I saw his eyes. They were amazed. I thought he'd fall on me. Then crash, loud, like a load of boards, just next to me, everything broken, ragdoll legs, blood bubbling out of his mouth . . . He pulled on air as he looked at us around him. Then like you said. Nothing.

She was silent then. She drank some more.

I left. I started to walk. Then the rain . . . then you . . .

She looked desperately alone. He moved his chair to be beside her. He took her hands in his.

You should stay close to that, he said.

What do you say?

To him, to what you saw. Live with it. Let it do its worst.

And then?

Maybe it'll take its rightful place.

And I won't feel so bad?

. . . I don't know.

Is that what you did?

I didn't let it do its worst, at the time.

Why not? You didn't think like that?

I was too busy.

They stayed like that, hand in hand, in a precocious intimacy. Then she let go and swirled the dark liquid in her glass.

I never drank brandy before, she said.

I'll get us another.

He called for the drinks.

What will you do? he asked.

I'll walk a while.

I can go with you to your house. I can sit with you until you sleep.

I can't go there.

Because?

Srećko was there. Tonight before the show. The glass he drank wine from is there, his shoes. I can't look at that, not yet, not in the dark.

After their touch of hands the dead man seemed suddenly to him to be an intruder.

He passed her a handkerchief.

Here, he said.

For what?

With a finger he indicated where tracks of mascara ran down from her eyes. They were like the lines painted on the faces of clowns. There was a mirror beside her. She knelt on her chair, dabbed at the lines. A woman before a mirror, so often painted.

The storm's stopped, he said.

Yes.

He leaned towards her.

Would you trust me?

She looked for a moment as if she didn't.

I have a room, he went on. Not beautiful but clean. You can rest there. When you feel better you can go back home.

A room?

It's just to sleep. I promise you.

Their faces were close. He saw her eyes, the grass-like lashes, the depthless ovals, the blues and greens in the irises like crushed minerals. The room blurred and faded.

You are . . . unusual, she said.

They drank the brandy and stepped out. There was no wind now. The sky was clear. People were in the street or looking upwards from the fire escapes of the SRO hotels. There was a high quarter moon and a dome of stars. They began to walk. They didn't speak. He felt her height and rhythm, as she felt his. The air was cool and soft. He felt its touch on his face, saw her eyes wide and bright. He guided her by the arm around pools of rainwater.

Later, he lay on the floor of his room under a blanket. She was in his bed. The drawing of the bridesmaid was in his pocket. He might be painting it now had he not come upon her in the storm. Instead he'd turned the painting to the wall when they came in so she wouldn't see it. It felt alive still.

They were on their sides, facing each other, a man and a woman in a room acting like passengers waiting for a train. He saw her through the prism of his lashes, a glow around her of warm hues, traces of violet in the shadows. Night had led through alcohol and opium to day and back to night again. He'd slept very little. His consciousness dipped like a bird but rose again. Something in him held to this night.

Are you awake? she whispered.

Yes.

I'm sorry about the floor.

I've had worse, he said.

Like?

Iron foundry, graveyard, a cellar in an old mill . . . There were animals there I could hear but couldn't see.

She made an involuntary cry.

Culvert, he added.

What's that?

A drain by a road . . . The worst was a bathtub.

The worst has to be those animals.

He appeared to consider this.

A bathtub is very hard, he said.

The bells of her laughter chimed softly. It was the first time he'd heard her laugh. There was something rich and knowing in it, something

155

hedonistic. He'd have liked to hear it again but couldn't think of how to provoke it. They passed back into silence. Sleep moved around him like dancers with veils. He thought again of the dress and its absent brides-maid. He thought he might lose himself there, but he was aware of her. He couldn't shake this. He opened his eyes. A grey first light had leaked through the window and lay on the floor like a fog. She was still looking at him, the sheets up around her neck, her hand under her cheek. She seemed to be floating just over the pillow, waiting. The thought that she would not sleep, that she never had, ever in her life, briefly took him. Then he sensed light, intense and vibrant, in the space between them. All he could see were her eyes. She'd turned them on like lamps. The space between them was breached. There was for a moment nothing else. Was it a circus trick? Had he dreamed it? He felt a kind of vertigo. Then the lids came down like doors suddenly closing. He watched her, on guard.

That was the last he remembered of the night of the storm.

His phone buzzed against his hip. He opened his eyes. He saw his shoes, the legs of his easel and, above, the woman's hand, upturned, half-open, tattooed and at the end of the blue sleeve of the shirt he'd given her to wear. She was asleep, softly breathing. Her eyes were moving beneath the lids in a dream. Her head lay lightly on his pillow. The trouble of the night was absent from her face.

He took the phone into the bathroom so as not to wake her. It was Ming.

Sorry, Ryan. It's early for you, I know.

You're all right.

I need colours for the presentation at the Crane house.

Ryan saw his own bloodless face in the mirror. He drank water from the tap while Ming asked him to go to Pat Garrity's shop and mix whites, some with undertones of violet, others with Wedgwood blue, a few with green.

Your colours, please. Not chart.

They signed off. He stepped into a room not quite his. He caught the scent of her clothes, the faint warming of the air that came from her body. He wondered should he wake her now. She could be alarmed to open her eyes to an empty room. Her cheek was flushed. She was light and entirely still. She seemed as impersonal as a statue and yet vulnerable in an alien bed. He reached to touch her shoulder to tell her he had to leave but the daylight had made the night an unreachable world and he stopped.

The clock said 8.24. He wrote 'I'll be back at 10.30' on a page and left it on top of her jeans. As he made for the door he saw the painting, turned away from the room like a punished child. He took it from the easel and jammed it behind an ice machine in the corridor.

He drove south on the freeway, a little hungover. This was familiar. The metallic taste, the haunted mood. He thought of how he might rid himself of it. He thought of Garrity, Ming, the short time he had left with his painting, the woman and her grief and the meaning of their night. He'd like to see her eyes again. He'd like to hear her laugh. He had no inkling that his life was about to change.

He came off the freeway south of Daly City and drove through the neighbourhood of dollar stores and muffler shops where he used to live to Garrity's shop. In the back room where the machines were he spent an hour mixing and testing until he had all the colours asked for by Ming. He brought the formulas out to Garrity.

Well, Ryan, and how's the form?

Not bad. But I'm after two long nights.

You want to watch that.

He reached into a cabinet below the till and pulled out a bag full of carrots with the greens still sprouting from the tops.

What about these then? Hey, Ryan? Fresh from the garden this morning.

I'm not cooking these days, Pat.

Still in the hotel then.

I am.

That's hardcore, boy.

He ran a hand through his hair.

Here, come out to us one Sunday, will you? he said. I've put in a deck. We'll grill some steaks, play a few hands of cards. Do it now, at last. And lookit. Sheila's niece is coming over from Sligo. Computer whizz. She has a job down in Palo Alto. Pretty girl, Ryan. And smart.

He looked at Ryan, head cocked.

Sure, Pat. Just let me know.

He drove back downtown in the outside lane and when he got there bought croissants and coffee for them both and walked to the hotel. At the door he paused. She'd be asleep still, he thought. He inserted his key, turned the handle, let it fall open.

He got it then all at once, the thing that pushed him from bar to bar and out onto the open road and away from himself – the familiar emptiness and inertness of his room, the deadness of the things in it. He saw the light on the floorboards, the strip of carpet where he'd slept. She'd folded his blanket and made the bed. A window was open a little, the curtains waving like seaweed in a current. He saw all this from the threshold and then stepped over a slip of paper. She'd written a note under his – 'Thank you, whoever you are – Nicky xx.' He threw open the window, sat on the ledge and ate his breakfast. The day lay ahead of him, horizonless.

He didn't know what to do with himself just yet. He'd thought he'd pass the day with her. There was no reason for him to make anything of it. A stranger had been given shelter from a storm. She'd left a note. It had happened to him before, often enough, when he was younger, missed chances he'd inflated into something larger and then brooded over. He wouldn't do such a thing to himself now. But where had she gone? Why didn't she wait?

In the afternoon he slept and dreamed of the storm. When he woke he felt not well but clear. He put away the blanket and reached for the shirt. Beneath it, in a coil, was her belt. It was black, soft, worn, with silver studs along the whole of its length. He wouldn't have expected it, the muted eroticism of silver and black. He looked at her note. Nicky, and a little xx. He rolled the belt back into a spiral and sat on the window ledge, looking at it.

He'd been waiting for the night, but it was slow to arrive. In the evening with light still in the sky he felt the oppression of the room. But he had no appetite for anything outside. He feared the painting now that he must face it, but also wanted it. He took it from behind the ice machine and brought it into his room. He covered the blue phantom with a wash and sketched the bridesmaid's dress directly onto it. He put white wings with a purple hue at its back. The dress too became a canvas on which he drew lines and panels with pencil. He did as he wished. It went fast.

He stopped at midnight, sat on the floor and drank and watched. After a while he began again.

By four o'clock the painting seemed to be finished. It had in it something of what had led to it, something of the night of the storm and also something it seemed to have brought about itself, something that had nothing to do with him. There was only the last vacancy low and centre-right. He took the woman's belt and placed it on a chair next to the canvas, then painted it over the border of the dress, coiled like a serpent.

In the days and nights that came then he went on. He worked fast, making new dress paintings one after the other, waking with a feeling for it, the music up loud. He cut the paint with turpentine to keep the brush moving. Always a wash, then another dress sketched in. He put in things that happened to him, things he saw in the world or in his mind. He put in more things from the night of the storm, green light in the brandy glass, an acrobat on the high wire, the woman's eyes. He didn't keep any of these. He was looking for something beyond personal facts. He covered them with washes of yellow and grey and blue and started again. He put in dawn light, pictographs from a *National Geographic*, Michelangelo arms and legs, a blooming yucca from Generous's hothouse. He played music loud and incessantly, had his meals delivered. He forgot to drink. He painted in brown and pink and aquamarine. The brown was for a desert painting and he used a canvas with a broad weave that gave him a feeling of sandstone as he left clots of paint with long strokes.

In each painting was an empty dress.

The ideas and images came to him fast and he had little time. He left each painting before finishing it and moved on to the next. He intended to return but then decided to leave them as they were. They trailed off at the edges to white canvas or indistinctness. Ideas left partway between thought and execution were left as sketches. They showed their own composition and seemed still to be happening. They were paintings of themselves being made. They seemed to ask rather than tell.

He painted a cross. He painted wings on the crucified arms. He painted fish in a ring because whatever was in the painting seemed to have no end. The dress was like a musical phrase he could play according to what happened to him or how he felt. Each painting had its own atmosphere, its own feeling, made by its colours. He could go on, it seemed he could go on for years.

But then he came to a painting he knew would be the last of the empty dress. For the first time he put a figure in it, a version of the bridesmaid herself as he'd imagined her during the storm, long-necked, mournful, straining to see the dancers. He lay down a sketch of her in a dark underlay and let it dry. He worked in images in the background and foreground. Outstretched arms and white wings. He made the dress with alizarin red. He prepared a green for the bridesmaid's eyes and a white with yellow and grey for her skin. He stepped back to look at the set of the head. It was black, with spaces left for eyes and mouth where there was only the white of the canvas. Black and white, hollow-eyed, the bridesmaid was stark, like an X-ray, neither dead nor alive, skeleton nor flesh. But was such a thing allowed? The central figure an unfinished thing made of underlay? Who could he ask? The thought of the request and to whom it could be made caused him laugh. He looked at the paintings set out along his wall. He couldn't tell where they might go or what they would do. But he believed them, each line. He'd tasted that, at last. He'd never been there before. He might never be again.

The following morning he ascended north through the city to the house on Telegraph Hill.

A small Italian in a dove-grey waistcoat arrived at Cornell to lecture. Silvio Balotelli. Our Silvio. It wasn't so long ago you were godmother to his first child. At the time I was still without tenure and we were living in the type of apartment where graduate students lived. Lydia was six. Silvio was based in Milan but travelling around America promoting his ideas on the democratisation of architecture through collective computer-generated design. Digital Agency, he called it. A cod, Generous would say. Not an idea you could touch. But I'd long left those behind myself.

I sat near the front. I had to be seen by the tenure-granting committee. Silvio started out with a story. It was about a county fair in England a hundred years ago where an ox had been put up on a stage. People were invited to call out guesses of its weight. They were all wrong, but together, when the numbers were averaged, it was found they were correct to half a per cent. The many were therefore more accurate than the one. That was the idea. From there Silvio launched the proposition that groups rather than individuals should author our buildings. They could do it online in the same way that a Wikipedia page is built, slowly, with collective, anonymous refinements. It was communal and it was just. The single architect is a tyrant, he said, going up on his toes. He seemed to picture himself at a barricade with a bandana around his head.

But then he went on for another hour and a half. I drifted. At one point I looked down and saw a very beautiful hand resting on a knee, the fingers long, possibly arthritic, mahogany-coloured, lightening at the joints, a surgeon's hand, or harpist's, elegant and worldly. It belonged to an elderly Indian gentleman. The hand threw me back to another time, a romantic time, to the chapel at Ronchamp where I so wanted to be Le Corbusier as he drew that the air seemed to crackle and dance with my desire. I thought it was gone. I thought I'd killed it with the thousand cuts of small compromises. But there it was, or some of it, before it passed.

I left the theatre. In that moment I didn't care about tenure. I came home to our apartment and that night wrote it up – Silvio, Digital Agency, the elderly Indian with nails like the enamel on a watchface, Le Corbusier, my memory of Ronchamp, the glory of a hand that makes. *Behold the hands*, I quoted, *how they conjure, promise, appeal, menace, pray, supplicate, refuse, beckon, interrogate, admire, confess, mock and what else besides, with a variation that makes the tongue envious.* And *shoot*, I had the temerity to add, citing Generous about revolutions being for nothing unless they made new things. I paused then. The tenure committee came into view. I deleted 'shoot' and the line about Generous. But then on a wave that was almost thoughtless I went on. I celebrated the hand and inveighed against machines and saturating online connectivity and the dapper Silvio Balotelli. I wrote 'Le Corbusier's Hand' across the top. It found its way into a journal called *Prism*. I think it's the only thing I ever wrote, until this, connected with real feeling.

By chance an English television producer in need of a project and on a flight from London to Los Angeles opened the issue of *Prism* with my essay in it. Someone had left it in the pocket in front of her seat. She was drawn to the title, and then to the aura of combat between Silvio and me. She remembered a BBC controller saying he'd like a pitch for a series on ideas in contemporary architecture. A perfect storm broke. Article led to six-part series to book deal to international auction for rights. Silvio and I were paired in all of it, promoted like boxers in a title fight. We became stars, stars in a very small world, yes, one you never inordinately valued, but within this world it was spectacular. A collective flinch of envy, I learned, ran along the corridor of our department when they heard. In time our shelves became laden with awards, our diary was full, our accounts were engorged. Columbia called to offer their McIvor Chair. We came to this tower beside Lincoln Center where I am writing this to you.

I never told you what a fluke it all was. That would have taken the shine off it.

It helped to be Irish. The Good Friday Agreement had been signed. The soldiers were packing up, the prisoners were being released. They were probably digging up the arsenal buried on our land. We'd gone from being apes with hurling sticks to the charmers of Europe. At the first tests for the television series I was asked to bring up my accent. I had to practise a bit.

I think of it now, the hero-hailing warmth in the voices of editors when I'd call, the smiles of New York women with winter tans who sit on prize juries and museum boards. They keep throwing things at you when you are replete. No one ever warned me how quickly it could go cold.

PART III

Nemesis

CHAPTER FIVE

The House on Telegraph Hill

San Francisco, 2009

Ryan stepped through the front door of the house on Telegraph Hill into a wide hall of cedar and brick. Men in jumpsuits were moving around. He heard the whirring of drills and the banging of hammers. There were jigsaw shapes of plaster not yet cleared from the brick. In a corner was an old upright piano. Ming's voice came down from the floor above.

He walked slowly along the walls looking at the century-and-a-half-year-old bricks. He touched one as if it were an egg in a nest. He wondered how long he must be here. He arrived at the piano. He lifted the lid and looked at the keys. It was very like the piano in the house in Belmullet where Annaleena Brennan had taught him 'Begin the Beguine' and it took him there, the light coming into the room brightened by the sea falling on her fingers as she tried to teach him the tune. The metallic shine on the wet sand, the red blaze of the sunset. It was their last time together. How she could make him feel. That she was dead from a hundred bullets came to him more acutely than it had in years.

He picked out a few notes from the tune but didn't get very far. He tried again and faltered. He had only the beginning. He was looking at the keys when he heard a voice behind him.

Go ahead.

Ryan turned around at speed. He saw a man in a dress shirt, adjusting a cufflink.

Really, feel free, he said.

The man swept an arm in a long arc and smiled, his teeth sparkling in a shaft of light that came through a window.

Ryan stepped away.

That's my limit, he said.

The man went to the piano and took up the tune where Ryan had left it, his foot tapping out the rhythm.

'Begin the Beguine', he said over his shoulder. Haven't heard it in years.

He played with pace and style.

It's got that tropical night feel, he shouted over the notes. Everybody *loose*!

He bore down on the piano then, playing it louder and faster, his fingers on the keys like popping corn, singing the song this time into the ceiling, a full performance with a flourish at the end, and a bright laugh.

He walked towards Ryan, hand extended.

You're Ryan, right?

I am.

I'm Paul.

He was dark-haired, compact. His skin and his fingernails shone. A smooth Englishness moved through his voice like a mineral vein in stone, diffident in the foreground, an assumed status behind. The shoes were hand-stitched, the shirt worth nearly a day's wages at Ming's current rates. The cufflinks were square plates of gold with small rubies like drops of blood in the centre. He'd been smiling since Ryan first saw him, an affectedly shy, helpless, complicitous smile, created, thought Ryan, with the intention of making people like him. He had a dimpled chin, like Bobby Kennedy.

Heard a lot about you, he said.

Ryan nodded.

Paul stared at him. He seemed not to realise he was doing it.

You look . . . I don't know what. Familiar?

I can't say the same, said Ryan.

No . . . You from Belfast, somewhere like that?

The question always made him alert, especially when delivered with an English accent.

He nodded, then asked, Would you know where Ming is?

Ming? . . . Right, Ming. Upstairs, I think. With my wife.

Ryan moved towards the door but Paul stepped across his path. He placed a palm over the bricks.

Beautiful port wine colour, don't you think?

He touched a brick lightly, as Ryan had.

We've been nomadic, he said. London, Paris, Frankfurt, New York, Cleveland, God help us. But this is it, our last stop, the place we'll die in. It's the oldest house in the city they say. Well, that's what Ming says. I don't want to blow it.

He turned back to Ryan.

What would you do with it?

That's Ming's job.

I know. But what do you do to make a place *yours*?

Ryan thought of hedges, the backs of cars. The bathtub. He almost laughed.

I put up postcards, he said.

Paul Crane was born on the same day of the same month of the same year as Ryan, four thousand miles away in Gary, Indiana. This would make him feel that there was something fated in his and Ryan's encounter, something too in the mystery and magnetism of twins. His father worked the gantry in the Bethlehem steel mills, his mother changed sheets in a Howard Johnson's motel. He was their only child. They lived in a clapboard house with green shutters in the all-white suburb of Hobart. There was grey dust on the grass, and a yellow haze and the thick smell of sulphur from the mills in the air. He never knew it could be different until he went away.

What shaped and distinguished him from an early age was the prodigious facility he displayed with numbers. He loved to fill his head with them and place them in order. On his way to and from school he worked out square and cube roots. He memorised pi to thirty decimal places. By the time he was twelve he was already on a scholarship at Andrean High School, which was run by Basilian priests. Within a year he was doing partial differential equations.

His father had already left by then, 'ill from bourbon whiskey', his grandmother said. For two years they didn't know where he'd gone until he sent $2,000 from a Western Union office in Jacksonville, Florida, with the one-word message 'Sorry'. His mother tried to fill what she thought the boy would miss. She looked for things to defend him against, bought bicycles for each of them and took him on picnics at the lakeshore. Twice a year they went by bus to Chicago for concerts at the Orchestra Hall. He marvelled at the faces in the restaurants, the snow swirling in the canyons between the high buildings.

But the priests had in mind a grander stage for Paul than could be provided by the American Midwest. They had grown from a secret society that taught French boys during the Reign of Terror and by the time Paul was with them they had alumni all over the world. Father Arnaud, the headmaster, persuaded a group of bankers in Zug, Switzerland, to put the money together for him to study mathematics at Merton College in Oxford – Merton, where mathematics had been studied since the 1300s, when a group known as the Merton Calculators anticipated Galileo by formulating 'the law of falling bodies'.

Paul hesitated. England was so far away. He sensed that something could happen to him there, that he could lose who he was and be unable to find the way back. But Father Arnaud pushed him. So did his mother. Yet on the day he left she ran into the garden and turned away to hide her desperation. He could see the small yellow and blue flowers in her dress. Though he visited her during the summers and for long afterwards, and though she is still alive as I write this, he feels as if somehow he saw her then for the last time.

At Oxford, he found himself to be in a play for which he hadn't rehearsed. The food, the sizes of things, even the complexions of the faces were strange to him. But he watched and learned. Oxford began to insinuate itself into the formation of his words, his taste in desserts, his humour. He followed patterns, as he did with numbers. He went for long walks over the green hills, took up nicknames, the memorising of poems, Latin tags, drinking songs. He found friends and went away to their houses for weekends. Their parents were magistrates, surgeons, wing commanders, inventors, newsreaders, Members of Parliament. They set their children and their children's friends up on chairs in their living rooms and waited to be dazzled by them.

At the end of his first October he went out in sub-fusc with everyone else into the Fellows' Quad for the clock-changing Time Ceremony, walking backwards with a candle and drinking port. At one point he found his backward steps had become synchronised with those of a young man with strawberry blond hair. His name was Piers. Paul was the youngest at his college, so young as to still look androgynous. He had yet to kiss a girl or, until that night, drink alcohol. They drank port until they became dizzy and fell over onto a lawn in an entanglement of limbs and laughter. There followed a Sunday punt from Magdalen Bridge and two weeks after the Time Ceremony Paul was in receipt of half a page of handwritten verse, a week after that a pale blue silk shirt to match his eyes, and then the following week a clench and a kiss before they parted. Paul was a cloud, Piers the wind blowing him into uncertain territory. Finally, just before Paul flew home for Christmas, they were in a copse, a little drunk, a hand slipped down below his waistband, belts were unbuckled and the infatuation was consummated.

It was a single moment. He told himself he hadn't meant it to happen, that he was still in many ways a child. But he knew too that he had gone somewhere and that there was no clear way back to where he had been. He passed the Christmas with his mother and grandmother. He was unusually silent. He wondered who he was and feared who he might become. For the first time he began to yearn for his father.

In the summer before his final year Paul surprised him at the door of his trailer in Thibodaux, Louisiana, on the Bayou Lafourche. His father cried through the whole of the day. He got Paul a job beside him on a shrimp boat and they worked and lived together for three months. In the trailer at night his father taught him the accordion. It was cardinal red with pewter trim and black bellows, and had been made by Elton Doucet. His father kept it in a black silk bag. Paul saw music as if it were diagrammed in the air, whole numbers in the spaces between notes and chords. On Wednesday nights in a bar on the bayou where the shrimp boat workers went they had zydeco music and a raffle. High-velocity rifles were the prizes for men, breast implants for women.

That's something you won't see in Hobart, said his father.

By the end of the summer he was sitting in with the band.

He went back to Merton with the Doucet accordion.

It's yours now, his father said. You're better with it than I am.

He came out into Oxford streets thronged with bicycles, fluttering scarves, book bags, the bobbing hair of sauntering girls. Sometimes when he looked out he heard zydeco music in his head. The notes seemed to scatter over the scene like flecked paint.

In the spring of his final year he was invited with other gifted students drawn from the disciplines of language, history, economics and anthropology to a private recruitment dinner given by Matthew

Hayford, later assassinated by the IRA at his home in Mayfair but at the time a middle-ranking operative in the British intelligence service. Paul was tempted, but declined. He completed a thesis on thermodynamics and was given a double first. He packed books, clothes and his accordion and flew back to America, where he lived in the trailer with his father until he decided what to do.

When Ryan told him about the postcards, Paul checked his watch, said, Look at the time! Must collect my boy, and left. He found himself disarmed by the encounter, so brief. He'd grown used to dominance, through his money, or intellect, or what he took to be his charm. Ryan was evidently immune. He seemed to make a point of conveying this to him. But why should it bother him? He'd been talking with a housepainter. He skipped down the steps of Telegraph Hill pondering it.

Ryan went up to the kitchen and sat on a window ledge. He had the phials of sample paints he'd made at Garrity's and hoped he could soon hand them over and leave. Ming was on his feet, fingertips joined, in a black velvet suit and Chinese prayer cap, and was telling Charlotte Crane the story of Tom Merriweather. He gave him a blind right eye and a limp and described his journey from cabin boy to captain as though he'd been there for it all. Charlotte was a cloud of black hair, green eyes and black lace. Her feet were bare. Her gestures were slightly awkward and her voice too soft, as though she couldn't get the measure of the room. She listened, rapt.

Ming asked her to picture the scene, the newly married captain in a far-away port or out at sea in his cabin, missing his wife and yearning for solid ground and a home of his own at last. Like all captains and ship owners he wanted to live in a high place with a view of the water, he wanted to see ships coming and going, and he bought this plot of land. Gold miners laid down the brick base, carpenters raised walls of cedar and a wraparound walkway like on a ship. Big windows so the rooms would be saturated with light. He went to sea and brought back carpets, tapestries and stained glass and kept them in a warehouse until the house would be ready. The whole house was in his head from the time he bought the land. He informed the ship's owner that his next voyage would be his last.

Ming pointed to a window that looked onto the street.

That's where the tragedy happened, he said, right there at the corner. The Captain came up that hill straight from the ship. His wife was watching, from where you are now. He suddenly stopped, his hand went to his head, he looked confused, he stumbled, he fell.

He was dead, Charlotte. Brain haemorrhage. He never got to live in this house, not even for a night.

Charlotte gasped. She thought it would be a happy story. She'd seen the gold miners and carpenters and the raising of the house from the dirt of the hill. It moved her. She'd been with the Captain and then with his wife as she looked out the window.

I did the research, said Ming. I saw drawings *in the Captain's own hand*. He had a beautiful vision for this house. Break my heart how beautiful. I drove to Rodeo Beach. I sit in the sand. I think. I see. I draw. *I know* . . .

I ask one thing, Charlotte – let's do it together, you, me, Paul, Ryan. *Let's finish the Captain's house.*

Paul appeared in the doorway with his son, Oliver. Charlotte didn't see them. They'd arrived in time for Paul to hear that a man named Tom had fallen dead long ago outside his house. He didn't know who this man was or why his story was being told to his wife, but he could see the brightness in her eyes, a brightness he knew well.

He crossed the room with dread and tenderness and took his wife's head between his hands and kissed her on the crown. He held the kiss, eyes closed. She reached up without looking, familiar, pleased. Ryan wouldn't have expected the man who had made the small concert at the piano downstairs to make such a gesture. It was a degree too intimate to watch and he turned to the boy. He was pale, a trace of veins around his temples giving him a faint hue of blue, like a blue moon. He was eleven years old, but his pressed shirt, the carefully combed wave of hair and the seriousness and skeletal definition of his face made him seem an adult in miniature. He studied the room as if it were a puzzle. Paul beckoned to him, and finally the boy crossed the floor, tense under the eyes of the strangers. His mother sensed him and turned.

Ollie? . . . You're not at school?

Orthodontist, said Paul. Remember?

She saw the appointment card on the refrigerator door.

Damn, she said. Sorry, Paul. I forgot.

She embraced the boy. He gripped a handful of black lace at the shoulder of her dress and twisted it.

He wants to tell you what we just saw, said Paul.

Where?

Coming up the hill, that green house across the street.

She held her son at arm's length.

What did you see? she asked him.

A string quartet, he said in a whisper, his dark eyes widening. *Right in the window!*

Hard at it, said Paul. Full evening dress.

Beethoven, said the boy. The third Razumovsky.

The *Allegro molto*. Elbows going like pistons! said Paul.

You see? said Charlotte. You see what kind of place we picked to live in?

She made coffee for them all as she told her husband about the man who had made their house. Ming collected the samples from Ryan and arranged chairs around a table. Ryan sat apart, the boy was standing by his mother, his hand on the back of her chair. Ming spoke of a fossil-laden slab from the bottom of the sea for a shower. The boy seemed unwilling to leave his mother but could find nothing in the conversation to hold his attention. His eyes grew vague. The toe of one foot tapped against the heel of the other. Ryan watched him. He saw his isolation. He wondered what room there could be for this boy in a family with two such vivid parents drawing all the available air. The three at the table were leaning in towards one another. Paul had his hand over Charlotte's. Ming was making a list in a notebook as he described what he believed it would take to create the Captain's house. Ryan tugged at the boy's sleeve and, when the boy turned, pointed out the window to an apple tree in the garden, its blossoms white. Two Telegraph Hill wild parrots were sitting on a branch, the head of each inclined sideways towards the other, like two men trying to have a conversation in a church. They were dusty green with spots over their beaks, like the heads of matches. One flapped his wings suddenly, as if in agreement. The boy laughed. He looked at Ryan and then back again. There was a bang of a hammer from an upstairs room. The parrots, alarmed, stepped with speed away from each other, their beaks digging under their wings at either end of the limb. Then they looked around, alert. When they were calm they edged back to where they'd been and put their heads together again. It was as if they'd forgotten to mention something. The boy looked at Ryan and laughed again.

Have a seat, said Ryan.

The boy sat. He lifted one foot onto the ledge and a deck of cards edged out from his pocket. Ryan tapped the top of the box.

You're already at that?

The boy looked down at the cards and reddened.

I collect tricks, he said. It's about that. Would you—

He stopped.

Oh sorry. I'm Oliver.

He held out a hand.

Ryan.

My dad's brilliant at them. We've got this deal. If I get a certain projected grade, he teaches me a trick. I've already got six. And what I meant to say was, there's this trick, a really good one I think. Not from my dad. I learned it yesterday from an older boy at school – we get along pretty well – and, well, I haven't practised it much, but . . . would you like to see it?

The eyes of Paul Crane left the table where Ming's hands were moving and drifted towards Ryan and his son. He wore a faint, crooked smile.

Yes, said Ryan.

The boy took the cards from the packet. He fanned out the deck, his small hands making it difficult for him. Ryan selected a card. There was a rubber band, several complicated cuts, a slamming down of the deck and Ryan's card popped up like a ticket from a machine.

He laughed, the sound ringing around the room.

Outstanding, he said.

Charlotte looked up, expectancy on her face, as if she were about to rise. Her husband swivelled on his neck from Ryan and the boy to her, his smile a little more crooked. The boy kicked his heels off the wall beneath him, but his eyes stayed still. They were like rabbits' eyes at night, looking to Ryan, asking him for something, a smile waiting on his lips. Ryan whispered into the boy's ear. The boy nodded. Ming herded his parents back to the subject of their home. He spoke of drapery rods and chandeliers and taps. He added lines to a column of figures. Charlotte built the picture of the house in her mind. Paul deferred to her, but kept his eye too on his son as the boy crossed the room with a crystal bowl-like glass and a silver fork and handed them to Ryan, who seemed about to do a trick. Ming extolled Ryan's gifts – patinas, faux finishes. He paints iron so real you feel cold, he said. Ryan pinched the tongs of the fork to make it ring and then appeared to lift the note from the fork, transport it in his fingers to the glass and then drop it in, where it rang out like the call of a whale. The boy shot up in amazement. Charlotte and Paul looked to Ryan and their son.

Her lips parted. Her eyes were on Ryan. Over Paul's face small muscles moved like scurrying mice. *Wow*, said Oliver. The note thinned and died. Ming pulled Paul and Charlotte back again. The Persian knot is very fine, he said of rugs, and added them to the list. His last act was to sell them hand-scraped hardwood flooring he'd taken in payment from a bankrupt client and hadn't been able to get rid of. His pen moved across a page. He passed it to Paul, who signed. Ming clicked his pen closed, put it in his pocket, adjusted his prayer cap. Paul's new house would be Ming's, not his. They said goodbye and went out the door.

After Paul came back from Merton, he put together a punk zydeco band, Les Beaux Anarchistes of Butte La Rose. It swelled and contracted, at its grandest comprising fiddle, zither, bells, piano accordion, stand-up bass, drums, hurdy-gurdy, three kinds of guitar and tin whistle. Paul was on his Doucet button accordion and vocals. He stood at the microphone stripped to the waist in a Russian military hat and sang songs he'd written himself.

In Baton Rouge they played a club called the Full Nelson. He saw a dense mass of heads that bobbed and thrashed, faces red from exertion and shots, and then in the shadows at the side of the stage the pale, green-eyed and gently swaying figure of Charlotte Silver. No one in the band understood why she was there. She wore filigree earrings and linen dresses. They saw her at shows they did in New Iberia, Opelousas, Picayune. She'd take one drink at the bar and drive off afterwards in her convertible black Porsche, a scarf trailing behind her. The band went on a tour along the Gulf and she was at the last stop, a blockhouse bar set among the auto dealers on the highway leading into Biloxi, Mississippi, 150 miles from her home in Baton Rouge.

In the break he stepped into a space beside her at the bar.

So? he asked.

She turned. She suggested they take a table. He sensed he was out of his depth.

It's the music, she said. I find it hilarious.

Before the second set started he learned that she was married to an oil industry lawyer named Benjamin Silver. He thought she might have intended a diminishing in this, to express a dissatisfaction. He wasn't sure. He wasn't used to women like her. He knew a few at Oxford, mothers of friends who bought their clothes in Bond Street and knew the best restaurants. The women he knew now drank in the bars where his band played. He knew men sometimes too, furtively, intensely, anonymously. These moments came upon him unexpectedly. There was a code, he thought, for how to relate to a woman like Charlotte Silver, one known by other men, men older than himself, but not yet by him.

He watched her from the stage. Men approached her, men in suits, men in greasy T-shirts and baseball caps. She laughed, clinked glasses with them, let them spin her around a few times. There was a weightlessness in the way she moved over the floor that was unmissable, though she did nothing more than follow where she was led. After the show she gave him her keys and he drove with her through the night all the way back to Louisiana. She took off her shoes and put her feet up on the dashboard. Her dress fell around her thighs. Her car seemed to him a piece of jewellery.

She'd been dancing since she was five, ballet at first, but then moved of her own accord into modern dance. This displeased her father. When she was seen with her arm around a Black dancer from the company she'd joined in Baton Rouge, her father attempted to assert his authority. There was just enough left from her training in Southern Belledom for her to submit. The father, encouraged, steered her into a relationship with Benjamin Silver, a lawyer he knew from his country club, and her dancing career and her romance came to an end.

By the time Paul met her she'd lived through four years of silent breakfasts, silent dinners in restaurants, weekends when her husband worked on briefs and they played silent tennis matches at their private club. He went to bed each night at 9.30 and she began to walk the streets. It was on one of these nights that she heard from the sidewalk the ramped-up, train-wreck, vertiginous music of Les Beaux Anarchistes of Butte La Rose. She stepped into the back of a room that itself seemed to be sweating. One hundred and fifty drunk, pogoing, fist-pumping fans were being driven on by a band so populous that they were slipping from the stage, led by Paul, veins out on forehead and neck and with a Vladimir Lenin badge on his cap. It made her laugh. She fell for the relief it gave her from her life.

They came into their time. She picked him up on street corners. They went to roadhouses, for river walks, slow-step dancing in a piano bar in the Faubourg Marigny in New Orleans. He got his father to take them out on a shrimp run. Afternoons on the mattress on the floor of his room. Damp and twisted sheets and a tape machine playing Cajun dance tunes. Afterwards she put herself together with comb and make-up and stepped out in her sunglasses.

When her husband went away to Kuwait she took him to a house on stilts on the shore of Lake Pontchartrain. He saw her husband's monogrammed robe and Greek sandals in the bedroom. Oaks and cypress trees and tupelo gums crowded the perimeter. No one could see them there. When they went in she spread her arms and said to the rafters, *I can be whoever I want here.*

Later, when I met him in California, he told me about his time at this house.

I was twenty, he said. She was twenty-eight. That's a lot of difference at that age. I didn't know anything. I hardly knew I had a body. She was . . . well, it was her affliction, mine too indirectly . . . She was, she is, some kind of flame, or current. You'd get near and . . . How can I tell you? It was like being eaten alive by an epicure. See, in that house by Lake Pontchartrain, in those days, with her, there was no time. We just watched the colours change. Cool white from the moon at night, a green mist coming up from the base of the trees. I'd see her walk by a mirror fanning herself, there was a spark and we tangled up like fighting cats. She seemed sad when she was asleep. I'd wonder if I was enough. But she'd feel me, she'd wake, a little syrupy, then the blood flowed and she'd be fast, wicked, smart, full of some kind of malice. She'd hiss like a snake . . . It was too vivid to be real, you know, too much colour, too much force. There was this night, quite black, clouds over the moon, we'd eaten grilled crab, I walked across a room that smelled of night-blooming flowers and her sex. Her dress was on the floor beside a chair. That dress, I felt short of breath . . .

The bankers in Zug who had sponsored him through Merton watched their investment from a distance. They watched Charlotte leave her husband and their six-bedroom house and move into the room Paul had over an electrical shop. They watched as he tried and failed to get recording contracts, stocked supermarket shelves and did shifts as a doorman in an oversized coat with brass buttons and as Benjamin Silver closed his wife's access to their accounts. She made banquets on a student's budget which they ate on the floor. Paul tried not to think of what she had given up. But then one day he saw her downtown, hesitant before a window of Italian shoes. She went in, tried on a few pairs, came out. Then she walked home, empty-handed. He tried to see the expression on her face but she was too far away.

So when the bankers arranged for Paul to be offered a position at a small, Swiss-owned investment bank in London he took it, with relief but also with a sense of defeat which he tried to ignore. They rented a house, Charlotte bought shoes. Paul learned with great rapidity about delta hedging, martingales, implied volatility surfaces and Brownian models. He thought imaginatively, expansively, about risk and time. His maths ran true. His bonuses rose from five to six to seven figures. He started his own bank.

Some months after Oliver was born, Charlotte changed. The incandescence he'd earlier been thrilled by grew yet more luminous, and erratic. She disappeared at times. She could be found on a roof, thinking that she was about to receive an illumination, that its words were about to enter her mouth. She'd be brought back. She'd lie still in a dark room for a month. Sometimes it seemed to him that a hole had opened in her head into which random visions were poured, chairs she sat on as a child, messages from saints, the torsos of young men. It would pass. She'd be given lithium and would settle. But he lived in fear of its return.

They kept moving, city to city, through the world, until they arrived at last in San Francisco. By then she was sleeping apart from him, most of the time. It had started in her low times. She came back to him when she was better, but then less frequently, until it became their climate. She asked for his understanding. She loved him as ever, she said. He willingly offered it. He could live on nostalgia until she came back to him, if he must. But when she was high she seemed sex itself, and it was directed to the world rather than him. He felt her ebbing. He was terrified of losing her. He'd come out of a time of confusion and ambiguity through her, and become defined.

He worked in a small room filled with screens delivering market prices and exchange rates. One day he lost in the high six figures on the Singapore dollar. Just a blip, he told an investor. I'll make it up on the dinar or some damned thing.

Everywhere they went the Elton Doucet accordion came too, but it stayed in its box.

Ryan worked in the house of the Cranes through the spring and deep into the summer. Ming was there every day. This was unusual for him. He pursued effects he never had before, making textures with paint instead of metal or fabric. Walls were redone in search of ineffable hues. He wanted the house to be on the skin as well as in the eyes. He listened politely to Charlotte Crane's ideas, but then did not implement them. He was making his great work.

Charlotte danced through the house with the music up, catching light and disappearing like a trout in a stream. She thought all working there were geniuses, the plumbers, the French polishers, Ming and Ryan. She brought them bowls of fruit. The rooms filled with her nerve ends. Paul came out from his office and watched her. He knew she'd pay and that he would too for this elation by a descent into blackness that could last weeks. Her doctors had explained her ailment to her and predicted its rhythms. Sometimes she took the lithium they prescribed her but sometimes she didn't, for she liked the way the disease made her feel when she was high. She was high now, she rose with the warming weather like sap. The climb would be steady, exhilarating, risky, and the fall precipitous. She was halfway there. She'd walked one day like a tightrope artist along the edge of the roof. She began to write letters to Captain Merriweather.

Ryan finished his day with a game of chess with the boy Oliver on the gallery outside his room, then went home. Since early in the year he'd been used to the presence of the unfinished painting. The possibility of it was always there, if he walked or if he woke in the night. It was company, for better or worse. Now he'd finished it, and the feeling of its possibility was gone. It would not return. Would another replace it? He couldn't know. Something new would have to happen to him. He felt envy for the person who had made the painting of the dress, and the other dress paintings that had followed. Its absence was like the absence of the war.

He took his bike out and hit the twisting descent of Highway 1 from the height of Tamalpais. The road was like a length of ribbon that kept doubling back on itself. He went into it as if into a dive. He reached speeds beyond what he thought he could control. For a quarter hour the frame shook and the wheels balanced on their edges. The scream of the engine seemed to burn through his brain.

He walked with Alexis on a warm evening through streets of prosperity south of Market. They said nothing. Her arm was looped through his. The beat of her heels was the only sound. They saw waiters light candles in restaurants, families in the ample rooms of their homes. They moved past the scenes like a boat in a current.

They turned into Sixth and headed north. Darkness came down from the dome of the sky. The Tenderloin was like a small, stale room. A malarial light from the streetlamps reached to the undersides of the low clouds. They saw the iron-clad building and smelled the foetid food in the alleys. Residents of the SRO hotels were looking down from their windows at a bad night in the streets. There was crying in doorways, the sound of sirens, people falling. They heard the crack of bone as a fist met a face. There seemed no one sane or well here tonight, the mouths without teeth, the skulls misshapen, the eyes without sense. Faces looked around corners as if on sticks, lit by the blue flashes from a patrol car.

Alexis stopped and looked at Ryan.

What did you do that put you here? she said.

She searched his face.

You did some kind of sin?

They went into a restaurant on Larkin Street, but she got a call and had to go, there was a woman who'd been attending the clinic who was in a crisis, she didn't yet know from what.

Wait, please, she said. I'll be back.

She was there for all but for none in particular, except perhaps him. He was alone now with her questions. What had put him in such a forsaken place? Had he sinned? He did not believe that Francis had sinned. The state, British or Unionist, was and had ever been an instrument of violence in the country. He had seen it himself. Even Gandhi had said that violent resistance was preferable to dishonour. He'd been led to guns and been asked to use them and been thanked by those on whose behalf he had acted, as soldiers in their hundreds of millions had done through the ages in the name of causes honourable and dishonourable. The only war I can justify to myself is a war of liberation, Generous had said. With Francis he was at peace. But less so with the boy who had watched the cat on the wall and followed the melody of the piper and drawn the Russian priest. This boy was not permitted to kill. He violated the Sixth Commandment.

He would like at last to be known, by Alexis more than anyone because he loved her and trusted her. She could relieve him of the paradox of his absolved and unabsolved selves. She was strong enough. But the insurgent's rule against 'loose talk' was too deeply ingrained. He wouldn't tell her about the war.

Still, she had never before been so direct. He must answer her somehow. He tore a page from his notebook and began to draw the face of Generous McCabe. He left the eyes to last. In Generous's eyes, as in his own, there was the capacity to kill. After killing the Englishman in Keady Generous had killed detectives, Castle officials, spies, informers and soldiers, on street corners, in bars, in hotel rooms with women lying beside them and in back gardens where they were planting cabbages. He lamented these men. The lament was also in his eyes. What would Generous have been doing if the English hadn't been occupying his country? Playing the violin? Creating buildings? The loss of this time was also in his eyes. To kill is to make a sacrifice of yourself, though only those who have done it in defence of something would know it.

Alexis came back. He handed her the drawing, knowing that nothing of what he'd thought while making it would be visible to her.

Who's that? she asked.

Me as an old man, he said, and they laughed.

On a Sunday he couldn't otherwise fill he sat in the Museum of Modern Art through the afternoon in front of Mark Rothko's *Number 14, 1960*. It was a massive thing, more than nine feet tall, a rectangle of orange and a rectangle of blue. He was on a bench. A woman was beside him. He wasn't sure when she had arrived. She wore an old raincoat and her steel-coloured hair was held up by pins decorated with jade.

Rothko painted fast and then looked for hours at what he had done. Even days. He liked people to see his paintings at a distance of eighteen inches. He wanted immersion. Ryan tried to bring himself to the painting. He heard a guard move into another room. He saw that the light coming through the skylight had dimmed during the time he had been sitting there. His mind chased the things in the room. He couldn't be still. The woman next to him was motionless. She was looking intently at the orange and blue rectangles. He tried to force himself to look like her into the painting without recourse. There was an ache in his neck. An escalating boredom seemed to drain the life from the air.

Then there was a shift. He didn't notice it arriving, only that the softness of the painting had awakened. The vague edges of the rectangles, the bars of the prison window dissolved. The painting appeared now to have an inner light. It vibrated softly. *A painting lives in companionship.* Eighteen inches.

It moves, he said.

The woman jumped.

Bitte? she said.

Ryan turned quickly to her. He hadn't realised he'd spoken.

The painting moves, he said.

The woman was wearing steel spectacles and now she took them off.

Sprechen Sie Deutsch?

Nein.

Français?

Un peu, he said. *Un petit, petit peu.*

Qu'est-ce que vous dites, monsieur?

Rothko . . ., he began. He knew he hadn't the words to get through the thought. He started again. *La peinture est sur la* . . . uh . . . – He shrugged his shoulders – . . . canvas, *quarante-quatre années*. But it moves!

He vibrated his hand to show her.

Moves, *oui*, she said. *Je comprends.*

She put her spectacles on and looked again at the painting. Her brow descended in concentration over the steel rims of her spectacles. After a long pause she said, *Oui. C'est vrai. Comme un coeur battant.*

When he got back the porter in the lobby told him that a woman with hair nearly white had been waiting for him all evening and had only recently left. He handed over an envelope she'd left for him. Inside was a ticket decorated with Victorian machines, men with moustaches and women in bustiers and a note – 'I've been away. I wanted to thank you. Please come. Nicky x'.

When I came back from San Sebastián you and Lydia were both home because she had a throat infection and a temperature of 103 degrees. She had the glazed eyes and look of helplessness children have when they're sick. Their taut bodies rack with coughs, then they smile at you.

I stayed home with her, you went back to work. We had a slow, dreamy time. We played cards and had naps in the afternoon. I read to her. 'The Tell-Tale Heart'. *Huckleberry Finn*. She sat propped up by pillows, her eyes wide. We made fun of politicians who came on the television. Then around six we'd take a recipe from the *Times* and prepare dinner for when you came home.

I told you a little about Niall Dempsey, a family friend I'd met by chance who'd become a painter and put up an exhibition called Monaghan. I couldn't resist that, I said. I had to stay that extra day. You asked when at last I was going to introduce you to this place where I was born and I said something deflective and patronising. We had a good night at Niall Dempsey's house in the Labourd, I told you, sitting out under a beautiful sky drinking wine and reminiscing. I showed you the drawing he made of my eyes. Nothing of the corpses he'd left behind or the weapons he'd buried on our land or my brother blowing up a child in London. I put his envelopes away in a drawer. I didn't know yet what I'd do with him. Maybe I'd try to forget him. I felt him there, distantly, fleetingly.

The term ended. We had our summer as ever by the lake in Hämeenlinna where I first saw you. Bonfires, toasts of Terva Snapsi with neighbours and festooning the local bus, our car, a donkey and ourselves with birch branches. Then they all went away and we had it to ourselves. In the perpetual midsummer light we lost the distinctions in the day. We rose when we wished, we did what we wished, we had breakfast in the evening hours, walked at midnight, sailed at 3 a.m. Time stretched. I forgot everything. Birch leaves shimmered and whitecaps frothed, but mind and body moved as if through syrup. I watched Lydia's eyes follow a cat, you dropping onto our bed like a leaf.

In New York I cleaved to the Hämeenlinna rhythm. Maybe I knew that something was coming. A reckoning. Maybe I was trying to hold it off. I'd say I was. I lunched with friends, went down YouTube rabbit holes, walked around our apartment like it was an interactive museum, inspecting silverware, staring at photographs, browsing in magazines, looking at the city from our balcony.

Sometimes I went into Lydia's room. I felt her growing, slipping away from us into the world. I wanted to read the runes. Clothes, devices for the hair, posters, messages from friends I knew nothing of. They confer numbers on one another and swear fealty in sharpie on their trainers. I ♥ 42. Did you know that? I suppose you did.

Lydia's trainers brought me to the boy in London. Anything might have. The boy had been waiting for me since I first heard about him. Had he got as far along in his life as she had by then? I looked him up. He was Christopher Smyth, aged six. He'd been walking through the park with his aunt when Dermot's bomb went off. I read what his schoolfriends said about him. I saw a photograph of him squinting in the sun and holding his mother's hand. All the others killed that day came up too, the seven Guardsmen, their stories, interviews with their siblings and parents and friends and children left father-less, missing them, still living it, broken by it, still cursing my brother twenty years later, as it seems he cursed himself. I stayed with it through the whole of the afternoon.

The summer haze lifted. A snap came into the air. I set back to work. The television producer wanted another series from Silvio and me. We'd become Public Intellectuals, with a touch of Mutt and Jeff. I was on a prize jury, there was thesis supervising, mentoring, a seminar. At some point I'd have to write about the Plaza de la Constitución. That would write itself.

Our friends came back from their summers in Italy, London, Martha's Vineyard. The dinners and outings began. One was a little different. It was at our place. Silvio and Lucia were there, and that keeper of miniatures at the Met, I can't remember his name. His partner's Anthony. And Diane – teaching memoir writing at Bard – and her dog. And a few others. It doesn't matter much who. They were all people, I can see now, that I imposed on you, people who I imagined were a step on the way to a yet higher grade of guest. It began as it always did, the wine gradually warming us, the volume rising, the ingredients wit, insight and delight in one another's company. But then after the food and as we continued with the wine it began to look different to me. Something seemed suddenly to have altered my internal dials. What had seemed insightful now looked knowing, the wit sounded cruel. There was a striving to have the last word, to be exclusive, to rise in rank. No one listened. Some kind of desperation seemed to underlie it all. I didn't want to think like this. I'd been having a good time. But what could I do? Everything looked so insincere. I stopped speaking.

When was the last time any of us had ever spoken with a person who was different from us? When did we ever say, I don't know?

Not long after that I got a reminder note about the Plaza de la Constitución essay. I'd stuck with *Prism*, for luck. I went uptown to the campus with the Dictaphone on which I'd made my notes. It was a Friday afternoon, the corridor quiet, a workman buffing the linoleum. Jim Dix, lately specialising in the Chinese conception of space, went in through his door with a roll of biscuits. Fred Paltrow, in a red bow tie and with a polished head, had his feet up on his desk hoping someone would come in. The head checked her postbox. When I passed the secretary she pointed to a sign on her desk to remind me that I'd yet to buy a raffle ticket for her son's Boy Scout troop. Everything was as it had been, and would be.

I had a large office, larger even than the head's. You never saw it and now never will. It had high windows, a sofa and its own coffee-making machine. That picture of me receiving a state medal from Hillary Clinton was hanging by the door.

I turned on my computer, brewed coffee, selected the books I'd need from my shelf. I followed my ceremonial pattern, like a barris-ter getting into robes and wig.

I see the scene that followed now from very high and far away. I am like a figure in a doll's house. I open a book by an Italian philoso-pher, someone I'd long relied on, who could alight on the concepts of the day with a butterfly's grace. I am looking for a particular quote with which to begin. I find it. The unwritten essay is before me like a puzzle already solved. I turn on the Dictaphone. But instead of my observations on the Plaza de la Constitución I hear the voice of Ryan describing the killing of Corporal James Nealey. His voice moves slowly. There are spaces between the sentences and a kind of tender-ness. I hear the running water, the clinking of rocks from the stream in the Labourd. I hear my own breath. 'He flew back when the round hit him . . . his jaw came away . . . a jet of blood came out of the artery in his neck . . .' I stop it. I look out the window for a long time.

I rewind the recording. I find the spot. I press Play. I hear myself. I am in the Plaza de la Constitución. Then I am in my room in the hotel. I am used to my voice after hearing it so often on television, but now I don't like it. It sounds tinny, constructed. My observations sound so unimportant. Nevertheless, I manage to type out the Italian philosopher's statement and begin to write. Or try to write, for it is then that the thing happens to me. The words themselves paralyse me. 'Semiotics', 'plurality', 'historicism'. Always so reliable. I hear a voice, faint, neutral. Why don't you write as you speak? What are you afraid of? Is it Ryan? Lydia? Generous? My hands freeze. I see myself rise, walk around the room, lie on the sofa, get up, walk to the window, return to my desk. It was an aberration. It had to be. I place my hands on the keyboard. 'Negative dialectic.' They fly back as if repulsed. I know that I will not write a word about the Plaza de la Constitución, not then, not ever.

But if not this, then what?

CHAPTER SIX

A Night at the Circus

San Francisco, 2009

Ma Kettle's Autumn Dreams Circus played that Thursday night in a Dogpatch warehouse. Ryan sat in the back row. Stage and aisles were filled with wandering people in top hats, smoking jackets and vinyl bras, their faces decorated with lightning bolts and triangles. Music boomed through the speakers, a sound like a box of coins being shaken to a beat. A clown played a melancholy air on his accordion. In the heights a Marie Antoinette figure tiptoed on a wire under a blue umbrella. There were ukulele players, leaping poodles, a glass eater and mountaineering pigs in lederhosen who climbed on chairs.

Ryan looked for Nicky. She could be anyone or no one. He couldn't tell who were the audience and who the performers. The whiteface and masks made him doubt his memories of her. It had been four months since he had last seen her. He hoped he might know her by her eyes.

A trumpet sounded and people sat on benches or on the floor. A barker with implanted horns and black lips stepped into a pool of light.

Come all ye! Come all ye! he shrieked. Come and hear the sad and ridiculous story of Cyril, Human Dartboard and Unemployable Clown!

A beam moved onto the sorrowful figure of the clown with the accordion, shuffling among rubbish bins.

Mute from birth! called the barker – *they thought he was a tumour!* – failed schoolboy, failed sweeper, failed panhandler, a clown without pathos, a clown with a sense of humour too minuscule to be detected by the most modern scientific instruments, spurned in love, not once, not fifty times, *but every day through the four hundred and twenty-seven years of his negligible and putrefactious existence!*

A light hit the high wire, where Marie Antoinette sniffed a rose.

The Autumn Dreams Circus that night presented a profane and sentimental operetta involving fire-eating, Gypsy accordion tunes and a dumb-show Kama Sutra in which Cyril woos and is rebuffed by Marie Antoinette, but is revived when a giant moon rises and an Ice Queen appears, singing, *O moon, stand still / Tell me, O tell me, where is my lover?* In the blue light, she calls to him, they duet accordion to song, suitor to maiden, until he steps forth and sings the first and last words of his life, *Come to me now, white star in the night / Come to me now if it be life or if it be death!* They open their arms, they move towards each other, but the Ice Queen's touch is mortal. Cyril reels. He clutches his heart. They look at each other in horror and grief. He falls to the floor.

At this point the midway went to black. The audience stayed silent. Then a dim light crept along the floor like leaking water and shone on the clown's coffin. Circus members arrived in desultory fashion. They juggled phosphorescent balls, the barker folded himself into a small Perspex box and an angel with hooks through the skin of his back flew sadly over the coffin.

There was a sound then, sudden and stark, like the cry of an animal. The source could not be seen. A brightening light focused on a small door high above the stage and the performers looked up. A woman in white, with white hair and a white cello between her legs, came down through dry ice in a chair fixed to wires, the volume of her playing rising. It was hesitant, frustrated, a piece of music arguing with itself. She was folded around her instrument, looking for a single phrase in order to possess it. Ryan had the sense that the music was happening inside him, that it was describing something that had happened to him. It rolled through the crowd and shook him in his seat. *Too late . . . It's too late*, she sang. The barker came out of his box and took up the flute, the jugglers played guitars and the angel sang behind her, *Too late . . . It's too late.* She played on, harsh, tender, attacking, intelligent, the woman from the night of the storm.

They got into a bar beside the circus just before closing time and ordered brandies. Audience members were there, costumed and rehearsed for a play that was a continuation of what they had just seen. They performed illusions and played whistles and miniature guitars. Ryan was still in a condition of awe at what he had seen her do, but he hadn't the language to tell her. His face to her looked like flint. Hers to him was translucent.

She'd invited him to the circus because she wanted to explain to him where she had gone the morning she had stayed with him, and because of the way he'd looked after her when she was lost. She'd remembered his lurching, minimalistic speech, the way he'd slipped like a skater among the chairs of the bar he'd brought her to. She was curious about the canvas with its face to the wall in his room and why it was gone when she woke. Unlike her circus friends he appeared to possess qualities he didn't promote. She thought of these things now and then in the months she'd been away. The storm had thrown them into a sudden intimacy that was also anonymous. She wondered if there were an untold story in it. His face was not promising.

The bar music was cut. The staff were clearing the room. Would he go somewhere else with her? She wouldn't like this night to end so fast.

Ryan finished his brandy and went downstairs to the toilets. She followed him. When he came out he hooked his arm and pulled him into a closet full of buckets and brooms. She closed the door. Everything went to black.

What's going on? he whispered.

We're hiding.

Until when?

Until they go away.

They stood still, their faces inches apart. She could feel him breathing. They heard doors open and close. The lights went out. Locks rattled shut. There was silence.

They stepped out. It was as black as a well. She held onto the back of his shirt as they made their way along the corridor.

I've always wanted to do this, she said.

They came to a dim spill of light where the stairs were and ascended. They stopped at the threshold of the bar where they had just been sitting. It seemed a fairy tale world now, still but about to come to life, like a dollmaker's shop after midnight, the beer taps like sentinels, the bottles spectators at an event. A waiter's apron twisted in a draught.

She moved to enter the room but he held her back.

Movement sensors, he said, pointing to a wall.

They bent low under the beams and passed through swing doors into a kitchen. He checked the walls. They were sensor-free. He pressed a switch and a cruel grey-white light fell on blades and sinks and stainless-steel vaults. It was like an autopsy room. To be in a place where he was not meant to be was familiar to him, but she was high on the sense of trespass. She opened drawers and cabinets and fridges. She found racks of herbs, sherry, cookbooks, shelves of food and a little pouch of crystal meth stuffed into a crevice. She turned to him and he saw it again, her magic trick, the eyes suddenly switched on, her face vivid and magnified, everything else fading to indistinctness. It pulled at him like a siren song.

Would you eat with me? she asked him softly.

He stepped back. He'd lost for a moment the measure of her.

Do you cook? he asked.

I eat out.

Me too.

She took down a cookbook and picked out a recipe at random. Halibut with beurre blanc and grapefruit. They assembled what they needed to prepare it. They hadn't an idea what they were doing but followed the text. He chopped parsley and onion. She boiled the juice from an orange and whisked in cream. They put two fillets into a foil tent. He brought silverware and wine. She flavoured rice with vanilla and built towers of mushrooms and grapefruit salsa. They made a table with white linen and a dozen candles, turned out the lights and sat. It was like a private room in a brasserie.

I brought something for you, he said.

He handed her the silver-studded belt.

Oh yes, she said.

She unfurled it and then rolled it up again.

What would my aunt say?

Who's your aunt?

Polish Catholic. Very devout. Thinks priests don't use bathrooms.

What *would* she say?

She rolled her eyes, fanned her face.

She didn't know where her belt was until a strange man brought it back to her from his hotel room!

He could see the scene and laughed. She paid attention to the way he did it.

She told him how she'd awakened in his room. She saw a wall she didn't recognise. She was alone, in a man's shirt. Then the memory of the night came to her. The death of Srećko, the storm, their meeting with the rain pouring down over them.

All your things were there, she said, but no you. I heard voices. It was like a railway station outside your door. I picked up your note. I was hungry. I put on my clothes to go out. I thought I put the catch on the lock. Outside in the hall . . . it was amazing, like a carnival. There were people playing bongos. There was a woman dressed just in feathers. I went walking through the floors. I forgot I was hungry. I even forgot about Srećko. I looked and looked. Like for an hour. Every floor was a new show. Then when I got back your door was locked.

I see.

With my belt inside.

Yes.

I put the note under the door and left.

You did.

You must have thought me an awful ingrate.

I didn't. Where did you go?

To my apartment. I didn't have any choice. The circus people would want to talk about what happened to Srećko all the time. His shoes were there when I got home, like I knew they'd be. Our plates were still on the table. I know people die. But usually you don't have to see it happen. It was his eyes. Looking, not seeing. Like dead flies. He landed right next to my foot. His body looked like it had been beaten with bats. I'd only ever seen dead people in a coffin with make-up on. I couldn't stay there. So I went back to where I'm from for a while.

You ran away from the circus.

Yes!

And this place you're from, what is it?

You can't want to know about Allen Park, Michigan.

I'd like to know how you describe it.

Well, it's true. We spent the night together and haven't been introduced . . . Let's see, Allen Park. Everything there is beige. Like graham crackers. The houses are beige, the skin is beige. The thinking is beige. Everybody buys their clothes at Target, whether they're eighty or twelve. Lives of sensory deprivation in the beige suburbs of Detroit. I was so unsatisfied. Everyone I knew was unsatisfied. There were cutters, girls putting out cigarettes on their hands. There was a game people played, they covered their eyes and dropped a finger on a map and wherever it landed they went there. It caught on.

If I saw people do interesting things, like back flips, or playing the trombone, or even if they just wore weird interesting clothes, I wasn't just entertained, I coveted what they had. I plotted how to get it.

I was learning cello in a conservatory and was set to go to college like everyone else in my family didn't do. Then I saw the Back Porch Dogs. You couldn't have heard of them. Doesn't matter. They came through Allen Park and put on a wild, crazy circus show in the back of a club. Me and my friends went. I thought up until then that anything you really liked wasn't allowed. But the Back Porch Dogs weren't afraid. They did whatever they wanted. They didn't have to have a reason. They painted their faces, their clothes were Wild West or Berlin cabaret. They looked so interesting. The audience too. They were a tribe. We hung out with them. We got stoned in the back of their van. It was like being handed a free pass to your own life.

They took me on because I could play an unusual instrument.

We all lived together in a big brick warehouse in Austin, Texas. Barbecue and high wire. We had little curtained-off cubicles and when we woke we crawled out. Somebody was always there.

Ryan went to the refrigerator and scooped out two bowls of blueberries for them. He stood looking at the wall for a while. Then he came back and sat.

There was a painter, he said, who had to be with people all the time. He'd be at home wondering what was going on in some café he liked and he couldn't stand it. He had to go. If he had an idea going out it was gone by the time he got home. The need to be with people got so bad it felt like it was burning him alive.

Sounds like everyone I know, she said.

A friend told him that the only ideas that have any strength are the ones you get alone and stay with alone. They can't survive being talked about with other people because everyone understands things in a different way. The ideas break up, fly away.

Is that what you think? she asked.

I think I shouldn't take the chance of thinking otherwise.

She let him know she understood this answer and took some pleasure in it.

What did he do? she asked.

He stayed alone.

Did it work?

Yes. He was Delacroix.

I looked for your painting when I woke up.

There was nothing to see there, he said.

He leaned in over the table towards her.

What was that music? he asked.

You hear music?

The music you played on your cello.

Oh. That was Dvořák. His Concerto in B Minor. I just play a phrase. I go around it a different way each night. That phrase, you can revere it, parody it, argue with it, be tender towards it. I get a feeling and I play that.

Like the dress!

The dress?

Never mind. But what if you don't feel anything?

She laughed.

I remember something. Or blow fire. Or sing.

But what if there's nothing there?

She found this even funnier. He seemed in his guilelessness to be from another century.

It's just the circus, she said. Most of us are in it so we won't be bored. We like the audience, we hang out with them, but the show's for us. We're trying to get to a point where we don't know what's going to happen. It's a game we play. We try to throw each other off. I used to think you fixed a show and repeated it. But these people'd rather bag groceries than do that. We're not good enough anyway to be perfectionists. But we think we have some things to say. If you have that you don't have to be artful. We barely get paid. We sleep in the sleaziest hotels. It's not worth doing it unless it's a kick.

He looked like he was trying to work through a new technology.

What did you feel when you played . . . say, last night? he asked.

Last night? . . . I know. My grandma. How she's forgetting things. How I'm losing her.

And tonight?

I knew you'd be there. Or hoped so. So I tried to play the night we met.

He sat up, remembering the piper in the snow.

Did something happen? she said.

What do you mean?

You jumped.

No, nothing. I just remembered somebody else playing a night.

It's more inviting to play the night than the day. Did you like the way I did it?

It was big . . . it was gorgeous . . . it was breatht—Oh, God.

It felt good tonight.

He threw up his hands.

I'm not good at this . . . See, that painting I took away, I'd been throwing myself at it for months. I'm not even an amateur painter. I'd not made a painting. I was about to slice this one open with a blade. I went out. The sky opened up. I saw a bridesmaid's dress in a window. That could be it! I thought. I met you in the rain. You slept in my room. You were gone in the morning. I began to paint the dress. Everything was different this time. I felt such exhilaration. I actually tasted it. Whatever happens to me from now on, if I never paint again, that at least is mine. But there was still something missing. I'd found your belt. I put it into the painting, lower right. That was it.

He took a long drink of wine and went on.

There was another painter in Paris. Poussin. Delacroix couldn't abide him because he thought him too correct. His fussiness meant he couldn't make a sacrifice for something larger. His paintings were like barricades against the people looking at them. Delacroix wanted to let them in. *Living in the minds of others is what is intoxicating.* That's what he said. And he had to isolate himself to do it . . .

So what I mean to say is, you sounded that note at the top of the stage and you came down playing the phrase and it all seemed to have happened to me before and was happening again, *right inside my head.*

She passed the rim of her glass along her lower lip. Her breath fogged the bowl.

So maybe Delacroix's friend was wrong, she said.

How?

About having to be alone because people understand things in different ways.

You mean?

The music I felt and played described what happened to you.

Could be a coincidence, he said.

Maybe you should take the chance that it isn't.

He smiled, lifted his glass to her.

That was good, he said.

And what did the music say?

It said the making of the painting. Search. Failure. Argument. Despair. Discovery. That was the order. Then something after that. What . . .? Dancing?

Dancing, she said.

It was like dancing, with a canvas the size of . . . well, of you.

Their eyes locked. He reached for the bottle, shook it, found it empty.

It's done.

Get another.

He stood.

But don't be long, she said. You were long last time.

She watched him bend low and slip through the doors like a fish. She sat back into the shadows. She took small sips of wine and felt strangely lonely. For him? In a minute? She got up and put her ear to the door. There was no sound. She sat back down again. She pictured him crawling under the surveillance beams towards their new bottle like a recruit at a military training camp and began to laugh. She liked the sound she made but didn't want to be heard. She counted her breaths, became still. She couldn't abide a puny laugh in a man. What would his sound like? She didn't know. She hadn't heard him laugh yet, not really, not with all of himself. She'd watched the lines around his eyes and imagined it. Something with enough knowledge and author-ity and helplessness in it. But she couldn't be sure. She hoped it, though. She placed a spoonful of blueberries in her mouth. What would it be like to dance with him? His hips had slithered among the tables like they had radar. The first physical moment with a man. It could kill everything on the spot if it wasn't right. You feel them coming towards you through their chests with their hesitancy and ineptitude and needs. The blood turns cold. Thin, hard lips, self-important cologne. They mightn't know how to hold you, just slump on your shoulders like a wet coat. How would it be with him? She couldn't take her mind away from the desire to know. There he'd been, across from her, just minutes ago. He was older than her. He looked like he knew things. The gauzy light of the candles. Words braiding so elegantly it seemed over the linen. The space between them was liquid. But still a space, small and resolute. She'd like it breached, not by her, perhaps not by him either. Just dissolving of itself. She wanted music so she could dance with him, a dance almost motionless, his arms around her, her white and weightless on his chest. But there was no music. She'd already looked. Just to feel him for a moment. She waited. Still no sound from the bar. She took a long drink of wine. It was the wine as much as anything that was doing this to her. The wine. Their transgression. His eyes. His disarming, lazy glance. Blue jewels. She had eyes that didn't seek but instead called you to them. She knew that. She could make it happen when she wanted. But it was unfair that a man could also do it. She felt herself thinking along the cells of her skin.

He came in, water beads on the cold bottle. It was 5.10 and still dark. She took tealights from a box and made a galaxy of the kitchen. They sat. She poured wine. They clinked glasses, her hand grazing the back of his. She made a hook of her little finger, she was on the point of catching his and holding it, but she couldn't make herself go through with it. *How demure he makes me.* She softened her eyes and lowered her voice. This kept him close. Her words came to him tenderly, like scent. He moved around small spheres of oil on the table, making shapes. She kept his glass full and asked him questions. *What was the argument?* You're talking about that painting? *Yes.* With myself. *The discovery?* It was the dress. The dress seemed to say something. *What?* You'd have to see. *Can I?* He cut the patterns of oil with a knife. I guess so. *And the dancing?* Dancing's always better when you're a little drunk, isn't it? Painting them was like that. *What are you after?* I'd like to paint an ear that looked like it could listen . . . I'm a child in this. I read about what people do, or I see it. An unlaboured line or a very soft touch. You can get it in a song, a long note unfinished and unsatisfied. I'm far, far away from that . . . I'd like to paint that ear . . . I'd like to get to the secrets of colour. Did you know amethyst comes from 'not drunk'?

The colours and temperatures in the room were variants of those of flesh. Her hand moved towards his and his towards hers . . .

Very shortly after that their night came suddenly to an end. Hip-hop in Spanish shook the air. Chairs scraped, water drummed into buckets. They stepped away from each other. Two middle-aged Latino men with black moustaches and yellow T-shirts imprinted with 'BURTON'S CLEANERS' came through the swinging doors and turned on the overhead lights. They nodded a good morning to Ryan and Nicky and set to work. Out on the pavement of Dogpatch the sky was pink.

When I left my office the day my hands refused to type all seemed impossible. The feeling stayed with me, on the subway, in the lift, through the door of our home. No one was there. I decided to cook something elaborate in the hope it would absorb me. I can't remember what it was, only that it didn't turn out well. You seemed to sense that something was wrong. Lydia too. You looked at me with bright, encouraging faces. I knew somehow I was going to let you down and found I could hate you for it. This is not an honourable story.

The panic subsided, but the malaise did not. It settled in. I began to feel I was living with a ghost, a ghost that took my air, made me hesitant in my stride, snarled up words before they could get out of my mouth. The world kept making its offers and demands, but I turned away from them. I had lost belief. I kept showing up at my seminar, but let my students run it. I didn't answer calls from the head or the television producer or even from Silvio. The stream coming to me from the outside world began finally to constrict and lose force. People backed off. Perhaps, like you, they sensed something was wrong with me.

I got up with you in the mornings. I made you breakfast. Sometimes I'd go out with you and say I was heading uptown to my office. Then when you were out of sight I'd come back here. There were days I pulled down the shades and watched cartoons. There's a picture for you. But I didn't feel I was utterly lost. I felt I was waiting for something.

But what? And what had made this happen? It was him, it had to be, him and all that he brought before me, about my family, my evasions, my unasked questions and undone things of my past. He didn't mean to do it, but the effect was the same as if he'd had.

One late morning when I was alone at home I didn't turn away. I went to a bottom drawer in my study where his envelopes from San Francisco were. Maybe there I'd discover what I was waiting for. I took them out. I opened them. I found loose pages, discs, an address book, photographs of people you've been reading about if you're still with me, the drawings he'd made as a child that had been collected by Ambrose, twelve notebooks full of quotes, sums, dialogues, sketches, reports. *All paintings seem to me like prison windows in which the lines, precisely, are the bars . . . The imperialist is the bringer of violence into the mind and the home of the native . . . I know I can't paint a flower, but maybe with paint I can convey to you my experience of a flower.* There was a page, wine-stained, written in haste, about the throbbing edges of a rectangle in a painting by Mark Rothko, the dissolving boundaries of the self, between people and between the parts of Ireland, the word 'THINK' written under it, the pressure more intense here. I saw a drawing of Eimear, Generous's obituary. A street map made by hand of what I later learned was Crossmaglen, where he passed part of his war. The drawing he did of himself, too, the one you can see there at the beginning. Pages of colour mixes set out in rows with names in a woman's hand placed under them: Truck Tyre, Iron Ore, Flag Orange, Old Guitar, Embarrassment. Postcards: fifty-seven. One was Caravaggio's *Madonna of Loreto*, another Gerhard Richter's *Lesende*. Notes in various hands, one saying, 'Thank you, whoever you are – Nicky xx'. I saw drawings of her, a hundred photographs of open skies. There was page after page of failed drawings of the same image. I had the impression of a man throwing himself repeatedly against the stone wall of a fort.

The things of his life, intimate and distinct. They were not meant to be seen. They appeared to think in front of my eyes. His struggle to make something in which he could believe was intense and long. It was comprised almost entirely of failure. Yet he never let go of it. I'd seen the terms when I was still a boy, though I didn't understand what was at stake. His laugh at the funeral carried all the desolation of his war. What must it have been like to carry it? And yet he danced in the light among the trees. It was the picture of an artist as yet unable to make art. How could he get to it, dragging the weight that he did? How did he go from receiving from my brother the weapons he would kill with to living in the Labourd beside the baker Juliette? It all happened in the summer of 2009 in San Francisco.

I could tell you that I went in pursuit of this story for some therapeutic reason, to find the truth of my past, to bring me to my true self, to make myself worthy of you. But that wasn't really it, or all of it, not after I'd opened the envelopes. It was the only thing at the time that truly fascinated me.

I didn't leave at once. I felt like I was at the foot of a high dive. I approached with tentative steps. I already sensed the vertigo. That which we fear is that which we most need. How pompous that sounds. Especially to you I imagine in these circumstances. I say it because all my life I've turned away from it. I was afraid of making what I dreamed of making. I was afraid of uncertainty. I lived in the familiar. And as I suppose you noticed I passed most of my time among people like me for whom turning away is a perfectly plausible and respectable life strategy.

I stayed at home and thought about the risks. You could be one. Now I know that you were. The university was another. I didn't think I could find and tell his story with a clear mind and satisfy the engine that drove our lifestyle. I'd have to miss classes. I'd not write the things that 'bring such *lustre* to the department', as the head liked to say. I could be throwing it all away. I thought I'd take a last look at it before setting off.

I went out into a thin dirty rain. I took a cab uptown. I went up to the department floor and walked the halls. Students made models in studios. Adjuncts had the harried looks of commuters on overcrowded trains. A Black janitor moved among them unnoticed as he swept the floor. Along came Fred Paltrow, striding like a cardinal in his pomp. I looked at the office doors. They were decorated with surrealist collages, *New Yorker* cartoons, fragments of poetry. Mine was the same. Sometimes a revolutionary or inspiring message from someone who had risked all, as if someone dangerous lay just the other side of the door. I think no one here had risked all. Or much. Or anything. What was this place for? It could be for something. Informed people meeting curious ones. But the curious ones weren't in the equation. It was for us, so we could continue grazing contentedly in our pastureland. It all seemed so silly, so juvenile.

No one paid any attention to me as I passed except one, a small nervous man named Jason Garfield you never met who was moving along the wall fraught with facial tics. He seemed to recoil, as if red satanic lamps were shining from my eyes. What did he see? Something was happening to me. But I don't think I was mad, then or later.

I walked in the streets. The sky was low. People moved as if their shoes were waterlogged. A cab driver in a fez bared his teeth. A little dog in a tartan jacket looked around resentfully. It all seemed so funny. I felt it falling away, the mild pleasantness of my life, the fictiveness of my intellectual pursuits. In my head I was somewhere else, moving along a mountain range in clear Alpine air.

That afternoon I waited by the door to Lydia's school. She came out with her friend Maya, head to head over a phone.

What are you doing here? she said.

Her voice rebuked but her eyes smiled.

Just passing, I said.

I took her for hot chocolate. I did the imitation of your brother trying to whistle that always cracked her up when she was small. I took her hand. It was a long time since I'd done it. There was a special way we used to arrange it, something about thumbs or little fingers, the way they interlaced. I couldn't remember. Then I felt her moving her hand into the familiar position. She did a little skip as she walked.

That was the weekend we went to Saratoga Springs. All was yellow and orange and red. I bought you earrings from an antique shop. You put them on at the restaurant. Your long fingers, the tilt of your head. You looked so beautiful.

We came home and the next day I left for San Francisco.

I took a room in a small hotel in the Wharf District. It had by then been four years since all the things I've been telling you about took place. I only knew the people from what I found in Ryan's envelopes. They were phantoms there – phone numbers, sketches, snapshots, fragments in notebooks. It's a city of exquisite veneer but with a rawness underneath. Those who did not fit elsewhere in America washed up there and stayed. This was true for the people of that summer, rich or poor or in between. Paul, Nicky, Alexis, Ming, the boy Oliver and his mother Charlotte. I wondered would I find them all.

Ming was the easiest. His star was in the ascendant. Two style magazines in my hotel carried stories on him. He'd have been harder to avoid than to find. We met at a sushi bar in North Beach and drank saké. When I told him about the great weight borne by Ryan's laugh at the funeral in Carrachor, tears made runnels in the creases of his face.

I miss him, he said. It's not the same.

Afterwards I walked up the hill to the house on Telegraph Hill.

Plastic sheathed the scaffolding and rippled in the wind. Ming told me it had been like that for years. The catastrophe there had enhanced his reputation – a masterpiece traduced by an act of madness. But I'll come to that.

Alexis was still in the Bostonian Hotel, tending to the beleaguered, and Nicky was in Eureka to the north, her hair no longer white. Funny you saw him more recently than me, she said. How does he look? Did he say not to tell me where he is?

I found Paul Crane through an article in the *Wall Street Journal*, which concluded by saying that he was in Lompoc Federal Penitentiary in Santa Barbara County. I met him in a cinderblock room there. He had aged since his press pictures, his body had spread on a bad diet and he had a scar the size of a dinner plate that took away his right eye and ear. It was ribbed like cooled candlewax.

Go on, he said. Take a look. Touch it if you want. Then we can talk.

I went to San Francisco several times that autumn, gathering the story. On each occasion I told you a different lie. When Alexis told me a room was available in the Bostonian Hotel I took it. I came alive there in the Pacific light. I was finally doing something that had to do with my life. Of all the cities I believe it is the only one where such people could fly up into one another's lives. They clashed, they mingled. The sun poured down on them as they moved through that summer towards their fates.

CHAPTER SEVEN

Three Men

San Francisco, 2009

i

Three years before he and his family moved to San Francisco Paul was brought by a client at his bank to a dinner at a private house in Bolinas, a spit of land reaching into the Pacific Ocean thirty miles north of the city in Marin County. A small community of intensely private citizens lived there, so private that any time the county put up a sign showing the turnoff to their town, they tore it down. Five men and three women sat around a table beside a window the width of the wall. The sun descended towards the ocean, warm light fell on heather and dune grass, and the surf curled in. Paul thought he'd never seen a place so serene and beautiful. A rare plot of land overlooking the beach had come up for sale, the host told him. Paul bought it with a phone call the next day. He'd build a house there for Charlotte, in the hope it would bring her back to him.

He remembered, with a repetitive insistence, the house on Lake Pontchartrain she'd taken him to in the early days of their romance. *I can be whoever I want here*, she'd said when they arrived. This sentence had haunted and thrilled him since, but in that house in those days she'd been who she wanted to be with him. Any moment could combust into sex so pure and savage as to be more of the rainforest than the bedroom.

He made a sketch of the house on Lake Pontchartrain for an architect. He kept the details vague. He only wanted to evoke a faint memory. A team of builders began to assemble it. One was a Ukrainian, Vanko, ex-Special Forces, who lived in a hut in the marijuana fields to the north.

Paul had taken the loss on the Singapore dollar around the time he bought the land in Bolinas. He tried to tell himself it was bad luck, but knew it was a failure of maths. Nor was it an exception. His models began to break down. He tried to rebuild them, but found they were composed of a language he only partly understood. Career performance charts told him that mathematicians peak in their mid-twenties. By these standards he was already elderly. The young hedge fund managers he tracked were now out of his league.

He might have handed his money over to one of them, but he feared boredom. He began to place hunch bets on options. They were fast and entertaining. The bets were small compared to the possible rewards. He opened a brokerage account at J.P. Morgan. His credit was good and the well, he thought, was bottomless.

But he didn't entirely believe it. Lack of belief in general was seeping slowly towards him. It had begun with the arrival of his son and the receding of his wife. He thought it would cease, but it hadn't. He felt it in his body. The malaise was growing more sure of itself.

Among the trading screens in his room were others bringing CCTV images from his houses on Telegraph Hill and in Bolinas. The builders had offered the service and he'd assented. He told himself that the cameras were for the safety of his family and most particularly for Charlotte. He saw her dance weightlessly through the rooms, the music up. He saw her fervour and expressiveness and grace. He wanted her with a desperation that choked him. She could not reciprocate. Her illness was taking her. This time it revealed itself in the way the house and the story Ming had told her about it entered her and conquered her. She researched Captain Merriweather's routes and the artefacts he might have brought back from the countries he visited. She tried to talk with him through a small window in her room. She lit small fires to call him.

Paul turned with increasing frequency through the day to the images on his screen. He spent more time with them than with his trades. Five, six, nine hours in a single day, his logs told him. They were like an opiate.

The school year ended for the boy Oliver and he stayed at home to attend his mother. He watched her sleep, he brought trays of food to her bed, he hid matches and lighters. Sometimes he lay beside her and read to her. Paul saw their quiet, vibrant intimacy. When the boy rose to leave she held him to her, reluctant to let go, tears in her eyes, knowing she was slipping away from him and could do nothing to stop it. Paul watched on the screen with an envy that embarrassed him.

A poker player he'd met in the Bayou Lafourche told him that if a gambler is to become a professional they must first break their addiction. Paul had never had an addiction. He'd run his investments through his mathematical models with an effortlessly cold detachment. But the option bets were different. They were flings. Each one seemed to have a story and a promise. Probability calculations were irrelevant. That they so infrequently delivered for him did not reduce their allure. He pleaded and laughed with them as to a person. In the moment that preceded the revelation of the result of his bets he experienced exhilaration, fear and something like lust. He kept coming back for more.

By midsummer he was out of money. He felt breathless. He couldn't sleep. The walls of his room seemed to be moving in on him. In this condition he made the decision to set up a private equity company through which he would sell shares in a $50 million loan that would return at a guaranteed fifteen per cent. The company had a name, an email address and a representative named Justin Braithwaite, who had an English accent and was played by Paul. Paul made the calls, Justin Braithwaite dealt with the details. The loan did not exist.

From his room Paul heard sounds from the outer world, a clap, loud and sudden, a cry of delight, laughter. He thought he heard his son in it. He also heard a woman, but the woman, he felt, was not Charlotte. He spun in his chair and looked at his screens. He flicked through the rooms of his house until he found Ryan, his son Oliver and a young woman with white hair he didn't know. They were sitting on the floor. Everyday objects made strange by their randomness were before them. He watched Oliver place a balled handkerchief under an overturned cup, wave his hands abracadabra style over it, lift the cup, where there was magically no handkerchief now, and then pull the handkerchief from his pocket instead. It went back into his pocket and appeared again under the cup. The woman rocked back and clapped her hands. Then she took Oliver's handkerchief, placed a bread roll under it and made the small assemblage float upwards seemingly under its own power. They all laughed, Ryan too. Paul was surprised at how natural Ryan looked as he did it for he had never managed to draw laughter from him or even to be able to imagine it. The images flickered grey and white, the figures in them evanescent, even Oliver, perhaps particularly Oliver, the gestures more spontaneous, the laughter simpler, happier, freer than could be so in real life, as in silent films, or the Super 8 reels shot by Paul's father at home in Hobart, Paul blowing out the candles on his birthday cake, Paul charging in his cowboy clothes past the backyard tomato vines firing his toy pistols, his mother opening presents with him on Christmas mornings. All so far away and alluring. He watched the tricks. He didn't know any of them. He wondered how they were done.

He had been paying the builders in Bolinas to work evenings and weekends so that he could present the finished house to Charlotte in the hope that it would save them in time. By late July their work was complete. Under a vow of secrecy Ming was driven by Paul to Bolinas and offered an extension to his contract to design the new house. Ming accepted, but didn't let it get in the way of what he was doing on Telegraph Hill. His vision for the house there had continued to grow and be made visible. It was reaching sublimity, Ming believed, and he felt a sincerity in the work he'd never have thought possible. He sensed a darkness closing in on the house and wanted it finished and photographed before a calamity befell it. He advanced some ideas for Bolinas. He relied on tropes he'd used before. He sent Ryan there on his own to execute them.

Ming had seen by then that the escrow account that had been set up for him to draw on for the works had been nearly emptied by withdrawals in the tens of thousands made by Paul. This was curious, he thought. He'd understood from the reports he'd received that Paul's money had no end. He began to watch him. He'd seen the hidden cameras since the day they were installed. He made a remote link to his own computer and put a bug in Paul's office. He saw things that amazed him. One morning Paul lost $3 million and vomited in his wastebasket. In the afternoon he lost another million. Ming watched him vomit again, throw water over his face, breathe deeply and then he saw Paul live coming out of his room walking towards him, smiling, like he was about to greet an old friend. He's got guts, he thought.

As July turned to August the temperature rose into the nineties. Ryan painted his effects in Bolinas naked but for a T-shirt and slept on the roof. Paul watched him from his room. He watched Charlotte spiral upwards onto a rarefied plane not meant for him. He saw his son attend to her until she slept and then sit at the kitchen table with his head in his hands like an old man.

Paul drove up to Bolinas one evening with fish tacos, a bucket of steamed mussels and beer and wine on ice. He wasn't sure what he wanted there. Ryan was alone, as he knew he would be. Paul walked through the rooms, praising the effects. He laid a table on the terrace and lit candles in old railway lanterns. An extra button on his shirt was left undone. He ran his hand over his chest. He cocked his head to the side to listen. He told stories of zydeco bars and shrimp-boat men on the bayou he thought Ryan would like to hear. He'd built a fortune by limiting risk, but now played a high-risk game. He'd lately become inured to risk.

Around midnight Ryan rose to go to his bed on the roof. Paul rose with him, mist in his eyes and with a flushed face. He held out a tentative hand. In Ryan's eyes he thought he saw pity. Finally Paul stepped aside. Ryan went through the door leading to the roof and closed it. In the night Paul walked the floor.

Paul had a dream of a world without Ryan. The landscape had been emptied of him. He woke with a clear memory of it. Loneliness and failure lifted from him as he lived again through the dream. It became the destiny he had to bring about. He didn't stop to analyse what it meant or how he would do it. There was no time to analyse.

ii

Ryan was with Nicky every night since he went to see her at the circus. He ate and slept with her and left her in bed when he went to work. His days painting walls on Telegraph Hill funnelled towards the night when he could be with her again.

Yet still, within himself, he resisted her. He feared she might rearrange him in some way, and however badly arranged he was the arrangement was at least familiar and had produced the paintings of the dress. And she was so present. In the war the way out of an operation was of equal importance to the way in. What was the way out from her? There would have to be one sometime.

Then something happened to him. It was evening. They had arranged to meet at the edge of the Valencia Corridor and were walking towards each other in the street. The night was ahead. What he saw of her slowed and magnified. He saw the rhythmic slicing of her walk. The humour in her eyes that assumed they saw things the same way. The hands that pushed the bow and drew his face and body to hers. Her drive, her freedom, her absence of fear. The sun lit up her face. The word 'home' came to him. Strange word, he thought, even then, for two people forever passing through. Something broke and fell away, his edges came alive, grew permeable, osmotic. There was nothing complicated in it. It felt like love. He had never used this word before or believed he had earned the right to know what it meant.

The gap between them was narrowing. They met at mid-point. He held her by the shoulders and looked into her face.

I love you, he said.

Alexis

I missed him. I wondered what I'd done. Then one of the boys on the desk told me he was in love. I shouldn't have been surprised, in spite of what he'd said, a man like him in a city like this, he'd be approached, she'd be the right one, he'd reciprocate. I was happy for him, in an abstract way. But it left a hole. The evening would come on and I'd feel an ache. I never had someone like that in my life. No tricks, no wish to conquer. I didn't even know that existed.

He must have felt bad about me because he brought her down with a strawberry cheesecake tied up with a bow. He looked different. I saw it right away. He was all blood and oxygen. The empty plains of his eyes were full of her. I studied her. I wondered who it was could do this to him. She was right there, if she was interested. *Unnervingly* actual. Those eyes. She'd lift the lids slowly. Like opening a jewellery box. She did what she wanted and always seemed to know what that was. She'd go down and jam with wild boys in their rooms. Make fun of them, give them new names. Boys with long prison records who could have crumpled her up like a piece of paper in their fists. No fear. Everything was not *then*, or *maybe*, or *if*. It was *right now*. There are not so many women like that. You may not know. Women see the big picture. Or they feel it if they don't see it. They sacrifice their pawns. But she was dancing when she danced. Or loving. Or forgetting. She had the capacity to forget. She certainly did. He tasted that . . .

Ryan lay in the dark. A text had arrived at 10.15 – First half over. Miss you. xox. He'd been reading, he lay the book aside. Raw street sounds blew upwards to him. She was in Oakland doing a show. Pictures of her there came to him. Thinking. Watching. Drawing music from her instrument. One drink and then you, can't wait, warm kisses – said a message at 11.37. Head on a pillow, hair across her lips. She would arrive at one. That was his estimate. He adjusted himself to it. He went back to his book. At 12.50 he began to anticipate. What would be the beat of this encounter? He felt a minor tension. At 1.20 time began to move differently. It was slow, thick. Pictures of her crowded him and not all of them were benign. There was no room for the sentences in the book. He again lay it aside. He took off his clothes and went into his bed. The numbers on his clock advanced past two and then, as if time were a heavy load being dragged, past three. He wasn't used to this. He squinted in the dark at the forms in his room. He knew that he could put everything he needed into a suitcase. It would take fifteen minutes. It had always been thus, and it had worked in its way. No one waiting for him, and no one to wait for. Or if he'd waited it was without the sense of anything belonging to him being risked. Just desire, and whether or not it would be short-changed. He lay still in the dark. The minutes clustered like filings around a magnet. Time was moving differently for her. He knew this. 'A drink' in the mind of the drinker is of a different duration for the one waiting at home. Anticipation was succeeded by an injured sense of justice. He could not halt this. The jugglers, the horned barker. Men from the audience, intriguingly dressed, skilled at praise, men who had been stoked by her tilting on the wire, her embrace of the cello as if it were her lover, and who had nothing to lose. Frivolous-ness and gaiety and shots of vodka. He got up and drank a long glass of wine. He rarely drank naked and alone. The picture displeased him. He went back to bed. His chest was tight, the air less ample. A bad taste was in his mouth, as of old coins. He rolled onto his side and forgetting himself for a moment a tenderness in his chest and throat and arms rose to meet her who on this night was not there. He turned on the light. He got up and wrote into a notebook, 'Small dependencies accumulate.' He turned back to the bed but decided to stay up. He put on his clothes. What could he do with her now? All he could offer was bile. He hesitated at the door. Should he leave a note? Was he being infantile? He went out and didn't turn the lock in case she might come. He'd like her to see an empty room.

He came back three hours later. It was a dead time. He'd walked along Geary all the way to Richmond and in an all-night place had poured brandy from a flask into paper mugs full of coffee. Then he walked back again through a cold mist. He was calmer, until the room stirred him again. He looked for signs of her presence. The bed was cold. Shadows fell across rucks in the sheets. He looked at the patterns. He couldn't tell if she'd been there.

He peeled fruit and cut bread. He brewed a pot of coffee. He sat at his table and ate but the tastes were muted and dull. He felt foolish. He wished she was there to forgive him. He walked to the window. There was a broad blue sky.

It was a day they'd shot a rabid dog on Geary Street. The sanitation department had arrived. The streets were wet. People were depressed about the dog. He looked up through a wide shaft made by the buildings. The clouds were on a gigantic scale, huge cumulous anvils boiling upward. He watched them for a long time. They kept changing. The light was beating down on them and the clouds were climbing up. He couldn't figure out the light dynamics. He could see it wasn't just a matter of light shining on top of the clouds. That wasn't the evidence. There were grey clouds that should have been in light, there were others rimmed all the way around in silver. What were the lightlines? He stood there for an hour and a half. He couldn't get it. He thought if he put a sky on a canvas he might understand.

Right on time tonight, she said.
Yes.
She ignited her phone and looked at the clock.
Even a little early.
Right.
About last night . . .
Do you want a drink? he asked.
I kept trying to leave that bar in Oakland.
Do you want a drink? I want a drink.
Yes. Rum.
He brought drinks.
I knocked, she said. I turned the doorknob. I went in.

I wasn't there.

You weren't.

I went out.

I guess you did. I was sad. I was really sad that you weren't there. All the way in the cab I was so excited, I was lit up.

Well. I had to go out.

Yes. I sent messages.

That's right.

Didn't you know I'd come? I always come. Or you do.

. . .

Can I ask, she said, . . . am I allowed . . . Where did you go?

It's not important.

The reunion was worth the long night waiting in his room for her. She shut the shades, banished the world, dissolved the space and brought him back. The warmth of her body through her nightdress was more familiar to him than anything else in his life since the war. He was full of her.

Something had to happen for him to paint again, he'd thought, and something was.

The circus went dark, Ryan took a week off and went with Nicky into the mountains and deserts to look at skies. Yosemite, Mammoth, down into Death Valley and then east towards the Vermilion Cliffs. She shot skies with a camera from the back of the motorbike. They stayed in little hotels with heart-shaped beds. They went on through the Navajo lands and in Monument Valley drove lightly on a dirt track past the towering buttes and pinnacles. The sun was going down. It had rained in the afternoon. Stone, earth and scrub were newly washed, silver beads of rainwater were on new shoots. They stopped under a tower of rock, took off their shoes and walked in the red sand. The touch of the air and of the sand were exceptionally soft.

They stood still. The smell of fresh earth rose in waves. It seemed the ground was breathing.

Along the way he asked her what she saw, the colours, the shapes, the proportions, and what they made her feel. Did you see the rose, the green? What was the texture? She framed the scenes, she looked in the particular, she read what they made happen in her. They made paintings out of what they said and heard from each other and when they got back to the city he painted them.

After he'd seen Mark Rothko's humming rectangles he'd thought to paint abstracts and bought six-foot-high canvases. But lines now formed horizons and triangles evolved into clouds. The paintings became skyscapes. He pushed piles of paint towards each other until they met in the middle sky. He kept the clouds indistinct with the pass of a soft brush and a smear at the edges made by his finger. The making of the paintings moved through what they had seen and said. He liked the middle stages best, when the foundation was down and he didn't know what would happen next. They were still alive and forming. She broadened and particularised them. He could see her in the marks he made. Finishing them was an anti-climax.

iii

I flew to Ireland after the Thanksgiving break. I'd been with you and Lydia, mostly ignoring my classes and Silvio and concerned emails from the producer in England while filling my room with a webbing of storylines I'd gathered in San Francisco. Had you known what I was doing you'd have thought me mad. Eventually, you did. But I was beginning to get a sense of what it would have been like to do what I never did – to make a thing, rather than to comment.

At Dublin airport I stepped into a cab.

Can I hire you for five days? I asked.

You can, said the driver.

He was Peter Finnerty, from Cavan.

We drove north, towards Belfast. I asked him to take the old route and we moved up through farmland and towns. I hadn't been home, as we call it, since my father's funeral. Whenever I thought of it, it was usually with indifference, or disdain, or embarrassment. It looked different to me now. Those pale faces and quick, sympathetic eyes. Wet air and a whiff of turf smoke. Boys whacking balls with hurling sticks, yapping dogs, old men in their suits up on tractors. Familiar, yet new.

We came up to the border in a soft rain. I told Peter Finnerty about Ryan and my brother and our fields full of weapons and that I was there in pursuit of a mystery. The watchtowers were gone now and the roads dynamited by the British had been patched up. I saw a customs shed covered in vines and with an oak growing up through it. The border had evaporated since I had last seen it. The light came back and shone through the trees and we drove on into Belfast.

My father had taken me here when I was twelve on a visit to his brother in Andersonstown. I remember coming up through the centre of the city, the statues of British monarchs and generals, the City Hall, massive, imposing, like a disapproving prefect with folded arms, a Union Jack flying from the dome. We took a turn west, into the Falls Road. The scene changed suddenly, jarringly. It was as though footage from another movie had been spliced onto the one I had been watching. I saw pods of soldiers wrapped around police-men moving along the pavements, rifles out, looking down their scopes at the citizens, looking too at us. I saw the little o's at the ends of their barrels. Saracens sped. Watchtowers loomed. Hovering heli-copters came down from the clouds. The whole place seemed to be under siege.

Did something happen? I asked my father.

He drove on. His lips were drawn tight. Then he pulled over and looked at me.

The same thing that's been happening since they came here eight hundred years ago, he said. They're showing us who's boss. They want to crush us so we'll feel small.

He started driving again. We passed broken walls and wet wastegrounds, an abandoned mill with the windows out. Soldiers were on the pavements and in the roads in their vehicles. Barracks with barbed wire and lookouts. I saw it all as a hallucination in black and white, but through it, distantly, reds and blues and greens flaming up in paintings on walls. Women with their sleeves rolled up, a lark on an Armalite, clenched fists, Cuchulainn with a sword.

He pulled over again to speak to me.

But there are some here who are drawing the line, he said. No matter what it costs them.

I didn't know what he meant then, but I do now. It was Dermot he was proud of, not me. I was a kind of Martian who'd dropped down into their care. They were exalted by my triumphs, it even thrilled them that I bore their name, but I wasn't really one of them. Dermot was one who had drawn the line, and it had cost him. I was about to learn the price.

Now with Peter Finnerty I rode the same route. The soldiers and their installations had gone. Tricolours flew, the road signs were written in Irish. The wastegrounds were filled with houses and the abandoned mill with classrooms. They'd made things. The streets were theirs. I said so to Peter Finnerty.

It's not over yet, he said.

I put my headphones on and listened to Ryan. I saw his house as he described it to me, the wall where he'd watched the cat, the street where British soldiers beat Mr Doherty and humiliated Ambrose

McGuigan. I looked for the yard where the piper had played in the snow but couldn't find it. I walked through his words. I followed the lines of his war – his first shot from the cinema roof, the fusillade let loose from the barber shop, the attic window and the wall below where they'd shot him in the leg. The mural of Cuchulainn where the Para stood was nearby, a ghost now, faded almost to white. I followed the path of the hijacked lorry to the spot where he'd launched the mortars into the barracks. The barracks was gone. There was a GAA pitch and a republican mural in its place. All was gone – Saracens, men in masks, soldiers with nervous fingers on their triggers, watch-towers and helicopters – except as they still existed in the memories of those who had lived among them.

We went south and west then into the borderlands where I had been raised. It was all gone here too. We drove along. The border looped and twisted. We only knew it was there when Peter Finnerty's satellite navigator called out warnings. I listened to Ryan speak of massive attacks, the words lying eerily over the quiet land.

We arrived at the homeplace. It came to me differently than it had the first time around, the forms charged now by my desire to know them, both distant and familiar as if I were seeing them through two layers of time, through two sets of eyes. We walked the hills where the weapons had been buried and perhaps still were. We went on a long walk across the Blackwater River to Carrachor and I stood by the apple tree where I had first seen Ryan. We went into Generous's house by the conservatory entrance. Eimear lived there with a single wolfhound and a nurse from the Philippines. She was in a big arm-chair by the fire swathed in alpaca blankets, her hands twisted with arthritis, Ryan's portrait of her father spotlit above. She took my head in her hands and kissed me and wept. There won't be another time, she said. They gave us pheasant and put us up in twin beds in an upstairs room. We had tomorrow left, and then I was to return to New York. Peter Finnerty took down a book from Generous's shelves.

I put in my earphones and listened again to Ryan describe the final day of my brother Dermot's life.

It was Ryan's last operation in South Armagh before he was called back to Belfast, and it had been conceived by Dermot. He'd become aware of a cigarette smuggler named Evans who lived alone in a house just north of the border and was known to both the RUC and the Guards. They wanted him badly but hadn't yet found him with evidence. He was flash. He wore a tight leather jacket and no shirt and drove a car with orange flames stencilled on the sides. He thought he couldn't be touched.

Ryan's unit kidnapped him and packed his house with a dozen beer kegs filled with fertiliser and diesel, bound with cordite and primed with gelignite. The house became a live bomb. A command wire ran along overhead cables to a shed where they waited.

The idea was to lure British soldiers to the house and blow it up. Dermot drove Evans's car at speed over the border and along the lanes of Monaghan until the Guards spotted him and gave chase. He gunned it back north over the border, knowing that the Guards couldn't go further but would radio the RUC to say they thought Evans was carrying something. They'd go to the house accompanied by soldiers, enter the house, and Ryan would detonate the bomb.

Dermot dumped the car and got back to the shed. They watched the police and soldiers come down a small hill towards the house. Ryan had his finger on the detonator. But the soldiers stopped. They looked at the house through binoculars. They conferred. They watched for a long while. Then they withdrew.

They let Evans go under a threat that if he reported them they'd shoot him. Ryan and the others went back to their safe houses. But Dermot was quartermaster and he didn't want to lose the bomb. In the night he and another lad loaded the kegs into a van and drove back over the border to Bough to bury them on our land. But they'd been traced. Either there'd been an informer or the British had made an astute or lucky guess about the operation. The Guards were radioed and went after them. There was another chase through the lanes and the Guards were getting closer. Dermot abandoned the van. His partner jumped a wall and ran into the hills. The Guards followed. But Dermot slipped unseen down into a river. He stayed in it through the night. Nobody came for him. He was in the clear. In the early morning he came out.

I went out just before dawn to Generous's small lake. All was blue, pines, the lapping water, the air itself. I stood very still. A small ribbon of orange coloured the horizon. The water stirred the grasses. The pines a harp in the sough of the wind, the waterfall singing to the pool who receives her. Corncrake, heron, cuckoo, lark. *Étaín the queen flashes crimson and gold between the pines!* Don't get carried away, I said to myself, by stories told you by an old man when you were a boy. Quiet down. Still, something was happening. The tang of the pine. Mulch. The fear of the vole. Nature had always seemed so easeful, but not here by the lake. I left dead cells of skin and mind. Cold stormy air moved over my face. Musk rose from the ground. I drew in stinging air.

With Ryan's voice coming through to me I guided Peter Finnerty in the late morning to a bend in a borderland road above a river. Dermot had come up out of it wet and cold and strewn with rivergrasses and was struck by a cattle lorry that had gone out of control on a bend. My brother Paddy said Dermot hadn't seen it, that he never had a chance, it had hit him from behind. A man saw it though, a man who sold bottled gas out of his cottage across from the spot, where he still is, and where he told me through his half-door how a lorry which had come careening around the bend had smashed into a man who'd come out drenched from the river and how he'd bounced up and down like a child's ball between road and undercarriage and how the back wheels ran over his pelvis and left him crushed and dead face down in the road, blood running out of his ears and mouth. The peelers took him away in a bag. None of them ever asked this man what he'd seen and he'd told no one, and yet there was more to it, he said, something terrible, and it was that the man who'd come from the river hadn't been struck in the back but rather had seen the lorry, he was standing still soaking wet and his eyes swung that way and stayed on the lorry as it moved towards him and he took a step forward to meet it.

We went from the river on to Urbleshanny graveyard at Tedavnet. Peter Finnerty stayed close, minding me. He could see I wasn't far from falling apart. I walked among the stones breathless and shaking about what I had just heard, looking for Dermot and thinking of what a friend in New York once told me about his cousin, who'd come out of Vietnam and got a medical degree, set up a splendid, prospering practice as a dermatologist, had three children and a pretty wife, was the Division A champion at his golf club and an esteemed neighbour, and one day in his garage twenty years after coming back from Vietnam put a .45 to his mouth and blew out his brains. I couldn't understand it, said my friend, none of us could, until a little guy from his army unit, a machinist who'd flown in from Indiana for the funeral, leaned across at the lunch and said, Twenty years, the same voice in his head, 'What does it matter, What does it matter', it never stops, the same pictures, that hollowness, he couldn't carry it any more. No one has any idea. I wouldn't either except I was there too, he told them. I found Dermot under a Celtic cross made of grey stone. There was a laminated photograph of him embedded in the monument. He was smiling in an open-necked shirt, a smile with a lot of teeth, a smile some might call gormless, GAA banners strung up behind him and beer taps on the bar, someone's arm over his shoulder. Volunteer Dermot Treanor, killed in action. The same action maybe that blew up seven Guardsmen and a boy named

Christopher Smyth watching as the parade passed through a London park. But who am I to know?

Peter Finnerty dropped me back to Dublin airport. We said our goodbyes and I handed him €1,500. At a café there I tried to send $1,000 to the National Graves Association in thanks for looking after Dermot, and then I saw it, my brave march through our money, $24,367 in airfares and hotels and the rest since I first went to San Francisco. At this rate I'd spend over $200,000 in a year on a project designed to destroy our life as we have known it.

They called my flight. I walked to the gate. As I stood in line a text arrived from you – Where are you? What are you doing? Why don't you answer your phone?

Over the Atlantic, I began to have doubts. This thing I was doing, to you, to the three of us, suddenly seemed embarrassing, frightening, absurd. Could I not go back to how it was? I could fix it up with you, the department, write the next script, restore our accounts, accept accolades. We could resume our dinners with our friends and our summers in Hämeenlinna. It was nice there.

I lowered my table and tried to make some notes. I got some weak, familiar signals. But when I tried to write out what the signals were sending me I found they were dead in my hand. All of it was dead – the departmental meetings, Jim Dix with his ponytail and clenched fist railing against some change in conference expense accounts the dean wanted to make, and then Silvio and me – two rubber ducks made to squawk at each other in a bath. The door was shut. I had nothing to say. If you've lost belief there's nothing that can be done.

We began our descent. I saw the New York lights ahead. Soon I would face you.

Now, I said.

I lifted my hands as if to enclose something, then let them fall.

I got your text, I said. You have something to say, I think, or ask.

Yes, you said.

I'm with you.

Are you?

Entirely.

The Bostonian Hotel.

Yes.

I looked it up. It's a dive.

Yes. You could say that. But you mightn't if you stayed there. Would you like to stay there with me?

You drew in your breath sharply.

Do you get drugs there? you asked.

No.

Do you have somebody there? Are you sleeping with somebody in this hotel?

No.

You waited, so I spoke.

I can see how you might think that, I said. I can imagine how this looks.

Thank you.

I want to know the people there. There and elsewhere. People I didn't look at before.

We looked into each other's faces, I imploringly, inarticulately, you looking for coherence, sceptical. You have such beautiful, cool eyes.

Who are you? you asked.

Oh, Erica.

I look for you in Boston, you're in a prison in California. I look for you in London, you're in Ireland. I lived, breathed, thought and slept with you. Or so I thought. Your desk is full of crazy things. It's the desk of someone I don't know. Who are you?

. . . I don't know, yet.

You're forty-two.

Suddenly everything seemed a lie, I said – the university, the books I wrote, my past, my words, my breath.

I dreamed you were on a ship, you said, sailing away. We were waving from the shore.

I don't want to go.

But you are.

Yes. To the Bostonian Hotel.

What?

Here it is. The poorest offering. A request for patience. For faith, even more onerous than patience. I'm not mad. I'm incomplete. This all sounds so egotistical . . . I started something and the only thing I know is that I have to finish it.

How long?

I don't know.

I reached for you. You pulled back.

Will you wait? I would dearly love to hear you say you will wait.

You pulled back again and though you stayed in your chair it seemed you were still moving away. A shooting star. Nothing spoke, not hands, lips, eyes.

You went to bed. I saw the light spill from our room, then it went off. I was really frightened then. That light seemed terminal. I poured myself a brandy. I couldn't let go what I had started, as I had let every other thing go along the way, and then have to live with an everlastingly foul taste.

I wrote to Silvio to tell him I was pulling out of our double act. I wished him luck. I wanted to do something more decisive with the university, something that would bring me disgrace. I didn't want to leave a way back. I remembered an essay I'd sometimes feared could come back to haunt me. I'd written it under pressure to publish when we were at Cornell and with time running out and had put in a paragraph near the end I'd stolen from a German monograph. I didn't attribute it. I claimed its virtues as my own. It was peer-reviewed. No one noticed. Before I went to bed I sent both article and the plagiarised monograph anonymously to Jason Garfield, that aspirant assistant professor who was waiting on tenure. He'd know what to do with it.

CHAPTER EIGHT

Fire

San Francisco, 2009

Paul had the sensation that all that had been happening since they came to the house on Telegraph Hill was a dream with a malign air. Its portentousness, its faint connection with the familiar and his helplessness before it were like what transpired in dreams. Only the frantic movement of his bets, he found, relieved him of it.

In the two weeks since he'd begun selling shares in his fictitious loan he'd raised $30 million. He tapped professional investors and also people he'd known and worked with in the places where he and Charlotte had lived. The bankers in Zug who had sponsored him advanced him $18 million. There were still great reservoirs of faith in the mathematical genius who'd created and sold his own bank before he was forty. He'd heard their admiration over the phone when he was impersonating Justin Braithwaite. They were a receptive audience. They liked returns of fifteen per cent.

But he knew he was no longer this person. He was a felon yet to be found out. It gave him a sensation of vertigo, and yet he went on with it, making repayments to some with cash brought in from others. At some point it would crack, it would have to, he knew. Unless a miracle happened.

And then a miracle did happen. Dozens of options bets came good and he took in enough to pay off all the loan shares, with full interest, nobody the wiser, and still leave him with $25 million. But he was going down in a vortex, it seemed nothing could stop him, and he blew it all on wild hunches based on baseball results, whimsical word associations and the plucking of petals from a flower. The money burned and died.

The images on his screens came up like cards in a bad hand – his son looking with amused attention at Ryan painting a mural of parrots in his room, Ming walking the corridors of his home as if they belonged to him, Charlotte sleeping at midday in her separate room with her lipstick on. He was being displaced. He remembered his dream of a world without Ryan and how it had given him his only peace since the summer began. He sat in his chair and thought about it. He was accustomed to a favourable distribution of assets and deficits, and now they had reversed. How to flip it back again with regard to Ryan? He thought some more. Then he called Vanko, his Ukrainian builder.

Later that day he skipped up the stairs to Oliver's room and handed a set of keys to Ryan.

I want to thank you for all your work in the house in Bolinas, he said. Take a few days there, on me. Bring your white-haired girl.

Before a wall of glass that looked down on the beach at Bolinas, Ryan painted a sky they'd seen over Comb Ridge, Utah. He placed at her suggestion a stone in the foreground that flared in a shaft of sunlight. She stepped up to the canvas to take a look. Fish-scale silver, she said. She picked out daubs in the scrub and named them. Brown of an old guitar. Iron ore red. He told her the formulas. Iron ore is straight Indian red from the tube, he said. Rust suspended in oil. She went on. Confectionery turquoise like on a girl's nails (cerulean blue, viridian green, lemon yellow, titanium white and a dot of phthalo blue). The pink rash of embarrassment. Or the mortuary beige-pink of cheap make-up (Indian red with white, alizarin red, ultramarine blue to cut the intensity of the red). She wrote down the names in his notebook.

We'll come back to it later, she said.

She went down into the sea. He watched her slipping through the waves. Whites: sea foam, starched apron, flag white, blue-white on a child's temple. For the sea foam he'd use a bit of viridian and then alizarin crimson to cut it, hints of cadmium yellow and phthalo blue. Sea foam has a suggestion of mint. Blacks: truck tyres, onyx, new velvet. He'd tell her when she came back. Everybody loves blue, she'd said on the way out. I ask for blue light when I come down playing that cello piece you like so much. *There are connoisseurs of blue just as there are connoisseurs of wine.*

She stepped out from the wash of a wave, wringing her hair and putting one foot in front of the other on the wet sand. Everything shone in the sun. He watched her walk up the dune. These were their days. They had no home of their own, no plan, no possessions, no grocery list, only what they made fly up between them. The wall of glass. Moonlight on the waves. The murmur of brush on canvas, the sea, their speech.

She came up the step. She picked up a towel and dried her hair.

Paul spun in his chair. He watched the blue-grey CCTV image of the white-blonde girl coming through the deck door of his house on the coast, drying her hair with a towel. Ryan was by a window writing in a notebook. She moved towards him with quickening steps. He sensed her, he turned, he wrote a last line and lay down his pen. Then he rose to greet her. He took the towel from her and began to dry her hair. She moved her hands over his chest. Paul had placed a ceiling-to-floor mirror just where it had been in the house on Lake Pontchartrain and now saw Ryan and Nicky doubly, through the lens and through the mirror. He remembered watching Charlotte fan herself on that hot night, their clothes in heaps on the floor where they had thrown them off, the chair where he had been with her, their midnight meal. He saw this all again. But the panoramic image on his screen drove it away. Ryan and Nicky revolved, a single unit. Their mouths met. She moved Ryan back, back, slowly, and then down into a straight-backed chair, pulling his shirt over his head. Paul saw her sit astride him. He saw her slip her swimsuit to the side. He saw the jolt as Ryan entered her. He saw the tautness in her thighs as she drove down onto him.

He pressed a button and the screen went to black.

Paul had given the use of his house in Bolinas to Ryan and Nicky so that he could break into Ryan's room in the Bostonian Hotel. He went with Vanko. They'd had to wait in the stairwell all evening because of the crowds sitting out in the hall, then when it was clear Vanko picked the lock.

The room was a wonderland to Paul, so much life crowded into so small a space, pieces of wood and coloured glass, sheets of paper with daubs of colour, drawings and notes put straight on the wall. The dress paintings were stacked under the bed. He took his time. He sat in a chair and read Ryan's notebooks. He went through the clothes, Nicky's among them, hanging in the closet. He placed his hands in their pockets. He studied each of the tacked-up postcards Ryan said he used to make a place his own. He'd been there for two hours and was about to leave when he reached for a book on a high shelf and there spilled from it passports and driving licences, all in different names and all with photographs of Ryan in different forms – blond hair, dark hair, short hair, long hair, beard, no beard. Paul wondered not only why Ryan had these things, but also who he knew who would be able to replicate with such accuracy official government documents. He photographed each one. A newspaper clipping also fell from the book. It was from the *Andersonstown News* with a date in June 1981, and bore a photograph of a small group of winners at a school art competition. At the back was a tall, familiar boy holding a ribbon and with a gap in a front tooth where a triangular piece had once been. The caption named him and provided an address in the Ballymurphy Road. Paul later had a public records search done, which is how he learned that he and Ryan had come into the world on the same day. He photographed everything, he got Vanko to lift a fingerprint from a glass, then they put everything back where it had been and left.

When I went to see him in the Lompoc jail I asked him why he did it.

I wanted . . . I wasn't sure, exactly, what I wanted. I suppose it was to get a line on his price. Everybody has a price, as they say. I do, you do. But I hadn't found his.

Paul's loan campaign was mortally wounded by his own hand. He'd run through his address book. He turned to those who had been there for him. He got his father to hand over his pension account and his mother to mortgage her house in Hobart, but when he went back to the bankers at Zug a second time they sensed a crude Ponzi scheme and had it unpicked within an hour. With melancholy spirits they sent an emissary to the FBI in San Francisco with incriminating evidence about their protégé.

Ryan sent his sky canvas to the Bostonian Hotel and set off from Paul Crane's house on the coast a day earlier than he had expected. Nicky had left by bus the day before. She had a show, she said, in Palo Alto. Ryan let the air flow around him and the sun pour down on him. He thought about skies he wanted to paint. The waves rolled in, lacy and white.

He passed Sausalito, crossed the Golden Gate Bridge and turned east into the city. The traffic snagged as he entered Cow Hollow. He caught the red light at Lombard and Octavia. A luminescence of white and gold flared to his right. He turned to look at it. He saw a man and woman in an alcove by a blue door. The man, bare-legged, his beard neatly trimmed, his hair unkempt, faced the street in a white bathrobe. The woman, in an oyster coloured short silk dress that Ryan recognised, had her arms around the man's neck and was kissing him. She was barefoot. A pair of high-heeled shoes with gold straps was in her hand. She dropped the shoes to the pavement and put them on. The man laughed. She, too, seemed to laugh. Ryan heard the tinkling chimes. She kissed the man again, and turned. She was flushed with what Ryan sensed was the intensely private enjoyment of her laughter with the man and of the night she had evidently spent with him. It was Nicky. Her eyes rose to the street. They met Ryan's. Her face fell as if its entire structure had been taken away. She raised her hand in a gesture she can't remember the meaning of, a hello, a beckoning, a cancelling, but the light turned to green and Ryan drove away.

While Ryan was on Lombard Street and the FBI were at Paul's house with a warrant for his arrest, Paul was stepping through the doors of the Loews Regency Hotel following a breakfast meeting with a former board member at his bank. The man had agreed to take a cut of the loan at what seemed to Paul an unduly cautious quarter-million. Still, it quelled Paul. He whistled as he walked.

Earlier that morning he received a call from an old Oxford friend who had accepted Matthew Hayford's invitation and was now with MI5 in London. Paul had sent him the print Vanko had lifted from the glass in Ryan's room, the MI5 officer in turn sent it on general release to police services around the country, and Special Branch forensics experts in Belfast found a match on the stock of an AR-18 that had been retrieved from a chimney during the remodelling six years earlier of a house on the corner of the Falls and St James Roads. The gun, the same one Ryan had abandoned when an unexpected beam of sunlight had hit its tip on a winter morning, had since been linked to the shooting of sixty-seven security personnel between 1983 and 1986. We have a gun, a list of victims and the print of the probable shooter, the MI5 contact said to Paul. So who is he? Paul said he wasn't sure. There'd been a team of Irish electricians in the house. A painting had gone missing. He'd look into it.

Paul didn't know what he'd do with this information. He only knew that he was the only person in the world who could provide the missing link between the gun and Ryan, and that this gave him considerable power. When he'd had the idea to break into Ryan's room he hadn't thought he'd get so lucky. He picked up the pace as he walked up Sansome. He dispensed five-dollar bills to the homeless. He cut west to Montgomery and ascended Telegraph Hill.

As he turned into his street he sensed an altered atmosphere. Half a dozen people were running from different starting points in the direction of his house. There were shouts. He saw a black column of smoke. He too began to run. Neighbours rushed to his side. They gripped him by the arm. Your house is burning, they said.

Through a window at street level he saw fire on the stairs. There would be no way in or out through there. He went over railings into a passageway to the side of the house then over the garden wall, opening a wound on his hand and ripping his trousers from cuff to knee on shards of glass placed there to deter thieves. Oliver was running back and forth on the balcony outside his room, calling to him. He saw curtains, cupboards, chairs and walls burning in the kitchen, where Charlotte sat in perfect stillness. I'll be there for you, Ollie! he shouted before holding out his suit jacket as a shield and plunging through a wall of flame into the house. Smoke moved up the stairs and flames flickered on the banisters, but he would have time to get up to Oliver and bring him down. He did not do this. Instead, he turned towards his wife, crashed through the kitchen door, took her up in his arms, wrapped her in his jacket and ran. As he was about to pass through the door his frayed trousers hooked on the leg of an upended chair, throwing him forwards. He held onto Charlotte, but the right side of his face pressed against the burning doorframe. This is where he lost his eye. The flame singed shut the socket with the blackened skin of lid and brow. Dad! he heard. The sirens of the fire trucks sounded. If his way back to Oliver was blocked they would get him out with ladders. He attended to Charlotte. It was a warm day and the heat from their burning house reached them, but she was shivering. He laid his coat over her. There was a blast, a profound concussive sound, such as he had never heard, except distantly, from demolition or artillery practice or a plane breaking the sound barrier. He saw a section of his roof fly into the air, heard crashing boards and masonry as the upper floors of the house came down through the walls as if through a chute. He thought he saw Oliver's upraised arms descending.

They took Paul and Charlotte in an ambulance to the hospital. Surgeons removed Paul's right eye and cleaned and dressed his wound. Charlotte was physically intact but in shock. She managed, nevertheless, to tell Paul that men had arrived with a warrant for his arrest. Late that night he learned that his dead son had been found trapped under the rubble of a collapsed floor.

The next morning while the nurses were changing shifts he dressed in his flayed suit, slipped out the door of the hospital, withdrew in cash the quarter-million dollars he had received that morning from the board member at his bank, collected his car from where it had been left in front of his blackened, still smouldering house and drove south and east towards the Mojave Desert.

Ryan drove north, back over the bridge and onto the Shoreline Highway. The bike whined like a buzzsaw on the straights, the skin pulled back from his face like a surgical mask. He was trying to outrun the picture of Nicky and the man in the bathrobe that kept rising in his mind, of their lovers' laughter, braided limbs, of her opening herself to him, hunger in her eyes, welcome in her eyes, of the parts of her that he had drawn and touched and had now been touched by someone else. He looked for speed and for deep wilderness.

Far up the road he cut to the east and went back into the Mendocino National Forest. He'd been there on a spring morning, before he'd met the people who were now upending his life. He left the bike and walked. He walked for hours, under the canopy of trees, on mountain trails, on the banks of rivers. He left the marked paths and moved onto animal tracks. He came to a lake, clear, still, sapphire blue.

There was a man on the shore sitting on a stone and holding a fishing rod. This startled him. For the past hour and a half he had heard the warning calls of birds and the scurrying of ground animals. Once there was a heavy sound, something large, a bear perhaps. But he saw no human, nor even a footprint.

Ryan moved slowly around to the far side of the lake from where the man was sitting. He wanted to be in full view as he approached. He walked along the shore, stopped at a spot ten yards from the man and sat down.

The man had quick eyes, long grey hair and a white beard fine as cornsilk hanging from his chin.

The silence between them was long. The inhuman scale of the forest made them intimates, but they stared ahead as if they were fellow passengers on a train. Elsewhere, for others, it would be discomfiting, but not for Ryan, not now. He listened to the lugubrious buzzing of insects, the plink of the man's line entering the water, the fluttering of leaves high in the trees. The sun dropped further towards the distant ocean.

You all right? the man asked after half an hour.

Dappled light danced on his face.

I've been better, said Ryan.

Looks like.

Minutes passed between each sentence.

You in this deep, said the man, you must be a very ambitious hiker or a vet.

Ryan looked at the man, and at the high dome of the trees.

The latter, he said.

Thought so. Unit?

D Company, Second Battalion, Belfast Brigade, IRA.

What's that?

Irish Republican Army.

Don't know them . . . Oh wait. Yes I do. Like the VC, except you were sticking it to the Brits instead of us.

And you?

Second Battalion, Fourth Marines. The Magnificent Bastards.

The man leaned forward on the stone and the black butt of a handgun rose from his pocket. Ryan watched it, then turned back to the lake.

You're carrying, he said.

Sometimes I shoot the fish if they piss me off.

Must be big fish.

This is just a pea shooter.

That's a 1911, said Ryan, a .45 auto. Seven rounds. You could throw a man against a wall with it.

For the first time the man turned to look at Ryan.

That's right, he said.

He looked Ryan up and down.

You ever use the 1911?

Sometimes. Most engagements were long-range. We had Armalites.

They gave us M16s. Pieces of shit. Could have been made by Mattel Toys. Broke apart in your hands. Wouldn't fire. I thought the government gave them to us so we wouldn't come back and tell what we saw.

The man looked to the sky to sense the amount of light left.

I've got four regular and two sawn-off shotguns, ten handguns, a couple thirty-aught-thirties, let's see, an AR-15, I've got an AK in there and fifteen Chinese assault rifles I got in a swap. Nobody's going to fuck with me.

The call of a bird echoed operatically through the forest. Ryan let it fall to silence.

What was it like over there? he asked the man softly.

The man stayed mute so long Ryan thought he hadn't heard.

An uncle of mine asked me that Christmas Day 1969, he said then. Whole family was sitting around with their napkins tucked under their chins. I was just back from my third tour. I started talking and the room cleared in fifteen minutes. Left the food steaming on their plates. Only my little sister was left.

He swivelled his head towards Ryan.

What got to you? he asked.

A woman.

Figured. You're better off without.

It looks that way.

The line dipped and the man lifted a trout from the lake.

That's the first course right there, he said.

He unhooked the fish and laid it in a basket.

What did you say to them? asked Ryan.

What did I say to them? Let's see. I started at the beginning. First week. We hooked into an LZ on the Cambodian border. We were supposed to harass the Ho Chi Minh Trail. A Recon unit told our colonel there were suspected transfers of weapons and explosives going on at night at a particular spot. We set out in a line, marched two hours. I was on point. We got into firing position. And sure enough, there they were, shifting gear at four o'clock in the morning. We let loose, we threw everything at them, M60s, RPGs, M16s, total firepower, three minutes of deafening assault, never heard anything like it in my life. We emptied everything we carried from the LZ, every box of ammo. Then silence. Just cordite and smoke and burnt oil and the rotting jungle. We walked down at daylight. That's when we saw what we had done. A whole bunch of dead women and children and split bags of rice. They'd been loading it for a market. We killed every one of them . . . So I told them about that. About half the family got up and walked at that point. I went on with the story anyway. Don't worry about it, said the colonel. We'll take care of it. It's war. What the fuck were they doing there anyway? That's when my aunt and uncle walked. But I still had an audience. Body count! somebody in the unit shouted. We got body count! The Magnificent Bastards! Fucking A! Smoked them! That sent a few more out. When I told them there was an awards ceremony, that we got a unit citation and the colonel got a medal for killing all those women and children, the rest of them got up and left. All except my eight-year-old sister.

He checked the sky again.

Let's go, he said.

Right.

We can't be out here in the dark.

He collapsed his pole and lifted his basket. They walked the perimeter of the lake. Before they turned into the underbrush the man stopped. He gripped Ryan by the arm.

I'll tell you what it was like, he said. See that shoreline over there? Pretty. Innocent. Just right. Not in 'Nam. Could be anything. A sniper position. A camouflaged RPG. A sixteen-year-old girl could pop out of a hole and open you up with a blade from your balls right up to your heart. Dive back in like a ferret. You didn't know what anything was. A shoe, a poster, a Parker pen. They could all put your lights out. Anti-personnel. They had this one deal. A mine'd go off on one side of a path and if it didn't get you you'd dive for cover the other way into a bush. Only thing was you'd land on a board they'd fixed up with blades sticking out. Impale you in eight places. They'd figured it out just right.

We did that. But with bombs.

Fucking A.

He began to walk and Ryan followed.

Where are we going?

Home. I'm cooking you dinner.

The forest was peaceful, the air cooling. Low beams of light shot through the trees.

Total fear. Total hatred. Every step I took, said the man.

That's how the Brits were.

I bet they were. Poor fuckers. What'd you have against them?

Same thing the Vietnamese had against you.

The man stopped, looked at Ryan, then to the sky, filled his lungs and walked on.

The bastards never moved on us unless they had the advantage, he said.

We did that too.

They walked for an hour, Ryan following behind. They walked in silence. The man's calculation about the length of the journey had been precise. They arrived at his home in late dusk. It was sheathed in plastic and set among trees and bushes. Leaves and branches covered the roof. Vines ran up the sides. You'd have to be nearly on top of it to see it. A single brass padlock was on the door.

The man unlocked it and they stepped in. It was a single room with a loft for a bed. Everything old and worn but neatly arranged, water bottles set out on the floor, jars of fruit on the shelves, guns in racks of hewn branches.

The man turned to Ryan, fingertips pressed together in the shape of a tent.

You vegetarian, anything like that? he asked.

No.

I was thinking fillet of trout with herbs to start, then venison steaks. All right with you?

The man gutted and trimmed the fish. He marinated the cuts of venison. Ryan built a fire to cook the food. They set the table, lit candles and ate their meals. Afterwards the man cleared away the plates and brought a bowl each of forest fruits.

April 29, 1985, I came to with my hands around the neck of my six-year-old daughter. I was choking her. Thought she was VC. She looked at me like I'd risen up out of the deepest pit of hell. I walked out the door and kept going. Lived in my car. Lived in a chicken coop in Hungry Horse, Montana. This is my third one of these. Been here in this one four years, I think . . . I don't know about you, but I wasn't ready. Just a Catholic kid from Cedar Rapids, Iowa. Junior varsity track team. Sodality. We went into the poor neighbourhoods with food and clothes and taught arithmetic. The Corporal Works of Mercy. Next minute I'm burning people alive in their homes. I'm cutting off dicks and putting heads on poles. November 18, 1967. That's when it happened. I had a buddy, my best buddy, Joey Szymanski, a little overweight, big stupid smile, snored like a wrecking machine. He tried to tell jokes but he couldn't tell a joke to save his ass. Always there for you. People picked on him until they saw how beautiful he was. I did too. He didn't want to fight in the war. He'd put in for the chaplaincy. He was two days away from his transfer when a sniper's bullet went into his jaw and up into his brain. He was right beside me. He bled and spilled all over me, died in my arms. Far as I was concerned I was going to keep coming back until I killed every last human being in Vietnam.

He put a handful of berries into his mouth, hand and lip trembling.

I had seventy-two registered kills to my name. I don't count those rice haulers. I don't count those people in the hooches. Just VC and NVA.

Who registered them?

'The fuck. We did. And you? How many?

I don't know. That's all I did for fourteen years.

The man looked away. It seemed he was considering this. Then he turned back to Ryan.

Do you dream about them?

No.

I do. They come up from dark places in the room. One guy, I cut his head off, I see him in broad daylight. He wants me to bury him . . . I did those things. Nothing I can do about it now. It's *registered*. But it bewilders me. Who was that person who had that name? Who would do such things? I can't get back into his head. It all goes back to November 18, 1967. Up to then I was a member of the human race. I should have taken Joey's bullet. Because after that I defiled myself. You can't go lower. Thought I was made of dogshit. Totally and permanently contaminated. Time did not leaven, time did not ameliorate. I got so I didn't want anyone to see me, didn't want *me* to see me. I caught my reflection in the rear-view mirror on the door of my truck and drove my fist into it. Felt good for a minute. I came into the woods. Haven't caught sight of myself since. Won't let it happen. I'm sixty-seven years old and don't know what I look like.

You look magnificent.

Fuck you.

The man got up. He poured them each a glass of cool spring water and sat down again.

They don't play with your head, those people you wasted? he asked.

It was different for me. They were in our streets. They were shooting us. We weren't in theirs.

The man leaned forward. He studied Ryan. The furrows in his brow were like ripples in sand.

Will you let me draw you? asked Ryan.

'The fuck.

You don't have to look at it.

What do I have to do?

Just sit there.

The man shifted in his chair.

You have what you need? he asked.

Ryan searched his pockets.

No.

He was brought paper and a pencil. He lit more candles to throw light on the man's face. The man dipped his head and drove his eyes into Ryan.

Only another soldier could get me to do this, he said.

Ryan began to draw. He blocked out the overall shape. The left eye caught more light. The folds in the flesh were complex. He broke off from the main drawing and sketched the eye in on the chest to get it right on its own, away from its relation to the rest of the face. The man was disciplined, like a professional model, the head and torso held rigid as rock. The eyes bore with great force into Ryan.

I think about them, said Ryan.

What do you think?

That they had mothers, like they say . . .

Fucking right.

They all had people who loved them. I shot a man named Matthew Hayford in London. He was just reaching for his phone. I could see him very well. We'd made the call. His daughter came out when she heard him go down. I saw her face too. I saw her through the scope. I took her father away from her. I took a lot of people away . . . They come to mind. They seem close sometimes, like I could speak to them. I wish they could all rise up . . .

Fat chance, said the man.

He held his pose.

The drawing took two hours. They remained silent for most of it. The cuts and dabs with the pencil were the only sounds. When Ryan finished the drawing he held it up.

The man stood. He stepped forward. He took it from Ryan's fingers and looked at it with wonder.

I see, he said. So that's him.

He smiled, held out his hand.

I'm Vaughn Reynolds, he said.

[*Name withheld*], said Ryan.

Thank you, said Vaughn.

He made up a bed for Ryan on a bench and rose to his loft. The forest was silent. When Ryan slept it seemed he was descending through all of its depths.

There was the morning song of birds, then soft yellow light. Ryan got up, Vaughn descended from his loft. He brewed coffee and set out jam and bread he had made. The sun rose as they ate, the room became golden. They spoke of firefights, comrades, ballistics.

Put a few vets in the corner of a bar and you can hear the bullets flying, said Vaughn.

I've seen it, said Ryan.

He extended a hand with his drawing.

You want this? he asked.

I've seen enough of him, said Vaughn.

I'm going to make a painting of it.

That'll draw the crowds.

Vaughn stood.

I'll get you back to your bike.

They set out. Dew was on the leaves. The air was fresh. The animals were beginning to move.

I've been wondering, said Ryan. What's training like?

First three days they don't let you sleep. They pack the lines so tight that if you pass out you won't fall over. They walk on you, piss on you. One guy, they roasted him in an industrial clothes dryer. You're a maggot, then a puke. That's considered a step in the right direction. You're a cum-guzzler right up to the end. It's not, Be quiet. It's, Shut your cock holster! You could say they're fixated on homo-erotic oral love. You do push-ups in mud pits. They threw everything I had, clothes, pack, mattress, out the window and into the muck. At the end they set you loose with a fifty-pound load on your back for three days with one day's food. You beg, borrow and steal. It's based on Sparta. You've got to get up to the top of a near-vertical gradient called Mount Motherfucker on all fours. Up at the top is an officer who pins a Marine badge on you. You get to roll up your sleeves like a Marine for the first time and blouse your camis into your boots. There's hot food waiting for you in tents. It feels like heaven has come down out of the sky. You can hardly believe it's real. Everybody loves you. You're overwhelmed with gratitude. You're a Marine at last. People burst into tears.

Sounds like a cult, said Ryan.

The man stopped in his tracks.

A *cult*.

He held up his arms to the sky.

God damn. The United States Marine Corps. *Fuck you.*

A burst of laughter shot out of him like rapid fire.

He flinched at the sound, as if somebody had tried to jump him.

That's weird. Haven't heard myself laugh in fifteen years.

He turned to face Ryan. He jabbed an index finger into his chest, all the lines in his face animated, his chest still heaving.

Back in the day you'd get your brain rearranged for saying that. I could find a thousand guys to assist. The contract's written in blood . . . But man oh man. A cult. I can see it, that douchebag of a drill instructor up on top of Mount Motherfucker with a box of membership badges for the devotees like the Reverend Moon. Beautiful.

Laughter percolated, erupted. It sounded in the forest. They walked on.

Ryan's Notebook

After painting Generous from life I only worked from photographs. Didn't want to ask anyone to sit that long. Didn't want to stay with anyone that long either. What to say to them? Faces on paper, on screen. Flat, abstract, virtual. The photographed face is a collection of details, the living face is a unity. The photograph can pull you away into the details and you can get lost. I drew Nicky from life, then Vaughn. Better volume, better sense of light. More intensity. Vaughn's face was a canyon. I didn't understand at first how to look at such depths. It reacted to thought, to what I said. The drawing of Vaughn is a drawing of the two of us being there.

I will draw now from life.

EPILOGUE

The Birdcage

San Francisco, 2013

Ming

It got dark in the Crane house. Bad spirits, bad air. They got sick. I saw Charlotte leave food on shelves like there were gods living there. I saw the boy and the weight of it coming down very heavy on him. He thought he was the only one who could protect her. Too much too soon for him. You could see it in the eyes. I have a boy that age myself. I felt sorry.

I saw everything. I saw Paul pretend to be an Englishman, I saw him scam his own mother. I went to him. I told him I knew what he was doing. I had the evidence and it was locked away. I told him I wouldn't go to the police on one condition – that he let me finish the house. If he didn't have money to pay me, that was all right. He looked at me. He cocked his head like a bird. He didn't understand. OK, he said, before I changed my mind. By then I believed my own story about finishing the Captain's house. I still believe. I made a masterpiece.

He took a call one morning from England. I heard him talk about a fingerprint on a gun and some killings in Ireland a long time ago. Paul told the person on the other end he didn't know who the print belonged to. There were a lot of people going through his house.

He'd try to get a line on it. He hangs up, he opens his computer. I see a page of passports with photographs of different men with different names and all of them are Ryan.

I see very big danger for my friend. I go to him. I tell him.

Right, he said. Right, always Right with Ryan, like you'd asked him to pass the salt. But I see him making a decision. You know what it was.

An actor can see an actor. [*Pauses, looks at me, laughs a little, resumes.*] I knew Ryan had been somebody else, as he knew I had been. He asked me one question, very accurate –

Why do you never laugh, Ming?

How did he know?

Laugh? I laugh, I said to him. You see me laugh.

You pretend, he said. Your face moves, your shoulder shakes. But your eyes don't laugh.

I had a big laugh when I was a little boy in Gia Lai. You could hear it over the rice fields. Neighbours came just to hear it. Little Buddha, they called me. But the Americans sent everybody away. You know Free Fire Zones? They said we were in one of those. They burned the hooches, blew the wells, scorched everything. If something moves, they shoot.

But the people came back. They didn't mind about the houses, but they couldn't stand being away from the graves. The graves are more important than life. So we came in the night, built a little shelter with a hole under it to hide, and sat by the graves.

They saw us. They sent Koreans in to clear us out. I was in the bush collecting butterflies with my little sister Nah. My brother came for us, very nervous. He got us all into the hole. Nine of us, all lying on top of one another with me in the middle. Shhh, they say. We hear them walking, shooting. I think it's a game. I giggle into my grandmother's ribs. When my brother says, Bao – that was my name over there – Bao, keep quiet, that makes me laugh out loud. Then he starts praying and I think it's the funniest thing I ever saw. That was it. The Koreans heard it, the door opened and one of them emptied a whole clip into us, dropped a live grenade and walked on. Boom. The sound was soft, like an old man coughing. But it rattled my teeth. The walls came in. I was all right, though. Their bodies protected me. Like sandbags. I checked myself. Not a scratch. In the night I came out.

And your family? I asked.

All nine dead.

Because of . . .?

Yes. I killed them with my laugh. Then I walked to the graves and promised my ancestors I'd never laugh again.

I was silent.

Nobody knows you, Ming, Ryan said to me.

That's right, I said to him.

But I break the promise now. My little boy, he's very funny. I laugh and laugh. Go on, Ronan, tell me a joke, a good one. You'll see for yourself.

Paul Crane

I wandered in the desert. I stayed in little motels. I finally got a trailer on the edge of Pahrump, Nevada, a place full of meth labs and whorehouses and the walking dead. In San Francisco I still had some purchase, but it got pretty weird in that trailer. I admit that. I didn't have an eye. I barely had a face. I let my son get burned alive. My beautiful wife was and evidently is out of her mind. And even if she gets better she's out of my reach now and forever. There can be no forgiveness . . . Let me know, won't you, if you hear otherwise?

I'm working it all out with a shrink in here. We've got a line on it. She sees Pahrump as my Period of Atonement. I had a quarter of a million bucks stuffed behind the panels of my trailer and I gave myself a weekly budget of $57.65 to live on. No begging, no pilfering, just prudence and rectitude. I kept a record of every financial event that took place. They were all infinitesimally small. I took pride in them. If I found a coin on the pavement it would be noted, time, date, location, temperature. I'd fish out old milk cartons from neighbours' trash, cut them up and use them for drinking vessels. I used knives and forks from the Sonic Drive-In. The fastidiousness of it left me almost no time to sleep. My weight dropped, my beard grew, my eye socket was suppurating. Personal hygiene went into decline. Finally the FBI showed up. I thanked them. It was all I could do to stop myself from falling into their arms.

So here I am. I got seven years. Certain mitigating personality disorders connected with addiction were advanced at my trial and taken into account by the judge. I'm a different guy now. I run a maths class in here. I even got a little jailbird combo together, we do shows in prisons around the state. I'm on piano and back-up vocals. They'll let me out early for exemplary behaviour. I'm sure.

[Pause.]

Don't you get a touch of heartache when you see the round, open face of a child looking up with such innocent belief into the eyes of their father or mother? Don't you foresee all the disappointments and betrayals that child will suffer, often at the hands of that same parent? Like Ollie on his balcony, waiting there for me, believing in me, before I decided to save his mother instead of him. That was the last thing he ever saw in this world. Isn't it cruel?

[Pause.]

You'll let me know, won't you, if you hear anything about Ryan? [*I tell him I will.*] I sent him a text from the desert with his real name. I told him they'd found the gun he'd used to kill all those soldiers. That must have given him a jump. It got rid of him, anyway. And maybe impressed him.

[Pause.]

[I ask him what became of his father's Doucet accordion, with which he'd played his way into the heart of his wife.]
I have it here, he said. It was retrieved from Bolinas. It's one of the few things that were mine that I still have.
Do you play it?
It stays in the box. I look at it.
What stops you?
I fear it . . . Can you understand that?
[One half of his mouth lifts into a smile, the other is held rigid by the scar. I had not thought I was so transparent.]
I do, I said.
I thought so.

[Pause.]

Those last pictures. Charlotte so still in the kitchen, her hands in her lap. Her hair was burning. Oliver with his arms out imploring me to save him as any father must. They were my only ones. They were in my care. Whatever I'm spinning to you now, those pictures will chase me to the grave.

[Pause.]

Sometimes people come in, people like you, and I breathe in just to get the smell of the world outside, the air, the trees, cooking that isn't jail cooking, clothes not washed in the jail laundry. I want to smell

275

Charlotte again, I want to get that forest smell that came off her neck when she wanted me. I don't need anyone to tell me how over-crowded my liabilities column is. I've got no house, car, money, child, wife. My mother's in a Salvation Army hostel because I spent her house. I owe $46 million and the interest clock is ticking. And I'm deformed.

But if something can be changed, we change it. And in the sparsely populated assets column, I still have a brain. It may not be so diamond-cutting sharp and turbo-charged and dressed up as it was, but it may be more judicious. I have experience. You're not going to show me something I haven't seen. And I may have a glimmer of charm left, that thing I once heard described as 'subdued magic'. I charmed Charlotte Silver, the Belle of Baton Rouge.

I might come back. Watch me.

Charlotte Crane

I met Charlotte in a private nursing facility in Carmel. She was in a carefully ironed pale blue dress, sitting by the window. The blue sea rolled in. Dogs ran on the beach. The view was eerily similar to the one from the house Paul had built for her in Bolinas but which she had never seen. Her fingers moved but she had nothing in her hands. Her hair had gone white, the white of coal ash. Her lips quivered when she spoke. The ghost of a formidable beauty ran around the bones of her face. She seemed to have no consciousness of it. She cried, for her son, for herself, for her lost life. She let the tears run. She seemed used to it.

It started with the summer. Something terrible, fearsome. It walked, it had its own life, it was like a lizard hunting us down. The house sensed it. I felt it trying to warn me. The cedar in the walls was bleeding. Beads of resin coming through, garnet beads on the white walls like blood, on the white leaves Ryan painted so well, so beautifully. Something was going to happen to us. And it did, you know that, it broke in the morning when the police came for Paul. He wasn't there to save us. He hadn't any power. I wanted the Captain, he knew the codes to the house, he could make us safe. I believed that. Sometimes I still believe that. I tried to call to him. I lit fires to show him where we were . . .

[Pause.]

We don't deserve to live, Paul and I.

[Pause.]

I pray to be taken.

[Pause.]

I loved Paul. I never loved any other man. I loved him up on the stage with his shirt off and that Russian hat. It was such a thrill. All my life I'd been groomed for a Benjamin Silver. School in France, horses, tennis lessons. I had dance, I loved that, it was the only thing I loved then, I might have made something of it. They told me I was good. But Benjamin ground it out of me. I was suffocating. I was shrinking.

Then I loved that little room Paul had and our meals on the floor. We were free, we could be whoever we wanted to be. It felt like I'd taken off a straitjacket.

Then he stopped the music, he just gave it up. He went to the bank. Great sums of money came to us. I thought he did it because he didn't want to bag groceries and open doors for people any more. Now I see that he did it for me. He never said so but I know it. Why do people never speak of what is most important to them? It was all such a dreadful mistake, a waste, and it's gone now, eternally gone, I can't have it back.

Nicky

His name is Charles Poindexter. Good-looking guy. I can make him laugh. It wasn't like I'd just met him in a bar. I've known him since I was eighteen. We met at the conservatory in Detroit. Strings. He grew up in a castle in Bloomfield Hills with a monogrammed gate. The Prince and the Showgirl. It was never going to happen. He was going his way and I mine and every step we took we got farther apart. He's First Violin with the Berlin Philharmonic. He has a Japanese wife and speaks six languages. I wouldn't want that life. And he wouldn't want me in that life. Still, we have fun. He flies me into some city a couple of times a year when he's on tour. I stay the night.

I thought about it this time. I didn't really want, or not want, to go. I was so full of Ryan, we were up in that house by the sea, we were in a rapture like neither of us had ever known. But in my head Charles was something separate, in a different time zone or plane, just mine, nothing to do with Ryan, something that was in my life before him, like I was into origami or pony breeding, why should he mind, what's it got to do with him or anyone?

The mind provides . . .

Tell me what he's doing, will you? Does he still paint? Is he with someone?

I waited a couple of days after he saw us. I was hoping he'd call or come over. I should have known he wouldn't. So I went to see him. I went right up to his room. I was ready for him. I wasn't going to be judged. What did he expect from me, a picket fence and a dog at his feet? Did he think he owned me? I was in a travelling circus and he lived in the Tenderloin where people drop dead in the street. An extracurricular fling has to be small beer down there. You'd look kind of foolish getting worked up about it, wouldn't you? I loved him. I found out about love with him. I told him that and I meant it. Isn't that enough? . . . And what about Ireland? Maybe you can tell me? [*I declare ignorance.*] I never got to the bottom of that. You know, once he made this painting of a shoe, just a cheap child's sandal in the desert in Iraq. He'd seen a picture of it in a magazine. He said there always seemed to be a shoe left behind after a riot or a bomb. It looked so lonely and said so much. Just the shoe on yellow sand with a big streak of red he'd painted in for blood. The way he talked it seemed he was on intimate terms with riots and bombs and blood every day but if you asked him about it you'd get nowhere. Just driving his truck. I think he wanted to tell me. I saw it in his eyes. I think he was involved in things and he wanted me to know. Life and death things. What do you think? Come on, you're from there, you know him . . . Anyway, point is what's Charles Poindexter and me smooching in a doorway to that? I still wonder, even now.

I thought all that before I got there. But it never really plays out the way you think it will.

He wasn't angry. He didn't judge. He didn't ask for an explanation. I didn't expect that. I'd prepared for an attack with a counter-attack and he took that away from me. He had a kind of coolness, a far-awayness, that scared me. I could feel myself go pale. It gave me the idea that he'd already made up his mind to cut me off. It hadn't occurred to me that it could be the end. There'd be a scrap and we'd go to bed. It was too good to let go.

I moved towards him with my arms out. He stepped back. I had to stop. I couldn't crowd him. I stayed still. I saw how much he meant to me. I could go right into him, I could get lost in him, and then find myself. A self, let's say, of more than usual interest to me.

He could *say* me, as I could say him. We made paintings together. He showed me what my music was. It made me feel so thrillingly, so exquisitely alive. I never knew anything like that. Everything else looked so dull.

It was night. I wanted him with a kind of agony. I could taste him. I cried a little. Please let me stay, I said.

I can't do that, he said.

I'll sleep on the floor, like you did, the night we met.

His eyes softened a little. So much passed through them – he felt for me, I think, my abject begging, he was hurt, he hated me for what I'd done to him, he wanted me a little. Part of him didn't want to lose me. I thought he might give in.

That can't be, he said then.

It sounded more solid this time.

I asked him to pretend I was somebody he'd just met, somebody he'd found somewhere and brought back, like I'm sure he'd done with others, like I'd done, what would it matter, just for the night and then forget. I wouldn't bother him again if he didn't want me to. He was quiet. I watched him. I could see it all playing out in his mind, how he'd relent, we'd sleep together, I'd be back again, I'd have my little victory, and then I'd do it again, maybe not right away, but somewhere down the line when Charles called or someone caught my eye. He saw all that, he faced it directly, and decided he wouldn't let it happen to him. There was something in him he wouldn't let anyone touch . . .

And he was right. I would do it again. I wouldn't mean to, but I'd do it.

I came up here to Eureka. I'm all right. I have my diversions, I can have a good time. The show doesn't stop. I know what I lost, and that I did it to myself. He can be free of me because of what he saw in that doorway, he can burn me away to insignificance, make me a small thing in his past. But I don't have that. He's still there, I can see him.

Up at that man's house on the ocean, those were my days, my days of wine and roses. We went on his bike through the redwoods and into a forest where single men lived in shacks and there was a river called Mad. We slept there on a blanket. When we came back we lay in a bath on the deck until the water cooled. The bed was a dancefloor . . . I can't have it now . . . [*Sings.*] The days of wine and roses . . . I used to sing that in the circus after he went away.

Alexis

He came down, he told me about what happened. He looked like he'd taken a knife to the heart. It's the deepest cut. You shriek with amazement at the savage way it's treating you. Worse than someone dying on you. He put all his chips on her. But she's like a bird turning in shafts of light. She can't help it. She comes from a different world . . . I know a little about that pain. I went looking for love in terrible places, I got my ribs cracked, I cried over useless miscreant men. Better to love the world, everybody and nobody. That's what I do. Then they can't take you down. She wasted him for a while. It was a bitter thing to see. He's a stoic but not enough for that, not then anyway. Time will fix it, long as he's interested in himself. I believe he is. I believe in him. We had love, lovely and sweet. He listened to me, he cared for me, he looked after me, he wasn't afraid. He let me look after him. It was easy. That doesn't come around many times . . .

He came down here with his paintings. He told me he was leaving. There might be some trouble coming down from the past. That man he worked for in Telegraph Hill had something to do with it. I wasn't to worry, whatever I heard. He'd be all right. I believe he will. He'd miss me, he'd write when he got settled. He hasn't, but I don't mind. He doesn't live in words like I do.

He took me in his arms, he kissed the top of my head. He said goodbye.

Ryan walked in soft, warm rain. It was night. He had risked, and lost. The risk had been original for him. Either no opportunity for this type of risk had presented itself, or if it had it had made no sense to him to proceed. He had taken a risk on Nicky and now he was paying. The loss was acute. He could not turn from it. It threatened him because it defined him and he could not know when this would cease to be the case. He pictured her. He did not like what he saw. He saw calculation and deceit and a person who had casually wounded him. Other pictures more admirable and alluring had come to him in the past and would again in the future, but on this night that is what he saw. What, then, had he lost? He wondered about this as he walked in the rain. He was in the tight grid of streets south of Market. By the time he got to Mission Bay he had decided it was not the young woman from Detroit he had lost. It was what she had made him feel. A small quantity seemed to lift from his load.

It was to be his last night in America. He knew by then Paul Crane had uncovered him. Ming had warned him and he'd got Paul's triumphant text from the desert. He'd packed his suitcases and left them in the foyer cage. He had taken his dress and sky paintings to Alexis and said goodbye. He left Nicky's hairbrush and T-shirt and hat in his room, but after a battle of wills in which he had suffered defeat he'd dropped into a suitcase pocket a pair of earrings she'd left on a table beside his bed.

At midnight Pat Garrity would collect him from the front entrance of the Bostonian Hotel and drive him to Vancouver, where he would board a train to Toronto. From there a succession of flights would bring him to Marseille. French Basques would meet him off the flight. Money would be got to him from Ireland. For a year he would stay on the move. It was all familiar to him from the time he had hid there after shooting Matthew Hayford. In time he would meet the baker Juliette.

He walked as if aimlessly. This is how I imagine he would have looked to anyone he passed, head down, the eyes not registering, occupied with what was moving in his mind. But in fact he was headed for the circus.

He arrived at 10.30. He saw lights play on the canvas ceiling of the tent. He saw the silhouettes of the players and spectators. He heard the amplified shrieking insults of the barker. He stepped into the deserted midway. The show was entering its final act, the small opera of Cyril the Clown and the Ice Queen. He listened to their exchange, to her imploring of the moon to stay with her until its light could fall on her lover. *Light up his far-away place!* she sang. *O moon, don't disappear!* He remembered Nicky leaning over on the wire and peering through the gloom as Cyril stirred and rose and they beheld each other for the first time. *Come to me now, white star in the night! / Come to me if it be life or it be death*, he replied. Ryan remembered her flying down in her ice-blue dress and taking Cyril's face in her hands. Then the fall, the shock, the sudden death of the clown. How prophetic, he thought, how like he and Nicky, the ecstasy of discovery followed immediately by its theft.

The music faded. He would wait a little before going in. If it was her he'd lost there was nothing that could be done about it. He could not touch her now. And even if he could find a way to do it, it was clear to him that they could not be synchronised, their rhythms, their arcs were different, his long, hers short, his about endurance, hers about change.

The arena went to black. He entered and stood at the back. He watched the lights come up on Cyril's final rites. The clowns morosely juggled phosphorescent balls. The angel drifted through the air on hooks. The coffin was set down centre stage and the grieving barker folded himself into his box. Ryan braced himself. He had come for the moment that was about to happen and he did not know what it would do to him. The raw, piercing animal cry of the note was struck. The volume was up, the note arrived as an assault through speakers that encircled the crowd. A shaft of light shot from the back of the arena and struck a spot high above centre stage. Nicky came out, white and severe, with her cello between her legs. Something corrosive tore through him. She looked possessed, magnificent, magisterial. He would never have her now. Only her note was his. She began her descent through white smoke and tubes of silver light. She bent over her cello and drove the notes with her bow as if in a fury at them. It was as before a piece of attack and counter-attack, of a plea put before a core of resistance as the player searched for the form, as with the music and so with him and her. She had pleaded, he had resisted, she had won, and then lost. Now she played the score of what had happened and how they had lived it. He watched her. He watched her absorption in what she was doing. He understood everything about why he had loved her. The clowns and the angel moved into the shadows and they too watched. The audience watched, still and tense. If she was change and immediacy, and if these were the things that made it impossible for them to be together, then they were also what had brought him back from the dead. He remembered how he had been in the spring, before he met her, in a closed room with stale air, looking out through glass. In the summer he had painted with belief, and he had loved. He was alive again. She had brought him this, whether by accident or design. The windows of the room had opened and he was free. In the back row he raised his hand to her in a salute of gratitude. She was different from when he had first seen her play this music and had taken it for his own. She seemed unaware of anything around her. She was playing for herself this time, but what she played nevertheless moved beyond her. She played her grief, she played the story of their spring and summer. She was talking to him, though she didn't know he was there. The music was pitiless. It moved into him like surgical knives. It took its sustenance from their loss. It cared nothing for him or for her who played it, but only that it be rendered.

And it rendered itself before him and all the others. It found its form. Her chair touched the floor. The players came out, with flute and harp and guitars. Ryan turned away. He heard her voice as he walked, liquid crystal like before. *Too late*, she sang. *It's too late . . .*

You had to sign for the boxes of books they sent over from my office. Once they got the tip from that assistant professor they moved with efficacy and pace, charging me with flagrant negligence of my duties, plagiarism and bringing the university into disrepute. I put up no defence. They stopped my salary and benefits, put out a statement announcing my crimes and congratulating themselves on their vigilance and got the maintenance department to clear my office. I heard there was a brief squabble over who would get it, then calm settled back over the corridor.

When this happened, I suppose, you saw a future from which you felt you had to escape.

I'd met by then an elderly Pole who lived along the hall from me. His name is Witold. He'd been an ecclesiastical sculptor in wood but had been overtaken by vodka. He still did odd jobs out of a joinery workshop he rented by the hour. I started to go there with him. He taught me about moulding and planing, about measuring and the building of templates, the turns in stairs and the creation of arches.

He had a friend who lived on the fifth floor of the hotel, Legally Blind Maurice.

He can't see, said Witold, but it's the hearing that drives him crazy. All he hears are sirens.

He decided to buy Maurice a cockatiel so he could hear its singing instead and together we made a birdcage out of wood. It has a drawer-like base and strips of larch we bent over steam to make the cage's bars. They meet very elegantly, I think, under a round slotted ridge piece at the top. I made circular bands to bind it all together. It was the first thing I'd ever made in my life.

After that I began to draw. I drew small houses of increasing complexity. Sometimes I imagined us living in them. I can do this, I thought, I have the degree, I imagine they can't stop even a plagiarist, I want to do this, and maybe this time I actually will, draw houses for people and build them, in Finland, or Monaghan, somewhere away from New York, somewhere I'd touch wood or stone or you and not an abstraction on a screen in the *mariage blanc* of academic life. It had been twenty-five years, I counted, between the time Ryan made Generous's portrait and painting his empty dresses. I still had time. *It's not too late to become what you might have been.* I wanted to tell you this. I wondered how.

My birthday came. You let it pass. But a text came in from Lydia. Happy birthday, isukki 🥳

Where are you?

On a train from a piano lesson.

What did you play?

Scott Joplin . . . you're such a slow typist.

Record it for me, will you? I'm typing one-fingered. Trying not to make mistakes.

👍 to recording.

I suppose you're holding four simultaneous conversations.

No. Hanging on your every word . . . I JUST REALISED I FORGOT TO BUY A TICKET!!! They may catch me.

You'll have to use your charm.

I'll try.

Charm should be effortless. According to somebody I met in a jail. 😂😂😂😂

I remembered when she was a baby and I'd think of the tininess of her lungs and heart and wonder if she'd make it through the night.

The organism seemed so precarious. Now she designs lipsticks with her friends in an East Village shop. Or did. Has she found such a place in Turku? Has she made any friends? I thought of her shoes by her door, the bounce of her hair as she ran. The idea of not seeing the stages of her life, day by day, until she no longer needed us . . . But no, this is not the thing to say now. It's you I must address.

In the Bostonian Hotel I felt the familiar things falling away. My past, my work, my identity. You too, perhaps. That last night before I came to San Francisco you slid away from me when I finally came to bed. You stayed there at the edge with your back to me, motionless. I don't know if you slept. I didn't. It was a terrible night, phantoms fluttering around like moths. Then in the morning you left for work without breakfast. You didn't say anything. You put on your coat. There was something chilling about the meticulous way you closed the door.

In my last night in San Francisco I tried to write to you. Always in the night. I never got to the end of a letter. Words came down on me later at Gramercy Park on the night you left, maybe the right ones, maybe not. They're for you and only you can know if they've arrived. But I didn't have them then. It's easier to write a love letter to one ready to return your love than a petition to someone in the process of turning away. I'd write sentences with belief, I'd have been think-ing of them maybe as I ate or walked or drove, I could feel they carried a truth, and then I'd hear the whine of my explanations, my I, I, I, as you might hear them. These sentences were on pieces of paper strewn across my table in the Bostonian Hotel. They said that I'd let the best parts of my life wither on the vine and made a per-formance of the rest. It was a good enough performance to convince you, but it was simulacra. I controlled the presentation, as a PR agent would. I had in mind only the effect, on you above all, for once I had found you I felt, even at the best of our times, that I was play-ing for my life, because nothing had ever come to me that I valued as

I valued you. I feared that you would see that I was a fake. I feared even that I would see it, for an actor too needs belief. I kept faking until my whole system rose up in revolt. This revolt was one of those better parts of life that had been offered me, and for once I chose not to ignore it. Perhaps it is too late. But I wanted to say such things to you in order that I might hold you there before I lost you. I tried to find the words. Just to hold you there. For you to wait, just a moment.

Then your text arrived – I can't go on. I'm taking her to Turku. Don't call –

References

Unattributed quotations appear in the text, usually in italics. Their authors are as follows: page 81, '*The policeman's experience . . .*', Ryszard Kapuściński, *Shah of Shahs* (Picador, London, 1994); page 81, '*Let's analyse it . . .*', John Berger, *Bento's Sketchbook* (Verso, London, 2011); page 81, '*A rebel is a person who says No . . .*', Albert Camus, *The Rebel* (Vintage, New York, 1956); page 84, '*He of whom they never stopped saying . . .*', Frantz Fanon, *The Wretched of the Earth* (Penguin, London, 2001); page 84, '*Pacifism is a comfort to the powerful*', Leonard Cohen, spoken at a concert, most likely in Europe in 1972, introducing the song 'Kevin Barry'; page 85, quotes beginning '*Numerical weakness comes from . . .*', '*Rouse him, and learn . . .*', and '*He wins his battles . . .*' are all from Sun Tzu, *The Art of War* (Harper Press, London, 2011); page 90, '*I know I can't paint a flower . . .*', Georgia O'Keeffe, in a letter to William Milliken (quoted in *Portrait of an Artist: A Biography of Georgia O'Keeffe* by Laurie Lisle, Washington Square Press, New York, 1981); page 91, '*Every rebellion contains a demand for unity . . .*', Albert Camus, *The Rebel* (Vintage, New York, 1956); page 95, '*If you know the enemy and know yourself . . .*', Sun Tzu, *The Art of War* (Harper Press, London, 2011); page 95, '*For the guerrilla, the populace acts . . .*', Robert Taber, *The War of the Flea: Guerrilla Warfare Theory and Practice* (Paladin, London, 1972); page 95, '*War is based on leverage and deception*', adapted from words spoken by David Hawkins; page 97, '*The guerrilla fights the war of the flea . . .*', Robert Taber, *The War of the Flea: Guerrilla Warfare Theory and Practice* (Paladin, London, 1972); page 103, 'Aesthetics is for artists . . .', attributed to Barney Newman, based on words spoken at a conference in Woodstock, New York (1952); page 112, '*All paintings seem to me like prison windows . . .*', Yves Klein, *Long Live the Immaterial* (Delano Greenidge Editions, New York, 2000); page 163, '*Behold the hands . . .*', Michel de Montaigne, *The Complete Essays* (Penguin, London, 1991); page 189, '*A painting lives in companionship*', Mark Rothko, in an interview for *The Tiger's Eye* magazine (1947); pages 200 and 283, parts of the circus performance are based on the 'Song to the Moon' in Antonín Dvořák's opera *Rusalka*, libretto by Jaroslav Kvapil (1901); page 208, '*Living in the minds of others is what is intoxicating*', Eugène Delacroix, *The Journal of Eugène Delacroix* (Phaidon, New York, 1980); page 237, '*Étaín the queen flashes crimson and gold . . .*', Anonymous, 'The Wooing of Étaín' in *Early Irish Myths and Sagas* by Jeffrey Gantz (Penguin, London, 1981); page 247, '*There are connoisseurs of blue . . .*', Colette, *For a Flower Album* (David McKay, New York, 1959); pages 258–263, parts of Vaughn's dialogue are based on material from Jonathan Shay, *Achilles in Vietnam* (Touchstone, New York, 1995); page 286, '*It's not too late to become what you might have been*', attributed to George Eliot.

Acknowledgements

Novels tend to need assistance from people who know certain things their writers don't. This one, in my experience, needed and got more than most, all freely given. My first thanks is to the late Frank 'Lucas' Quigley, who came from Belfast to Poland to tell me with great candour of his experiences of war and art. I am also grateful to all of the following: Jim McNulty, Chris Hudgins, J. Dee Hill, Richard Romano, Christopher Erle, Robert Dorgan, Bríd Keenan, Serena Ng, Brian Patten, Michel Koven, the chefs at the now-closed Tommy Toy's in San Francisco, Patrick McCabe, Gary McKeone, Robert and Jan Gregory, Miguel Juantegui, Cynthia Kienitz, Aleksandra Jacuńska, Lamar Herrin, Patrick Mongoven, the late Heathcote Williams, Dan Rodriguez of the Magic Center, the late Randy King, Vu Tran, Niall Walton, Jim Gibney, Tom Hartley, Danny Morrison, Máirtín Ó Muilleoir, Patrick Magee, Séanna Walsh at Áras Uí Chonghaile, Belfast, Hank Pate, Louis Harper, Gareth Evans, Tom Overton, Ronan Sheehan, Hisham Matar, Brendan Lambe, Bill Rolston, Ian Cobain, Tay Kheng Soon, the late John Berger, Nicola Bruce, Graham Swift, John Kearns, William T. Vollmann, the Black Mountain Institute in Las Vegas, Janine Roux, the late Graham Swannell, David Ashton, Sasha Hails, Michael Clifford, Beatriz O'Grady, the San Francisco Fire Department, Nick O'Donnell, Mark McCauley, David Hawkins, Vuk Krakovic, Steve and Nic Pyke, the late Erich Maria Remarque. I've never had such attentive, acute editing as I've had with this book from Elizabeth Garner, Marissa Constantinou, DeAndra Lupu and Tamsin Shelton at Unbound. Thank you to everyone there, especially John Mitchinson, for his friendship and commitment, and Rina Gill. I'm grateful to all the people who bought this book long before it was published. I met Anthony Lott in a garden in Bluff, Utah, and was immediately taken by the humour, imagination and empathy present in his drawings and paintings. His engagement with this book has astonished me and I am very grateful for it. My wife, Hanna O'Grady, listened and reacted to each scene here with an unnerving objectivity.

Unbound is a publisher which champions bold, unexpected books.

We give readers the opportunity to support books directly, so our authors are empowered to take creative risks and write the books they really want to write. We help readers to discover new writing they won't find anywhere else.

We are building a community in which authors engage directly with people who love what they do. It's a place where readers and writers can connect with and support one another, enjoy unique experiences and benefits, and make books that matter.

This book is in your hands because readers made it possible. Everyone who pledged their support is listed below. Join them by visiting unbound.com and supporting a book today.

Douglas Adams
Drithle Adams
Gerry Adams
Enrique Alda
Kirk Annett
James Aylett
Barbara
Caroline Beimford
Mardi Bessellieu
Paddy Bolger
Jennifer Brady

Damien Brennan
Michael Brewster
Geoffrey Brock & Padma
    Viswanathan
Fiona Burns
Garrett Carr
Jay Clancy
Philip Connor
Francis Costello
William Cox
Pat Coyle

Elizabeth Cragg-Wright
Maggie Cronin
Jane Croughton
John Darcy
Patricia Davidson
Philip de Jersey
Louis de Paor
Maura Dooley
Megan Downey
Nick Drake
Dominic Dromgoole
Sean Dromgoole
John Duggan
Sonia Nic Giolla Easbuig
Catherine Eccles
Irish Echo
Gareth Evans
Martina Evans
Jim Ferrin
Andrew Fitzsimons
William Flanagan
Aidan Flood
Aidan Flynn
Jim Frawley
Joe Gannon
Jim Gibney
Rina Gill
Shauna Gilligan
Seán Golden
Robert Gregory
Dana Gynther
Adrian Harte

Anne Haverty
Helen Gillard Healy
Matthew Herbert
Tadhg Hickey
Rossa Horgan
Chris Hudgins
Sharon Iberle
Paul Johnson
Richard Johnston
Neil Jordan
Rick Jordan
Bill Karnovsky
Katey
John Kearns
Marion Kelly
Louise Kennedy
Tim Kerr
Anthony Kieran
Randy King
Mit Lahiri
Robert Lennon
Jane Levine
Kaye Lichtenstein
John Lynch
Jonathan Macartney
Phil MacGiollabhain
Joe Mackin
Patrick Magee
David Zane Mairowitz
Mary
Shaun Mc Carroll
Richard McAuley

Adrian McBride
Patrick McCabe
Mark McCauley
Maria McCourt
Hilary McDaniel
Seamus McGarvey
Angela Mcgrath
    (RIP Frank)
Gary McKeone
Michael Mckernon
John McMillan
Brian Meara
Chuck Meara
Danny Meara
Ineke Meijer
John Mitchinson
Patrick Mongoven
Deirdre Morgan
Danny Morrison
Kevin Morrison
Paul Murphy
Mairtin O Muilleoir
Matthew O'Brien
Peter O'Connor
Nick O'Donnell
Ruan O'Donnell
Sean O'Dowd
Ursula Helen O'Hare

Ann Oliveri
Brian Patten
Will Pittam
Paula Polley
Peter Power-Hynes
Steve Pyke
Gerard Francis Quigley
Lucas Quigley
Ciaran Quinn
Terry Quinn
Tessa Radcliiffe
Angela Ritchie
Alistair Rush
Peter Sheridan
Dáithí Mac Shim
Lorna Simes
Sarah Spankie
Lou Stein
Merle Taber
Jayne Tansey-Patron
Laura Thompson
Mark Vent
Ashley J Wintjens
Tristan Wood
Tom Woodhead
Peter Woods
Ian Young
Trisha Ziff

TIMOTHY O'GRADY was born in Chicago and has lived in Ireland, London, Spain and Poland. He is the author of four works of non-fiction and four novels. His novel *Motherland* won the David Higham Prize for the best first novel in 1989. His novel *I Could Read the Sky*, a collaboration with photographer Steve Pyke, won the Encore Award for best second novel of 1997. It was filmed and also travelled as a stage show. *I Could Read the Sky, Children of Las Vegas* and *Monaghan* are published by Unbound.

ANTHONY LOTT is originally from Salt Lake City, Utah, and now lives in the small frontier town of Bluff, along the shallow meanders of the San Juan River. He has been painting the people and landscapes of the desert southwest for twenty years as an associate professor of Art at Utah State University and as an artist-in-residence at Arches and Canyonlands National Parks